Twelve Beds

a novel

D. R. KNUDSON

BEAVER'S
POND
PRESS

Twelve Beds

a novel

Deb,

"Whatever it takes!"

Love & Peace,

Edited by Kerry Stapley
Book design and typesetting by jamesmonroedesign.com
Project management by Becca Hart

ISBN: 978-1-64343-668-5

Library of Congress Number: 2023905077

Printed in the United States of America

First Edition: 2023

27 26 25 24 23   5 4 3 2 1

Beaver's Pond Press
939 West Seventh Street
Saint Paul, MN 55102
(952) 829-8818
www.BeaversPondPress.com

BEAVER'S
POND
PRESS

To my mother and father, who taught me to live a curious life and to value the words, "Whatever It Takes."

—D. K.

CONTENTS

1

FIRE

Ben couldn't breathe. The air around him was thick and oily. Particulates of upholstery, burnt sofa, and carpets floated past. He felt his face burning as a wave of fire rushed toward him. His throat and lungs tasted of soot and smoke. The intense smells caused him to gag.

Ben was making eye contact with death as he grabbed his orange tabby and ran to the only window. Several coats of paint refused to surrender; opening the window was impossible.

He felt permeated by panic and dominated by survival instincts. He threw a nightstand at the window and leaped from the second story through the shredded glass with Junior still in hand. The crunch of ice and snow sounded like a car wreck. He felt a stabbing in his back. Excruciating pain seared his arms and legs. Fear of paralysis rocketed into his brain as he began a primitive examination by moving each of his extremities.

Sirens, loud horns, and flashing lights filled the night sky as Ben looked up at the red-and-orange glow shooting from his shattered upstairs window. He struggled to stand. He was a conglomerate of cold, pain, and fear. Two firefighters appeared, lifted him to his feet, threw a blanket around him, and yelled, "Anyone still in the house?"

"No," Ben said as he squeezed Junior, sliding the cat under his shirt. Ben was trembling. His perspiration froze on his arms and legs. He saw blood on his arm and wondered where it was from.

Cradling Junior, he realized his highly verbal cat hadn't made a sound since the free fall. Ben slid Junior out from his shirt. Junior meowed, and Ben hugged him, relieved.

Ben was fixated on a blazing red-and-orange mirage. His home was on fire. He was shaking head to foot. He had survived the fire. Watching flames and sparks shooting skyward, he saw his roof collapse and the walls crumble. He heard a loud *whoosh*. Then his home vanished. He shouted up to the sky, "Everything! I lost everything!" The firefighters continued spraying water at the flames. Ice chips crunched as they peppered the ground.

Glancing to his left, he read *December 27, 2022, 2:47 AM* on the officer's hip phone. The date and time would become indelible in his mind. Never in his life could he recall feeling so shaken and unsettled. His bruised, bleeding body was intact, but his anxious mind was blank. He shook like the epicenter of an earthquake.

Frigid wind slapped one side of his face while heat from the fire burned the other.

Ben looked down and saw a stream of blood coagulating on his arm. He wondered if the blood was freezing. *Damn.* He shook his head. *It was cold.* Wrapped in a blanket, he stood barefoot in his underwear and a Guinness T-shirt on the snowy sidewalk. He stared at the remnants of 10 Water Street as the firefighters struggled to protect his neighbors' houses.

The moment seemed surreal. His mind wandered to *what the hell a person should grab when they only have ten seconds to get out of their house.* He had grabbed Junior Walker.

He tried to make sense of the chaos. *The tabby saved my ass. Many times, he annoyed me in the wee hours of the morning. This time, he saved my life.*

He held Junior tightly. The miniature saxophone on his collar jingled. He had adopted Junior from the Blues Saloon, and Junior's name and the saxophone stuck. Ben had saved Junior from euthanasia, and Junior had just repaid in full.

"Can you hear me, Mr. Raymond?" The voice and firm touch on his shoulder startled Ben. He looked over at the blue uniform and Minneapolis Police badge 1656. "Sir, I have asked you three times to get in my cruiser. It's fifteen degrees, and you're barefoot. Get into my

2

cruiser before you get frostbite. Don't worry about Zipper; he won't bother you. He's a friendly dog until he's not. Start thinking about who you can call. Sooner than later, OK?"

Ben shouted, "Who the hell can I call? Nobody!" The perplexed officer looked at him.

Junior and Ben crawled into the back seat of the black-and-white cruiser. Its red and blue lights flashed like a carnival ride. Ben had no idea where they could bring him.

He was simultaneously freezing cold and sweating. *If ever starting from scratch meant anything, this was it.* His only possessions included a T-shirt, a pair of boxers, and his cat. He felt queasy.

An EMT knocked on the window. "Sir, I would like to check you out, if that's OK?"

Ben opened the door, and she got into the back seat. "If it weren't so cold, we could go to the emergency vehicle, but the fire trucks are blocking the street. If you are OK with this, I would like to check your arm and vitals."

Ben nodded. *I can't believe I am sitting in the back of a police cruiser in my underwear.*

Not knowing whether to laugh or cry, he said, "I am OK, just need some clothes and a chance to warm up."

"I would strongly recommend a tetanus shot. Who knows where that cut came from. I am going to put a couple of butterflies and a bandage on it. You might benefit from a stitch or two."

"Thanks, I'll go first thing in the morning. I guess this is morning, so in a few hours."

After checking his vitals, looking at his pupils, and checking his oxygen levels, the EMT smiled. "Sorry about your house, sir, but in my business, you are a lucky man. You've been through a hot slice of hell and ended outside in a freezer, but it could have been worse. After a little rest, go get that shot ASAP," she said, exiting the car.

Ben's thoughts were scattered. *Everything I owned is gone! I am sitting in the cage of a Minneapolis Police cruiser. And who even cares? Nobody! What about that German shepherd in the front seat? What's he think of my predicament? He doesn't care either.*

Junior kept his eyes on Zipper, licked Ben's ear, and meowed, clearly not wanting to be there. Zipper and Junior seemed to acknowledge a mutual tolerance.

Ben was more unsettled than Junior.

He glanced out the window, surmising that Officer 1656 would be relieved to drop him somewhere and go home. *Home!* Sadness crept into every inch of him. *Stay in control.*

He focused on his immediate priority—to get warm. *Where am I going to go at three in the morning? How the hell did my house burn down? Thank God for Junior's nudge. And that we survived that fifteen-foot tumble out the window. Did I really yell Geronimo? Once a paratrooper, always a paratrooper.*

Ben was used to being alone. But now, that loneliness was on display. *Who can I call? Where can I go? How pathetic I am! I have no one to call. His mantra of a solitary life stared him in the face. Being alone works until you need help.*

After considering his options, he decided to call Louie.

"Unusual Louie" would be awake. Louie was a nocturnal beast who slept from the early morning hours to the afternoon. They had been friends since high school.

Ben asked Officer 1656 if he could use his phone. Officer Johnson handed him a cell with *MPD* printed into the face. "Press seven-four-four and you can get information for any metro person."

After punching in the number, he noticed the black soot on his fingers and more dried blood on his arm.

"Name or address."

"Louie Larson, Laurel Avenue South."

Immediately, the operator said, "Push two to connect."

The next sound Ben heard was, "Wassup?"

Louie was consistent. Even at 3:00 a.m., Ben had to give him that.

"Louie, this is Ben. Man, I need a place to stay. My house burned down an hour ago."

"Hell of a story, amigo. You know the doors always open. Tomorrow, you can tell me the details. Sorry for not waiting up. I'm spent, in bed, and going to sleep. Let yourself in. Talk tomorrow. Sleep in."

Ben heard a click before he could respond. He appreciated that Louie asked no questions. He didn't want to talk. He just wanted to get warm and have some solitude.

As he hung up, he thought, *Haven't I made any friends since high school?*

Officer 1656 knocked on the window. "Mr. Raymond, Fire Chief Jones wants to speak with you. Obviously, the cause of the fire is under investigation. It seemed to ignite outside in the back of your home or garage. Did you have any flammable containers inside your garage? The investigators are focused on that area."

Before Ben could respond, the officer said, "Chief Jones is here."

Jones crawled into the back seat of the cruiser. "Mr. Raymond, we have identified the source of the fire inside the garage. There was an explosion of a flammable liquid that spread to the house." He paused, looked directly at Ben, and said, "We need you to stay in Minneapolis until the lab results are completed. Is that a problem?"

Ben was speechless. *Do they think I started the fire?*

After a few seconds, Jones continued, "Can you share any information that would help me understand? Do you have any idea how or why this happened?"

Ben shook his head. He felt a shiver go down his spine, and it wasn't from the cold. His mind was racing. *How is this possible? I have no idea.*

Fire Chief Jones said, "I'm going to need you to be available tomorrow. Officer Johnson said that you will be staying at the Larson residence. Is that correct? I am going to ask you to call me at ten tomorrow morning, or preferably, you can come to city hall." He handed Ben a card. "We'll talk in the morning. Make sure you call or show up at ten sharp. Do not forget. Do not leave town."

No pleasantries, no *goodbye*, no *sorry*. Fire Chief Jones simply got out of the car and walked away.

Ben thought, *Social skills of a honey badger.*

Seeing the fire chief leave, Minneapolis officer 1656 got into the cruiser and began the journey to the Larson residence. Neither spoke a word.

Ben was wrapped in a blanket when he crawled out of the MPD cruiser and ambled to his new residence for what was left of a short night. He was relieved to find the door unlocked and the light on. Louie's place was a calm reprieve from the past couple of hours. Both Junior and Ben were finally at peace.

Louie's home was clean and orderly, just as it had been when Ben had visited a few weeks ago. He saw the pinball machine in the dining room and a four-foot square picture of Jesus over the kitchen counter. He recalled Louie saying, "Jesus gives my home some ambiance, peace, and warmth. Jesus and I would have been buds."

Every room was multipurpose and undefined. Each had spaces to sleep, eat, and frolic. Ben lay down on a futon in the mannequin room. Alice, the mannequin, had been with Louie since college. As with the Jesus photo, Louie said, "Alice is special, always upbeat. She converts my house into a wonderland."

Ben understood Louie. Compared to the rest of the evening, sharing a room with Alice seemed normal. He watched Junior jump on a chair and look around. He wondered if Junior remembered staying here.

His mind returned to recent events. *What the hell just happened? If I could just wake up! This can't be real! God, I wish this were just another nightmare. I'm experienced with nightmares.*

Nothing made sense. Alone in the dark with a pizza sign flashing across the street, Ben began to relive the last twelve hours, hoping to make sense of the calamity.

He had come home from a dinner party at about ten. He'd crawled into bed and fallen asleep around midnight. A couple of hours later, his sleep had been interrupted as Junior jumped back and forth from the floor to the bed. The third or fourth time, Ben had sat up and yelled, "Junior, knock it off!"

He had seen a red glow under the bedroom door. He had jumped up and run to the door. Putting his hand on it, he'd felt heat and heard a crackle from fire.

The only way downstairs was through that door. His indecision lasted three or four seconds. Then the door had blown off the hinges, and the flames had shot into the bedroom as the alarm from the smoke detector squealed. He ran to the only window and tried to open it. When that failed, he'd tossed the nightstand through the window, grabbed Junior, and jumped.

Fifteen feet is not exactly a skydive, but both were thankful for the snowbank below. Ben had looked up at the window and seen flames shooting out. He'd heard howling sirens.

The shock of seeing flames had forced him to mumble to himself, "How could my house have started to burn? Who would have lit my house on fire? Why?"

A shiver moseyed down his spine. Stressed enough for one evening, he tried to rest and recoup. He was unable to sleep, so he lay quietly, trying to be satisfied with survival. Junior jumped up next to him, and they both fell asleep around quarter after five.

A nightmare that had never left Ben returned. He was on top of someone, fighting to live. He reached and found his knife, a military-issue Ka-Bar. He stared into the man's eyes.

"Wake up, wake up, rise and shine. You look like death warmed over." The voice was Louie's. "You having a nightmare? So, you left your abode and brought Junior along. This must be a great story."

He transitioned from the nightmare to Louie's smiling face.

"No story, Louie. My house was torched. You almost got to be a pallbearer. I would have only needed one after being incinerated. Lucky to be alive, thanks to this big ole orange friend. A miracle the whole block didn't go; those firefighters are pros. They saved my neighbors' houses, but I lost everything—10 Water Street is gone! The whole night was surreal. The chief thinks the fire started in the garage. They suspect arson. Makes no sense. Anybody you know trying to kill me, Louie? Who wants me dead?"

Louie looked shocked. "That's a crazy-ass question. I don't even know what the hell to say. Man, you look rough."

Ben noticed he smelled of smoke. He needed a shower. On the floor lay a Red Cross card. A stark reminder. *My family mantra of "Trust no one and you will never be disappointed" just landed. People who have no one to call end up with the Red Cross.*

Louie could see the sadness in Ben's eyes. "You're good here for as long as you need, amigo." Ben knew that no man approaching fifty wants his high school buddy moving in over the holidays. However, Louie was all he had, and if Ben hadn't been naked, he might have hugged him.

"You are gold, Louie." Ben tried not to get choked up even though neither man would have cared. They had cried together before losing their dads during their sophomore year in high school. *Nothing like a shared loss*, he thought, *to bring boys together.*

Louie said, "I have some calls to make. You collect yourself, shower, and then we'll take care of business. OK?"

Alone, Ben looked around the room, thinking, *Louie's phone beeped five or six times. That's a week's quota for me.*

Seeing Louie's tattered gopher sweatshirt recalled their past. He reminisced about when they were roommates at the University of Minnesota. They lived in a fleabag apartment for three years until Louie met Shelby. She was Louie's first love, and he fell hard. She was sexy and smart. Louie was helpless.

They married in January of their senior year. The marriage ended six months later when Shelby cheated. Louie had been completing an internship in Chicago. He was devastated. Louie forgave but couldn't forget. They divorced.

Ben's guilt returned. He had seen Shelby with another man. He'd taken the coward's path and never told Louie until later. It wounded their friendship. Ben was ashamed. His head was filled with secrets. His family had taught him well.

But that was then, and this was now. He had his own issues. He had nothing but a smoky T-shirt, underwear, and a cat. He needed some basics: a shower, toothbrush, shoes, clothes, and a phone. All his credit cards were with his phone, melted with the rest of his belongings. Ben had no money, ID, car, shoes, shirt, or anything left to lose.

"Louie, can you bring me to my bank? Any chance you have underwear, a T-shirt, sweatpants, some socks, and any kind of shoes?"

Since Louie was three inches taller, forty pounds heavier, and wore a size-thirteen shoe, a perfect fit was not in the cards. A half hour later, looking like an off-duty clown, Ben ambled into the bank and was instructed to have a seat.

He was greeted and led to an office. "How can I be of help?"

"My home burned down last night, and I lost everything. I need a credit card and to withdraw some cash to begin to put things together."

The woman demonstrated real empathy. "How awful. The house at 10 Water Street? I am so relieved you are OK. I will do whatever possible to help. By the way, are you the author of *Hearts on Fire*? I loved that novella; it was just too short, ended too quick."

"I am. Thank you." This was not the time to talk about his novella. "Too short."

After a few minutes, Ben walked out of the bank with $1,000 and a temporary credit card. It had been a relatively painless process. Next, a stop at Verizon put him back on the grid.

There were three texts on his new phone. The word was out that 10 Water Street was gone. His sister, daughter, and ex-girlfriend Eva had heard the news.

Ben went to Target for a toothbrush, electric razor, deodorant, a six-pack of socks, a four-pack of underwear, jeans, running shoes, and a hoodie. Louie reminded him that he was wearing his favorite winter coat, so he went to REI to buy a down jacket. *It's amazing what you need and more amazing what you don't need. I can't believe how empty I feel. None of the stuff I need really matters. Bottom line, I am alone, and I deserve it.*

Riding shotgun in Louie's car, Ben could feel his pulse in his temple. His hands were trembling. Something had to give.

"Louie, how can a forty-nine-year-old man be so lost and dysfunctional? I'm a mess."

"I'm not playing psychiatrist today. Face it, you're good at being a lone wolf."

"What d'ya mean, lone wolf, Louie?"

"Don't get all bent over it. People used to call you that. Most people didn't understand your aloofness. Some saw it as arrogance. I've always liked you, but it wasn't always easy. But when your dad died, I . . . With my dad dying a few months earlier, I got it. Knew what you were going through. Man, driving and drinking. Bad stuff."

Ben hit the dash. "Don't talk about my family! I don't need that speech today."

"OK. Sorry. But it is no secret that your dad drank. Most dads did. Most people were relieved that no one else got hurt."

"Stop the car. I'm getting out!"

Louie pulled over. "What the hell is wrong with you, man?"

Ben was living up to his old nickname. His face was wet, his teeth were gritted, and his hands shook. He put his face in his hands as Louie started driving. After a minute or two, Louie said, "Listen, man, maybe I was out of bounds. No, I *was* out of bounds. But your reaction was crazy. We'll hash this out later."

Ben nodded in compliance. "Almost dying, no place to live, short on money, writing a book that nobody will read. I'm out of luck, Louie. I'm a loser at everything, except Lily. And you're right about my dad. He was a drunk. For the record, Alison hated my family too."

Neither said a word as they drove back to Louie's. Each went to different areas of the house. Neither was sure how to get out of the funk.

Alone in Alice's room, Ben couldn't help thinking it was a blunder to quit his job and become a full-time author. *I'm an idiot. How stupid.*

Ben knew there was no turning back. After minimal financial success with the novella, he was feeling pressure from his agent and publisher. For a few minutes, he escaped the looming question of who'd started the fire.

Louie walked in carrying two beers. "Can we talk?"

Ben and Louie sat facing each other, beers in hand, and talked for an hour. Their years of friendship were an asset.

Louie was not holding back. "Maybe I'm one of the few who really knows you. Do you want to go through life with hardly anybody really knowing you? Can you name one good friend besides me?"

"What the hell, Louie? Give me a break."

"My point exactly—no straight answers. That's why nobody knows you. You've bopped in and out of my life for years. No goodbye, you just disappear, then magically reappear."

Ben was on his heels. He looked at the floor, then the ceiling, then at the only friend he had. He shrugged and blew a huge exhalation.

"My family did a lot of window dressing. Covered up every problem. It was a team effort. My parents tried to make us look like a normal family. Even Anne and I played along. We never spoke about my dad's drinking or my mom's depression. Shame lived with us. It still does. I always thought if anyone really knew, they wouldn't like me. Keeping a distance was safer. Now, all I have is distance. Maybe this is another mistake, Louie, but I need to be alone."

Louie left the room without saying anything.

The conversation was an aha moment. Louie's words were spot-on. He realized if he wanted something different, he had to do something different. Memories of his family flooded his mind. There was never a family reunion, and he didn't really know his relatives. Alone in the school library, Ben had searched for the two uncles he had never met. Both were incarcerated, one for assault and battery, one for drug smuggling. *My genes are flawed. I am flawed. Keep the secrets.*

Ben's family was secretive. Louie's family was the opposite. But there were similarities. They came from blue-collar, hardworking parents. Louie was an ordinary-looking, extraordinary man. At about six foot, four inches and 240 pounds, Louie had a soft-looking body. He wore horn-rimmed glasses and had retired at thirty-five years old. Ben was ordinary. Six feet tall, and 180 pounds. But somehow, they connected.

Ben admired Louie's heart and soul. He'd stood beside Ben in a bar fight, a trivia game, and as a godparent for his daughter, Lily. Louie was his man. *Louie is safe.*

Louie and Ben never spoke further about the blowup. Ben Ubered, made phone calls, and pushed Louie's painful words underground. He became ultra-pragmatic. It was easier.

After consulting with his insurance company, architect, and bank, Ben concluded there was only one choice—to rebuild. His insurance agent informed him there would be no financial settlement without closure in the arson investigation. The process could be a long journey.

He thought of the quote: "Sometimes the journey is the destination." *My whole life has been a journey. No destination. Louie is so much more grounded than I am. You get what you deserve.*

Given the events of the past twenty-four hours, he preferred a face-to-face meeting and drove Louie's car to city hall. He was escorted into Chief Jones's office. The chief was reading and didn't look up for one to two minutes. Without a greeting, handshake, or acknowledgment, he started to blather.

"I would like to fill you in on a few details, and then I have some questions. I completed a background check and want you to substantiate the facts. You were previously married to Alison Wilson and are now divorced. You have one daughter, Lily and spent eight years in the army, where you were honorably discharged, following one tour in Afghanistan and one in Iraq. You were awarded a Bronze Star with Valor, an Army Commendation Medal, an Infantry Combat Badge, and a Purple Heart. I guess you're kind of a war hero, huh? No criminal record, not even a speeding or parking ticket. Is this all accurate? Oh, and I am recording this, OK? Our background check identified a substantial home equity loan. Anything you want to share about that, Ben?"

Ben bristled, blood rushed into his face, and his palms were sweaty.

The word *hero* antagonized him. He had a bad taste in his mouth from the flippant synopsis of his life. *Control your genes. Don't become Dad.*

"Guess you have my whole life in front of you. Chief Jones, we just met; I'd prefer you call me *Mr. Raymond.*"

"Fine, Mr. Raymond. I wanted to join the military too, but somehow never got around to it."

Having heard that many times, Ben thought, *If Jones were on the* Titanic, *he would have been wearing a wig trying to weasel into a lifeboat.*

He found the chief's efforts to put himself on equal footing with the men and women who enlisted cringeworthy. He knew there were men and women, and then there were Men and Women. Jones wasn't remotely close to being the latter. Ben had looked into the eyes of soldiers and saw fear riding on the back of bravery.

Fire Chief Jones continued, "We have confirmed the fire was ignited from a gas can found in the garage. The police have begun searching the area for evidence. This includes abandoned vehicles, potential witnesses, phone records, and social media. We would like permission to access your social media. Which do you use?"

"I'm not on social media."

"None?"

"Zero."

"We need to find this arsonist, even if it's you. Am I being clear? All cards are on the table. Again, is there any explanation you can offer?"

Ben stood up, leaned forward, put his hands on the desk, and looked directly into the chief's eyes. He knew about interrogation and had an aversion to being manipulated. "Let me make something crystal clear. Last night, I lost everything in what could have been an attempt on my life. I'm confused about what you are asking me."

Every hair on Ben's body stood up. *I am a suspect.*

"You're expecting me to believe that someone might have been trying to kill you and you don't have a clue?"

"Why would anyone want to kill me? This conversation is over."

"Keep us informed of your whereabouts, Mr. Raymond," the chief called after him.

Walking out of city hall, Ben thought, *Reprobate.* Chills went down his spine as the frigid December wind greeted his face. He tried to refocus on 10 Water Street. He called his insurance agent and a builder. "I want to rebuild as soon as possible."

Estimates said the rebuild would take a year. Ben was low on cash and living on a home equity loan. He had a book to write and needed to escape. *Belize! San Pedro.* Louie would keep JW. They were compatible friends, having similar personalities.

After a deep breath, Ben touched his ex-wife's name in his contacts.

"Hello." He recognized the voice of Alison's husband. He had met Ted on occasion, and the conversations were awkward. This one was no different.

"May I please speak with Alison?"

"Who may I say is calling?"

"Hello, Ted, this is Ben. Is Alison available?"

There was no response from Ted. Then, thirty seconds of silence ensued before Ben heard Alison's voice. "Hi, Ben. We heard about the fire. So terrible. Relieved you are safe. Is there anything we can do?"

Will I ever be immune to the sting of her voice, always a raw reminder of my failure?

"Yes, Alison, everything is OK—well, sort of. My home is gone. I'm in a bit of a fix. It will be close to a year before it is rebuilt. I am wondering if the Palms is vacant and whether you would consider renting it to me for January while I sort things out."

"Let me talk with Ted, and I'll call you back tonight, if that works."

"Thanks. Appreciate it. And, of course, I'll pay whatever you want. I look forward to your call. Thanks again. Goodbye."

Ben hung up, never mentioning the arson. *She's not surprised. Bad things happen to bad people.*

Relief arrived around midnight. Alison texted. "Go to the Palms. It's yours until January 31. We'll talk money later."

Ben called Sun Country and booked a flight for New Year's Eve. Second, he called the Minneapolis Police and gave them his contact information in San Pedro. *They can tell Jones.*

He had one day to put closure on the issues at hand. He was in the shower rinsing shampoo from his hair when he had a brainstorm. *Maybe this could work. I don't have a plan B.*

With nothing to lose, he reviewed his contacts and began writing an email. *I have a bed for January. February seems light-years away. Maybe I can find eleven more beds available this year.* He swallowed hard and hit Send.

2

QUE SERÁ, SERÁ

Ben found the familiar trek to Belize City uncomfortable. Running from the fire and the unknown perpetrator didn't sit well. He knew he was running from his problems in Minneapolis. *Disappearing, like Louie said.*

Leaving Minnesota's weather was a no-brainer for Ben. He hated January. He appreciated seasons, but January was long, cold, and often coupled with a cluster of holiday-hangover blues.

From his window seat, he spent the entire flight staring into the sky. He wondered whether the fire was a murder attempt. That thought seemed absurd but not discountable. He craved information that made sense of the unsensible.

Then there was the book he was trying to write. He had never considered himself an author and didn't believe there was anything novel about a novel. He was more lucky than talented. A friend had connected him with a literary magazine after his novella was published. That interview and publisher's social media sold more copies of his little book than anyone had expected.

Ben doubted there was a novel in him. The pressure from his publisher and scant money up front felt like strong headwinds. He wasn't destitute, but he couldn't help second-guessing his career change. His private-therapy business had just gotten out of the red when he decided to leave it. *Another bad decision on the bottom of a long list.*

Looking out the window at the lush green landscape surrounding Philip S. W. Goldson International, Ben was melancholy. He had been alone in Belize once before and vowed never to do it again. Yet here he was. *I'll never learn.*

He knew that weather and locale could only do so much for the soul. Happiness had been evasive for a long time. The wheels squealed onto the runway.

On the ground, immigration and customs were quick. He was distracted by the humidity and tropical aroma. His mind was foggy from too many short nights.

Making his way down to the Tropic Air booth, he accessed a quick jump to Ambergris Caye, the island where the condo sat a hundred feet from the Caribbean. He sat next to the pilot in the one-engine Cessna during the twenty-minute ride to San Pedro.

"First time to San Pedro?"

Ben could barely mutter a response. "Been here before. Looking forward to some sun."

He had made this flight many times and was always mesmerized by the murals of color in the water. He settled into silence and stared at the turquoise Caribbean.

He usually liked landing at the small San Pedro airport. The experience had never previously failed to exhilarate, but this was different. He planted himself on a stool at the Runway Bar, pulled the napkin off the top of his Belikin, took a sip, and began watching alternating Tropic Air and Mayan Air takeoffs and landings. The warm air, the whirl of propellers, and the cold beer was a brief mental vacation.

Alison and Ted were the owners of the condo. Ben couldn't recall any discussion about how that happened. At the time, money and property were incidental. The divorce was a blur. Now, Alison was with her husband, a man who introduced money into every conversation. *How did Alison ever choose Ted, after being married to a guy who hadn't balanced his checkbook in thirty years?* He wondered how Alison and Ted described him.

Being solo allowed him to transform the one-mile journey to the condo into two miles. Ben had his luggage picked up by Wayo from the Palms. They had known each other for years. Then he opted to walk the rest of the way to the condo.

He meandered mindlessly along the beach, caressed by a salty sea breeze. He stopped at the Purple Hibiscus for a quick fix of conch ceviche and a second Belikin. The people, air, water, and sunshine were what lured Ben and Alison to buy the condo in San Pedro. Ben's mood slanted upward, and he thought about writing, which had taken a back seat since the fire. The opening sentence to his novel read, "Our brains make decisions before we are conscious of them. Before we are prepared."

He was glad he'd uploaded his manuscript to the cloud before his laptop had melted. If his writings had burned, he would have given up on his nebulous journey to become a writer. *Is San Pedro a good decision? Will the change of scenery free my mind?*

Finishing his ceviche and Belikin, he ambled along the beach, shoes in hand. He and Alison had traced these steps through the shallow, warm water many times. Ben vowed he'd never experience another breakup. He'd rather revisit combat than face another divorce.

He hadn't been there for Alison. He had left his wife and daughter. The divorce was on him. A life of loneliness and solitude. *My well-deserved fate.*

The Palms looked welcoming and fresh. The property was one of the quaintest on Ambergris Caye. The Palms's appearance was alluring, even to a veteran of the island. He stopped by the office and got a key from Nina, a gracious manager with a big smile and large brown eyes to match. Nina didn't know Ben, and she gave him a full rundown on the property, pool, and neighborhood. He allowed her to introduce him to all the familiar details.

Once inside, Ben realized how long it had been. Ten years. The paint was new, and the condo had been updated. They'd gotten satellite TV, internet, and fresh furniture, but the beautiful rooftop view of the ocean and its coral reef remained intact. The vista was spectacular, just as he'd remembered. He decided to grab some dinner and unpack later.

He stumbled onto a Cuban street vendor selling rice, beans, and mouthwatering barbecued chicken. He bought all three and headed home.

The geographic separation from his troubles helped. Here, he didn't have to talk about the turmoil from the fire. A late-night swim in the pool followed by a long, hot shower prepared him for a perfect night's sleep. Dog-tired, he crawled into bed. He tossed and turned for about seven seconds.

He spent his days in a trance of exercise and sunshine and devouring fresh fruits, vegetables, and seafood. None of it eliminated his sense of loss. His father's confirmation Bible, his parents' wedding rings, and countless family photos had been destroyed in the fire. He hiked, snorkeled, biked, and wrote every evening, trying to find inspiration for his novel. There were days when life was calm. But the questions around the fire lingered, tormenting him every night.

After a full day of visiting Caye Caulker, his second-favorite island, he dozed with his laptop on his stomach.

A loud beeping pulled him from sleep. He flew from his bed, fearing another fire, and ran into the living room. The front door was open, and a person was standing in the doorway. She was holding two suitcases.

Ben pushed the security system's code into the panel, stopping the beeping.

"What is going on?" She was as shocked as he was. "My guess is that one of us are in the wrong condo, but tell me what you think."

"I rented number 902 on VRBO. I got the key from the lockbox and thought I was in the right place."

It was 3:10 a.m. He was in his boxers, talking to a stranger who looked just as confused as he was. "One second." He retreated to his bedroom to put on a pair of shorts and a T-shirt. The woman looked frustrated and was shaking her head. "Please, have a seat. Let's try to figure this out." She handed Ben her reservation email. "The Palms #902 Jan. 15–Jan. 31." She was in the right spot.

"Well, there are two bedrooms, and it's three in the morning. We might delay this conversation until tomorrow."

The stranger didn't respond, laugh, or smile.

Ben explained that he was a previous owner and had made last-minute plans with the present owner, his ex-wife, to spend January here. "If it's OK with you, maybe we should close the door and come up with a plan."

The woman nodded in resignation.

"My name is Benjamin Raymond. I'm from Minneapolis."

"I'm Dahlia Karlsen from Toronto."

Ben offered his hand, and she reluctantly shook it. She looked exhausted. "It's after three and the birds start chirping in a couple of hours. This condo has two bedrooms and two bathrooms. I know you have only known me for a few minutes, but you're welcome to stay tonight, and we can figure this out in the morning. I don't have a better idea. If you do, I am all ears."

She shrugged and nodded. Ben picked up her luggage and carried it into the vacant bedroom.

"I'm very sorry about this, Dahlia. I hope you're able to sleep."

She didn't respond.

He started to walk away, stopped, looked back at her, and said, "I probably don't have to say this, but you are safe here. I am the father of a twenty-one-year-old daughter and have a high regard for women. Tomorrow, we will find a solution. Fair enough?"

Dahlia nodded.

Ben turned and left her room, wondering what was next. For a second time, he tossed and turned before he was out for the count. He dreamed the familiar nightmare and woke up in a sweat. Immediately, his thoughts returned to the fire. *Who is crazy enough to want to kill me?* He returned to an uneasy sleep.

The interrupted sleep messed with Ben's mind. He awoke several times, looking for Junior, the mannequin, and even thinking he smelled smoke. He fell back asleep until the sun reflected off the mirror and woke him. He wondered if he had a roommate or if that too had been a dream. He listened carefully. There was not a sound.

He wondered if the strange woman had already hit the road. That would have been OK with Ben. He didn't need another complication. The solitary life in San Pedro had been working.

He decided to approach the day normally. That meant a shower and a robust cup of coffee. He congratulated himself for having the foresight to bring three bags of Dunn Brothers Sumatran coffee beans.

Post shower, though the apartment was still quiet, Ben noticed the second bedroom door was open.

"Hello? Hello? Dahlia?"

He walked toward the door. Dahlia was not there, but her luggage was in the corner. The front door opened, and Ben was relieved to have left the security system disarmed. The intruder walked in looking like she had been on a jog.

"Good morning, Dahlia. I'm about to make some coffee. Would you like a cup?"

"Thank you! That run was a challenge! I'm not used to the heat and humidity. Feels good to get back home. Whoops, this is hardly my home. I will start looking for a place after I shower. Is that OK with you?"

"Sure! I'm familiar with the island; I might be able to help. The difficulty will be vacancies. January is the busiest month, for obvious reasons. Let's have a coffee on the balcony and talk."

Ben noticed Dahlia's physical prowess. She was tall, five feet, nine inches, and muscular. She reminded him of a biathlon gold-medal winner he had met in Norway years ago. She looked like a cover woman for *Optimal Health* magazine. Ben noticed her running shirt said *CANSOFCOM* on the back. He was familiar with those capital letters from his time in Iraq. *This is not the time for that talk.* He went to the balcony and waited for her to join him after her shower.

"So, Dahlia from Toronto, what brings you to Belize? Tell me whatever you want. I'll never know if it's true anyway."

For the first time, she showed a little smile, laughing slightly. "I'm not much for small talk, Ben, so I'll get right to it. I am a vascular surgeon at the U of Toronto Medical Center. I've worked there for three years and plan to marry my boyfriend, one of my colleagues, next summer. For complicated reasons, Ben and I—yes, my fiancé's name is also Ben—agreed that I deserved some time away. I haven't taken a vacation in two years, so Ben made this trip happen. I didn't want to go on vacation alone, but he made the reservations, and here I am. He would feel terrible if he knew about this predicament. I would rather figure it out myself. So, that's it. Wish I could have been more creative or dishonest, but that's why I am here. What's your story, Ben?"

"Pretty boring stuff compared to you. In a nutshell, I'm a divorced psychologist with one daughter who is in Spain for a semester and graduates from college in June. I worked a couple of different jobs and am trying to write a book. I'm rebuilding my house in Minneapolis because it was destroyed in a fire last month. That will take several months, so I decided to spend January in the warmth of San Pedro. There you have it. Belize it or not! I know of a couple of rentals if you want some inside info. I can help you check out some options if you want. Or I can just get out of your way. I feel a little responsible since I am living in the property you rented."

"Sounds good, Ben. Give me fifteen minutes. Appreciate your help. I will find a place today."

Eight minutes later, Dahlia reemerged in key lime–colored beachwear. She was strikingly attractive. Her long, ebony hair was in a ponytail.

Dahlia was an unexpected diversion from his personal turmoil. The fire was absent from his mind, and he felt normal. Still, he wanted the diversion to be short-lived.

They stopped at the Parakeet, a five-star, exclusive, all-inclusive resort. It was the pride and joy of Ambergris Caye. No children were allowed. It was an uppity resort for beautiful people who needed to spend money to feel important. Ben was hoping Dahlia would snag a rare cancellation.

Dahlia seemed lackadaisical, like she was going through the motions, wishing she were somewhere else. Ben excused her mood, figuring that being thousands of miles from someone you love and hanging out with a stranger instead would cloud anyone's spirit. He gave her a pass but decided his time with Dahlia would be limited to one day. He had a full plate of his own.

The best the Parakeet could do was to put Dahlia on the wait list. Julio, a handsome lad, seemed willing to try magic to find a vacancy even though none existed. He couldn't take his eyes off her. She took his attention in stride, unmoved, yet uninterested.

Casa De Conch, a glistening white resort with a palapa that reached a hundred yards offshore, was their second stop. Casa De Conch seemed more to Dahlia's taste, but at this point, a perfect match was not the goal. Maria, the manager, spoke encouragingly about a couple that might cancel by the following evening. Again, Dahlia shared her contact info, and Ben crossed his fingers. Then they went for some nourishment.

He searched for the Purple Orchid, a place he remembered for their banana pancakes, Belizean eggs, and café con leche. Even after ten years, the menu looked identical. He thought the same people might even have been working there. Dahlia and Ben were seated at a table in the sand facing the turquoise water. The hostess handed them two menus on conch shells.

"With a view like this, anything they serve me will be delicious." Ben was pleased to hear a positive comment from Dahlia. She had been serious all morning.

Their conversation was light and centered around Belize. Dahlia was a veteran traveler, but this was her first trip to Belize. Her choice of words was charming and deep. She was endlessly curious.

Dahlia inquired about the government, the English connection that ended British Honduras and gave birth to Belize in 1981. She was interested in the country's diverse population. Ben quickly realized she didn't need his help.

"Sometimes I think culture can be a fallacy used to magnify differences between humans when they really don't exist. The notion that you must first learn about one's culture to respect someone is based in distrust. Is there any reason not to respect a culture simply because it exists?"

Ben was keenly aware of Dahlia's intelligence. Their conversation was fast paced and electric. Breakfast was delicious but secondary to their conversation. Dahlia enjoyed Belizean eggs, fry jacks, and a latte. Ben had banana pancakes and a café Cubano. He kept thinking, *She eats like a surgeon.* Every knife and fork move were delicate and with purpose. Dahlia, he realized, was one multifaceted, unique human being.

After breakfast, they decided to hang tight and wait to hear from either of the two seemingly best options. The day was sunny and warm. Ben had tasks, a book to write, phone calls to make, and a Zoom scheduled with Lily.

"I want to call Ben and let him know what's up. I texted him last night but want to talk with him. I am sure you need a break from my problems too."

They agreed to meet back at the condo in a couple of hours.

As Ben walked away, he wondered whether Dahlia had enjoyed their conversation. Both of his needs had been met in the last hour. He'd had fresh, earthy food and stimulating conversation. His mind quickly turned to his situation in Minneapolis, and he called Louie.

"Hi, Louie. How are you, mi amigo? And how is my orange companion?"

"All is good here, Ben. You know, Junior is one fine feline. Every time JW has stayed here has been a delight. I'm keeping this little furry friend. So, how's San Pedro? Everything OK?"

"Yes, all good, smooth trip, just have some loose ends to tie down regarding my insurance, architect, and builder. Looking forward to Zooming with Lily later. But listen to this, Louie—my insurance agent told me that because the fire included arson, they must rule me out as a suspect before moving forward with a settlement. Can you believe it? I still am so baffled and unsettled about this. Why would someone want to burn down my house?"

"It's unbelievable. Why someone would want to end you is the bigger question. But there are loonies everywhere; maybe the moron didn't even know you, just wanted to torch a house. Who knows? Eventually, it will be solved. Being in San Pedro is a good thing for now. I can be your lead man up here with anything. Keep me in the loop, bro."

"You're the best, Louie, always have been. Talk soon. Will check back in a couple of days."

Hanging up, Ben reflected on why he didn't share more. He began self-talk evaluation. *At this age, a man's life should begin to stabilize instead of being in turmoil. A psychologist should be better at living.* Finding the answers were his responsibility if he had the courage to uncover them.

He had always advised clients, "Live the life you wish for, but first, answer the question, *What do you wish for?*" In an unsettling way, he knew his decisions created his life. He craved excitement and change. *I'm my dad.*

He felt his phone vibrating. It was his insurance agent.

Before the fire, he'd disliked insurance, although he'd understood the necessity. The agent shared that the company was considering every aspect of the fire and the value of his property. Of course, there was the continued investigation into the cause of the fire. Although Ben had been a valued customer for years, his agent again referenced the MFD's conclusion of arson and reminded him the FBI was doing a background check on him.

Ben remained passive. What he wanted to say wasn't going to be effective. He felt a quiver of butterflies in his stomach.

He wanted to change gears. He decided to Zoom with Lily. It would be eight hours ahead in Spain, close to eight o'clock at night in Lily's world. He hit the Zoom icon and immediately smiled in anticipation. Lily had been the only consistent person in Ben's life, unplanned and simply a delight from birth onward.

"Lily, you look great! So good to see your mug again. How are you?"

"Good, Dad, really good. I am loving it here. But first, I am so sorry about the fire and so relieved you and Junior are safe. Mom told me about it. I am so worried about who would have done this. Do you know any more?"

"Everything is fine, Lily, and the investigation is ongoing. It will be resolved soon. I have a hunch the person had some personal issues and didn't even know me. More important, you'll have a new house to visit in December. Tell me about Spain."

"I was pretty sad and homesick at first, but it helped to be really busy with my classes, figuring out my host family, a new room, a 'sister' who spoke zero English, and a new diet. The time is flying by. I'm so glad to be here for a semester. Thank you so much for encouraging me to do this. But when I get home, I'm probably never leaving Minneapolis again. How are you, and where are you? That doesn't look like Bde Maka Ska behind you. As I recall, there aren't any palm trees in Minnesota. Where the heck are you?"

"I'm in San Pedro, Lily, staying at the condo. If you weren't in Spain, I would want you here too. I am attempting to write, and with the house gone, San Pedro seemed like the best option. So far, so good, but I wish it would rain so I would want to write. I still wonder about being able to write this book or whether anyone will read it. Lily, my connection is fading, can't see you . . . Can you hear me?"

"Barely."

"Let's say goodbye while we can. Talk again soon, love you to the moon."

"Bye, Dad. I love you too."

The internet service in San Pedro left a little to be desired. Palm. com was unpredictable, dropping service at the most inopportune times. Ben hadn't been able to access his emails since arriving, and although February was several days away, he was curious about his lifeline email. He wondered if anyone had responded.

He worried that writing his book was improbable. In Minneapolis, he contemplated the Hemingway method: get up early, make a large pot of coffee, and write until noon. Have lunch, take a nap, and head to a palapa bar. But he wasn't one for excess drinking. *Alcohol ended my dad's life.*

When he got back to unit 902, the door was unlocked. Dahlia had let herself in. It was quiet, so he assumed she was in the second bedroom. He could hear a voice. She was on the phone. Not wanting to interrupt, Ben went out on the balcony.

After about ten minutes, he heard noise in the kitchen and decided to wait for her to notice the balcony door was open. Soon after, Dahlia came out looking frustrated.

"Do you have a minute, Ben?" Before he could answer, she sat down on the chair next to him, took a deep breath, and said, "I am going to go back to Toronto tomorrow. Both rental possibilities called, and there are no vacancies. Talking to Ben made the decision easy. So, if you can tolerate me one more night, I will leave tomorrow.

I am sorry for the inconvenience, but I really don't know what else to do. I will pay you whatever I owe."

"I am sorry. This is a predicament you didn't deserve. Of course, you can stay here tonight. Never mind the money."

Dahlia turned and stared into the sea.

"Do you want to talk or be left alone? I can do either. Whatever you want is OK."

Dahlia's voice was cracking. Raw emotions poured out. "I can't believe this is happening." She continued to talk, got up, stood at the railing, and sat back down, never once camouflaging her emotions. She paid them no attention.

She looked Ben straight in the eyes. "I didn't tell you that my sister was critically injured in a car accident last year and died in my hospital a year ago today. My parents and I sat with her until she passed the next morning.

"Sarah was two years older than I was. I admired everything about her, and I always tried to emulate her. Every tough decision, I would ask myself, *what would Sarah do?* The anniversary of her death was the reason for me to get away. She was my best friend. I miss her so much. My parents only have me now.

"Aside from my grief, my conversation with Ben was a disaster. I was honest with him about the mix-up, and he couldn't believe I stayed here last night. At a time when I was looking for support, I had to spend the conversation defending myself. It didn't end well. I am disappointed and angry with him. I must get back to Toronto." She took a deep breath and continued.

"The decision to come here was ridiculous. It was a stupid idea. I never wanted to come here. So, there you have it. Aren't you glad you asked? I guess you never asked, I guess I just had to unload, and you were the only one in range."

There was fire in her eyes. Ben admired her mettle. She was strong, tough, and had the heart of a lioness.

"I'm having a glass of wine. Want one?"

"Sure, why not?" Ben responded.

A minute later, Dahlia came out on the balcony with a bottle and two glasses. She pulled the cork out in one motion and poured the two glasses nearly to the top. She handed him one and sat down.

"You just never know when your life is going to change forever. I never knew until I lost Sarah. Now, I wonder, what next? So enough about me. How about you? What do you think of me?" She smirked. "If I ever run into you again, I will deny ever meeting you. In my thirty-nine years, I have never been so fraught with dysfunction, and I can't believe I am sharing it with a stranger."

"Do you believe in predestination, Dahlia? Do you think there is a higher power with a plan, and are we simply going through the motions? Or do you believe human beings have control over their lives and decide which paths to pursue?"

Dahlia looked at Ben with a nebulous expression. "What's with the Dr. Phil impression? What the hell are you talking about?"

"Good and bad events happen to everyone. I am asking you how you put that together. Are our lives orchestrated by a higher power, or are we in a free fall? Do you believe our choices make a difference or not?"

"I am a doctor and believe that our choices are paramount. In surgery, I am hoping that the patient's life can be extended with a higher quality. Without it, the result may be decreased quality or death."

"It looks like you and I may only share a brief time together. I like you. You're interesting. I was hoping we could have a meaningful conversation. But I'm OK just hanging out, looking at the ocean, sipping some wine, and chatting about the sunset or whatever."

"You are an unusual man, Ben Raymond. I haven't decided if that's good or bad. I do give you this, you have a complex soul. You ask provoking questions. Being totally up front, I don't like the company of most men. Some men just like to hear their own voice." Dahlia sipped her wine, looking at the coral reef. "You're either different or one hell of an actor. To be honest, I think it's uncanny that I am sitting here tonight. It's interesting that the only two men I have seemed to trust in the past few years are named Ben. You know quite a bit about me, my family, my fiancé, and my profession. All I know is your name and that you have a daughter. Oh, and you are from Minneapolis. So, if we are going to have a real conversation, how about you share a little more. What makes you tick, Ben Raymond?"

"Well, you know the basics. After the army, I wanted a different focus other than being a therapist and started writing in my free time. A friend liked what I wrote and connected me with a publisher. I wrote a novella, was very mildly successful, signed with a publisher who advanced me to write a novel . . . Honestly, I am a duck out of water. I haven't a clue whether I will ever write a book, let alone one that's worth reading. Time will tell."

Ben wanted to share more with her. She was safe since they would never see each other again. "I have only been hurt twice. Broke my arm playing football at twelve and broke my heart at forty-three. I have only joined two things in my life: the army and a book club. My blood type is A positive, my rank was major, my MOS was 37A, psychological operations. When I was analyzed for my job, I was told I have four dominant personality traits. I'm loyal, resilient, self-controlled, and secretive. I was assigned the code name 'Manimal Seasons,' and my dominant traits from my psych testing are passion, humor, physicality, and compassion. My family was dysfunctional. That's who I am."

"Hmm, there's more to you than meets the eye," Dahlia said. "You didn't share much about your family's dysfunction, but that's OK. I was deployed to Iraq too. My uncle died in the South Tower on 9/11. Over twenty Canadians died on 9/11. I was nineteen and in my first year of college. His death was devastating to my family. Uncle Bob was a wonderful husband and father. He was my only uncle. Uncle Bob's grandfather died in Dachau. As a child, I heard several stories about my mother's relatives who were murdered in the Holocaust.

"A month after 9/11, I quit college, joined the army, and deployed in '03. My parents supported my decision 100 percent because they understood that I had to respond. I couldn't be a spectator. I was assigned to an air mobile unit designed to medevac. I saw lives being saved every day. That experience motivated me back to college and eventually med school."

"If I may use your line," Ben said, "there is a lot more to you than meets the eye. You are the real deal, Dahlia, a quality human being. You saw a cause bigger than yourself and chose to step up. I recognized CANSOFCOM on your T-shirt, having spent time with Canadian Special Operations around Tikrit with the Fifth Special Forces Group out of Fort Campbell."

"Thank you, Major. But tell me—your code name—Manimal? The army can be a crazy place, but what the hell is that about?"

"I am not much for military talk, but my survival training instructor was British Special Forces. His favorite play was *A Man for All Seasons*, so he said his goal was to turn us into men, able to cope with any contingency, exhibiting appropriate behavior in every situation. At the end of training, he said we were 'men for all seasons.' He code-named everyone. My certificate said, 'Ben Raymond is unafraid of being afraid. He is a Manimal Seasons.'"

"Not afraid of being afraid?" Dahlia looked inquisitively. "How about when your house burned down?"

Ben declined to respond, then said, "Yes, my house burned to the ground. I was scared to death. My cat, JW, saved my life. It was arson and is being investigated. I've been afraid all my life. I'm just good at keeping it secret."

"Well, well, well." Dahlia took a gulp of wine. "I am getting a clearer picture of Ben Raymond, that's for sure. We share some history, huh?"

"Yes, we do," Ben said. "But regarding my family dysfunction— my dad had a drinking problem and died in a car accident. Both my uncles went to prison. Always makes me question who I am. But let's talk about the here and now, if that's OK with you. The past is gone, right?"

"Fair enough. Where do we start, Major Raymond?"

Ben had a sip of wine and looked at her. "Every living creature experiences birth and death. Do you see evidence of a higher power? What do you believe?"

Dahlia said, "It is incredible what we know and even more incredible what we don't. For me, the questions are more important than answers. Especially when there isn't an answer. When the body has a disease or malfunction, we can't understand why. We know what happens but have no idea why."

Dahlia kept talking, and Ben slipped back into being a therapist, dissecting every spoken word as well as the unspoken eye movements and shifts in body language.

"I am of the Jewish faith. My father is Lutheran Norwegian, and my mother Jewish Hungarian. I attend the synagogue regularly. I find comfort believing in God. Comfort is reason enough for me. The argument for atheism is as weak as the argument for God. How can one know the answer by saying there are no answers? Atheists contend, without scientific proof, that God doesn't exist. This doesn't hold up, because we are constantly finding new information in a myriad of scientific areas.

"There was a time when people thought the world was flat and at the center of the universe. Why is there life on earth as opposed to other planets? To claim there is no God because we haven't found proof runs counter to science.

"Perhaps, we are the evidence for the existence of a higher power. But as my dad used to say, 'If you aren't hungry for God, you are probably full of yourself.' Faith in a higher power is believing some-thing is more important than myself."

For the next few hours, Ben and Dahlia connected, massaging each other's minds and hearts, reminiscing about their lives without revisiting the war.

Dahlia asked, "How many times have you been in love? Tell me about who and how someone broke your heart."

"I have been in love four times. Strange as it sounds, I am still in love with all four. Not sure they would say the same. I think love is like a tattoo—difficult to remove." Then Ben took a bigger risk. "My overseas tours, months apart, damaged me. And although I tried everything, I ruined our marriage. Afterward, I lost confidence in myself, and every relationship since has suffered. Hard to admit, but I don't think I've recovered yet. In fact, my life is in shambles, loveless. Sometimes, I feel hopeless. Tough to admit."

When Dahlia asked specifics about his dad's drinking, Ben told her. When she asked about his uncles, he shared what he knew openly and honestly for the first time in his life. Dahila continued, seemingly thinking aloud.

"How does one know if they're in love? Or when love is enough for marriage, a decision that promises the rest of your life. And what is love? Is love simply physical desire with someone biologically compatible?"

Ben could tell she had more to say and remained quiet. Dahlia continued.

"For me, it's more than physical attraction, quite complicated, and each of us experiences love differently. Love is personal, defined by each of us. I think if you are open and let it happen, you know, because of the unique feeling. What is more beautiful than making love? Love coupled with physical intimacy might be the best human experience of all."

Both stopped talking and looked at a passing sailboat. Dahlia stood up, stretching. She turned, looked at Ben, and said, "This is so good for me." Then she sat back down, pouring another glass of wine for them both.

Dahlia briefly touched his arm. "Ben, would you live differently if fear didn't exist and you couldn't fail?"

"Quite the philosophical question, Dahlia. Off the top of my head, minimizing fear of failure would be a worthy goal. Easier said than done. I have had my share of fear and failure."

It was quiet again for a few minutes before Ben spoke. "What are five things in life that you think are beautiful?"

Without hesitating, Dahlia said, "Sleeping babies, snowcapped mountains, sunset over water, children holding a grandparent's hand, a genuine smile." They asked question after question of each other, probing their own hearts and minds, as well as the other's.

"What are five things you find beautiful, Ben?"

"A sweet sound from Billie Holiday, a salty ocean breeze, sun dogs in a winter sky, a passionate kiss, and holding a small child in my arms."

"Hmm. You surprised me again, Ben Raymond." Dahlia moved closer to Ben to get out of the sun.

Their conversation included their parents, families, childhoods, trust, friendships, sex, the existence of heaven, and their dreams, hopes, and fears. Without hesitation, they shared personal intimacies for almost six hours. During their personal revelations, Ben and Dahlia connected in ways that were magical. For Ben, the conversation was transformational.

Out of the blue, Dahlia said, "Sometimes I sense the presence of my sister. I feel Sarah's presence tonight. Feeling her near is reassuring. Do I sound crazy, Ben?"

"Not in the least. You're embracing free thoughts. That's empowering stuff."

Maybe the Malbec loosened their inhibitions, but the connection felt more momentous and mystical than the impact of wine. The moon and stars aligned. Two strangers were on a single carpet ride, uniting their souls. They were perplexed and astonished, loving every second of being together. Ben and Dahlia were in uncharted territory. Especially Ben. *I have never felt like this, ever.*

When time suggested sleep, they walked to the doors of the two bedrooms, cradling each other's faces in their fingers, looking into each other's eyes. With every ounce of self-control, Ben struggled with his desire for more. He kissed her hand softly, slowly, tenderly, twice.

They smiled into each other's eyes—no kiss, no embrace. Ben and Dahlia masked their desires, surrendered to their confusion, and regretfully walked to separate rooms.

Ben stood in the silent darkness. He was certain this evening would always be a part of him. A gift from the fire. He opened to Dahlia and had no regrets.

The next morning, he woke early for a swim. Pulling on his suit, grabbing a towel, and entering the water three minutes after opening his eyes reminded him of the military. Rough and ready! It still amazed him how one could get dressed in less than two minutes. The military goal was ninety seconds, and that was fast enough.

Early on a San Pedro morning, the water was warmer than the air. Gliding through the water slowly and quietly, he wondered about the time. Was it five, six, or seven? He didn't have a clue. He reminded himself that Dahlia was leaving, and his butterflies returned. It had been an amazing thirty-six-hour connection. But it was ending as quickly as it began. Knowing she was leaving shortened his swim. He grabbed his towel and looked up. Dahlia was sitting on the balcony, phone in hand.

Heading up the stairs, he ran into an acquaintance from a decade earlier. Kevin and his wife, Margaret, owned the condo across the hall. Except for the addition of ten pounds and his thinning hair, Kevin looked as he always had.

"Good morning." Kevin set a suitcase on the steps to shake his hand. "Haven't seen you for ages, Ben. You look great. Margaret and I think of you from time to time. We miss the times with you and Alison. Unfortunately, we are leaving in a few minutes. Got a phone call during the night from Margaret's mother. Her dad has a heart issue and has been hospitalized, so we are headed back to Boston. Hate to drop this on you, but we were having a new hot-water heater installed today. If I gave you the lockbox combo, could you let him in at ten? Just lock it up when he is done. You wouldn't have to do anything else. It would be a great help."

"Of course, Kevin. No problem. Just give me your cell so I can update you. Medical care in Boston is as good as anywhere in the world. Tell Margaret I wish her dad the best."

Ben put the lockbox number in his phone, exchanged cell numbers with Kevin, and headed up the stairs. Dahlia was still on the phone, so Ben decided to make coffee. He loved rich, dark, earthy coffee, topped with cinnamon froth.

"Top of the morning to you, Major. Just made a reservation, wheels up at 1600, sir." Her words seemed forcibly cheerful.

Ben thought, *I adore this woman's zest for life*, then asked, "Coffee, black or better?"

"Make it like yours, it looks scrumptious."

Taking two beautiful cups of coffee onto the balcony, Ben said, "Let's return to the scene of the crime. The sunrise has made the ocean seem like millions of diamonds floating toward San Pedro."

"I have to tell you, Ben, last night was exhilarating. I couldn't fall asleep until about five this morning. I've never had a conversation quite like that. The Malbec must have been infused with truth serum. You must have been quite the interrogator!"

"I cherish the unpredictable moments of life. Meeting you unplanned, in the middle of the night, and having our time together evolve into an evening of wonder . . . I was so comfortable sharing with you. Something special happened. I thank you for that gift."

With that, Ben realized that he still had no idea what time it might be. He relished in the no-clock lifestyle of San Pedro. However, at this moment, time mattered. This remarkable woman was leaving. He didn't like the feel of it. In fact, it felt awful.

Dahlia excused herself when her phone rang. Ben showered, deciding he'd start writing again later that day. He felt a familiar queasiness. He'd had the feeling when he deployed overseas, and again when he finalized his divorce. Briefly, he second-guessed spending time with Dahlia. He had only known her for two days. He put on shorts, a shirt, and sandals and walked into the living room. Dahlia was sitting on the sofa.

"Is life unpredictable or what? Ben has an interview at General Hospital in Boston. He is a UMass guy and has always looked forward to moving back. He is leaving tomorrow and will be there for two to three days so he can visit his parents. There's a snowstorm predicted in Toronto, so he is looking into flights to come to Belize after Boston as long as I can find a rental property. He is calling me back within the hour. As of now, I have a flight out of San Pedro at four and Belize City on to Toronto at six."

There is good and bad in most everything, Ben thought, quoting his mother. "Guess we have an hour to kill. The rooftop is one of my favorite hangouts. An exceptional view of San Pedro. Wanna see it?"

She nodded. "Sure, I will make us another coffee."

Dahlia made the lattes, and up the stairs they went.

"Oh my! The blues and greens of the water are so incredible, the skyline is amazing. Look at all the boats. I could have left, never seeing this. Thank you, Ben. I am going to miss this—and you." Dahlia giggled. "Last night, you joked that fun follows you around. I am starting to think it might be true. I could have used someone like you during my deployment in Fallujah. Whoops, we agreed . . . no more war talk. You are like a refreshing Caribbean breeze."

She squeezed Ben's hand. Dahlia's touch was electric.

Her phone rang. "Hi, Ben, what do you know? Hmm, really, are you sure? So, I must move quickly and see what is possible—yes, yes, I know. It would be great if we could spend some time here. You would love it. But . . . where to stay . . . that is the issue. Let me see what I can do, and we can talk in an hour or two. I am packed, ready to go, and that might still be what must happen. I love you too . . . Call you soon. Bye-bye."

Dahlia had two hours to make a second attempt to find housing. Knowing the odds were long, she retreated to her room. Ben stayed on the roof, staring at the ocean. He wondered about the option of renting Kevin and Margaret's condo, but he was wise enough to question the decision.

He decided to let the chips fall as they may. Maybe Dahlia would find a vacancy. Maybe she would decide to go to Toronto, snowstorm or not. Que será, será.

He retreated to the balcony to reconnect with his manuscript. He hadn't looked at it in a week. He needed a focused mind, and Dahlia was not conducive for his writing. He went to the kitchen, grabbed a Belikin, and headed back to the rooftop.

A half hour later, when he was about to get his second beer, Dahlia emerged from the steps. "OK, I am headed north. It won't be my first snowstorm and probably not my last. I have looked on every website and called every possible hotel. Do you know a decent cab company, Ben? I need a pickup in about ninety minutes, 1530."

"My neighbor Kevin and his wife had to go back to the US today because of a family issue. I just found out this morning. If you want, I will inquire whether they would rent their condo out for the remainder of January. This is your call."

"Hmm. Let me call Ben." He answered and said he found tickets from Boston to Miami to Belize City round trip, next Wednesday, leaving Sunday.

"Is this a good idea?" Dahlia looked puzzled.

"Why not?" He had taken bigger risks and was certain she had too. He dialed Kevin's number, but there was no answer. He hung up and looked at Dahlia. His phone rang immediately. "Hi, Kevin. No, there isn't a problem. I just wondered if you have any interest in renting your place for the rest of January. There is a party here, some mix-up with my place being double rented, and I thought to ask if your place is available. I understand, Kevin. I could vouch for her; she is a doctor from Toronto."

Ben swallowed hard as he finished that sentence. Their eyes met again. He looked up and took a deep breath, sighed, and said, "OK, Kevin, she will do the formalities with the office. By the way, the water heater is in and working. So, problem solved. Safe travels, Kevin. Goodbye." He turned to Dahlia. "Unit 901 is available, if you think this is a good idea."

"Why does this feel so weird? Guess because the whole trip has been weird. I will call Ben and let him know and get registered at the office."

Dahlia went downstairs to make another call. Ben went to the balcony. Within ten minutes, she reappeared. "The way this trip began makes me wonder if this is a good idea. Oh well, I'm going for it."

Dahlia went to the office and registered for unit 901. The process was simple and quick, done in less than fifteen minutes. She exited the office, keys in hand, and headed up the stairs.

"Well, at least I'm packed. Moving won't take long since it's about ten steps across the hall. We might as well move now."

Ben grabbed two suitcases, and she grabbed a carry-on as they exited 902 and entered 901. The condo was cozy. Kevin and Margaret were spending at least six months a year there, so it was lived in and well equipped.

"Nice view for the two of you." Ben stepped toward the door. "I plan on going to a happy hour later. There's a palapa where people play guitar and watch the sunset. I'll knock on your door. Don't feel obligated. See ya later, Dahlia."

"OK, Ben. I can't thank you enough."

Ben went back home and checked his email, hoping to find options for future months.

He got on a Zoom with his builder and architect. They wouldn't let the builder disturb anything until the investigation was complete, but all the permits and plans were on track. Then he called his insurance company. They said the investigation was wrapping up and builders could start as soon as next Monday.

Ben FaceTimed Louie, but it went unanswered. He called back and left a message. He decided to have a rare third beer. He feared his predisposition to alcoholism even through college and deployments, but this day was different. He was unsettled and confused, which made alcohol feel like an apt companion.

When the time came for happy hour, he passed her door without knocking and went alone to Harry's Hurricane Lounge. Harry's had a crowd. There were twenty to twenty-five people picking guitars of all shapes. Ben slunk into a chair, looking forward to his almond-crusted snapper bites and a fourth Belikin. An island waitress delivered both, making his wishes come true.

The band was playing "Samba Pa Ti." Ben was seeking peace with the world. Succulent food, cold beer, an ocean breeze, and Latin music were his nirvana. Glancing down at the dock, he read one of the beams. "Plant Trees, Save Bees, Punch Nazis." *Good one!*

Swaying with the music, drifting with the tide, watching the sun melt into the horizon, his mind wandered from his childhood, his parents, and college, to Lily and questions about why he was still alone. Dahlia having a Ben of her own rubbed him the wrong way. He ordered a double shot of Jameson.

He cradled his glass in both hands and stared at the dark ocean. *Live in the present, the past is behind you, and you can't see the future.*

He walked the beach before heading home. There was still light escaping from beneath the door of apartment 901. He didn't knock.

The next morning was steeped in a hangover-induced funk. Through his pounding head, he looked around the room. A Monet print of San Giorgio Maggiore from Venice hung on the wall opposite the bed. He and Alison had honeymooned in Venice. It was enough to rouse him from bed. He opened the drapes and thought of Dahlia.

He decided he'd speak to her after coffee and a morning swim.

Dahlia was lying by the pool reading *Pillars of the Earth*. He couldn't get away without her noticing.

"Good morning, Dahlia. Sleep well?"

"Not really. I got stood up."

He nodded but didn't say anything. He took a step back, turned, and dove into the pool, not much caring if he made a splash. He swam several laps until his lungs were burning. He couldn't stop looking up to see if she was still there.

"Can we talk?" he asked, pulling a chair beside hers. She looked at Ben. "Affirmative, Major."

"I should have knocked. I've got my own shit going on, and it got to be too much for me. Besides, your fiancé's coming and . . ." He trailed off.

"I get it, Major!"

"Please stop calling me Major! That part of my life is in the rear-view mirror."

"OK. Sorry for that. Understood. You're not a regular guy, Ben, but that doesn't make you special. You're different, but different can be a plus or a minus. Not sure which it is for you. Arrogance is a sign of faulty intelligence. And your little temper tantrum isn't impressive."

Ben didn't respond. *She sees me for who I am. Flawed.*

"Early on, I thought we could be forty-eight-hour soulmates. Do you believe in soulmates, Ben?"

"Not anymore. My first one divorced me."

Dahlia didn't laugh. "Maybe I've been living in the moment, not thinking about tomorrow, because I was enjoying a new adventure with you. But I know this isn't real life. This is a vacation. I need today to get my coordinates back. Could we have coffee tomorrow morning?"

He felt ambivalent about waiting another day to put closure on their conversation, but he was the one who'd stood her up. "I will knock on your door at 0900. Promise."

He wanted to reach for her hand but caught himself. Ben turned to leave. Suddenly, he was incapacitated as Dahlia gripped his neck with a hold from behind. Then she let go.

"No goodbye, just walk away. Were you raised by wolves or poodles? See you tomorrow or there will be more where that came from."

He walked back to his condo wishing he had never met her.

How could I be so concerned about a relationship with such a short life span? He was miserable and felt stupid.

The next day, he was up with the roosters and out the door running five minutes later, heading north along the beach. The warmth of the sun, the sea-salty air, and the rhythm of the surf created a runner's paradise. He ran for about two miles before turning around.

At 0900 sharp, Ben knocked on her door. Shortly thereafter, Dahlia, phone in hand, motioned him in. He sat down on the couch and waited as she paced.

"Sorry, work stuff." Once again, he was mesmerized by her smile and green eyes. He suggested the Yoga Café.

"Another beautiful day. What a view! So much of my life has been so damn real," Dahlia said. "I need more vacations. Work has dominated my life so long. I can do better."

Ben was unsure of what to say or how to act. They stood in silence amid palm trees.

Finally, Dahlia spoke. "I'm not sure I need to analyze these last two days. I need to go home."

They walked out to a palapa, sat down, and gazed at the ocean, barely speaking.

Back at the condo, she said, "I'm leaving tomorrow. I've told Ben to cancel his flight."

Ben said, "I'll take you to the airport."

He and Dahlia embraced at the top of the stairs. She turned left, he right, and they entered their separate apartments. *No one looks back on their life and remembers the night they got plenty of sleep*, he told himself.

Morning came too quickly. They loaded her luggage on Ben's four-wheeler and arrived at the airport. In silence, he waited as Dahlia checked her luggage.

She turned, walked down the ramp, and disappeared. He contemplated watching her plane lift off but drove north instead. Feeling his phone vibrate, he pulled over to read the text, hoping her flight had changed. The text was from Dahlia. It was blank.

He closed his phone. The palm trees seemed dry and needy. Dust blew in his face as he looked at the clouds covering the sun. He would return to Minneapolis the next morning.

Crazy as the thought was, Ben believed losing his home was worth it because of the time he'd spent with Dahlia. Back at the condo, he took his writings, looked at them for a minute, and tossed them.

3

ABERRATION

The temperature was negative six degrees when Ben deboarded in Minneapolis. He had neglected to unpack his jacket. He shivered on the concourse. He stumbled as he exited the escalator to claim his baggage.

Russ and Twila Curtis, childhood friends of Ben's who had grown up to marry each other, offered him a roof in Maple Grove for February.

He looked forward to seeing Russ and his family. He called to let them know he was spending the night at Louie's and suggested they all go for dinner the following night. They agreed to meet at a favorite supper club.

Russ was still muscular with thick red hair. He dressed conservatively in business wear. Twila remained sassy. She had pearl-white skin that made her look younger than the rest of them. She looked bohemian in a flowing, silky floral-print blouse and dangling turquoise earrings. Louie was wearing a Twins cap, flannel shirt, and khakis. Ben had on the Levi's he'd bought the day after the fire and a black sweater, which was still on loan from Louie.

Ben's subduedness was contagious. Uncomfortable silences were broken only by the clinking of silverware. Everyone felt relieved when the check came.

Louie headed east to Minneapolis. Ben, in a rented Jeep Cherokee, followed Russ and Twila home. Looking at the minus-ten-degree temperature reading on the dashboard, he second-guessed his decision to return to Minnesota in February. *It's only weather.*

Russ and Twila managed a health-club business. They had recently built a home about an hour west of Minneapolis. The somewhat-remote location would be a good place for Ben to write while still having proximity to the city.

I might be a little old for this, Ben thought. *I should have my own place.*

He was greeted by Elias and Leah, whom he hadn't seen for years. Their home was charming. It felt lived in, the way a home should. A stone fireplace surrounded a crackling fire. For a few seconds, he recalled that same sound the night of his house fire.

Russ took Ben downstairs to an area that had a bedroom, dining area, small kitchen, and bathroom. Russ and Twila had designed the space for their elderly parents.

"I feel a little like the crazy uncle who just moved in with relatives that lost the coin toss."

Russ laughed. "Good night, Ben. We'll talk more tomorrow."

Being back felt odd. He couldn't stop thinking about Dahlia's reentry to Canadian life.

Ben's first few days were mildly productive. He started over with trying to develop a story line.

The following week flew by. It was cold, and Ben continued to write. On Friday night, Russ and Twila invited their friend Jill over for dinner and asked Ben to join them.

Russ prepared a curry, naan, tikka masala, and jasmine rice. Twila joked, "I only cook to keep the kids alive." Jill, in her midthirties, was funny, cute, and a couple of miles to the political right of Ben. Jill kicked off the discussion with, "Wealthy people pay most of the taxes. If we dumped all the welfare programs, we'd be doing our country a favor."

Ben said nothing, thinking, *Arguing with a fool only proves there are two.*

The weekend was busy in the Curtis household, and Ben was alone for most of the time. He had good focus and was engaged in productive writing but still questioned whether he would ever finish the novel. On occasion, he found satisfaction in a sentence such as, "Love is a dubious fire, able to warm your heart or destroy your house. You never know which!"

Russ called Ben saying a few of the guys wanted to get together the following weekend. Ben declined, blaming the writing.

While on the phone with Russ, he received a voice mail from a Colorado number.

"Hi, Dr. Raymond. This is Denise Harbin. You might remember me. I was briefly in therapy with you a few years ago. I would appreciate it if you could call me at your convenience. No rush—whenever you can. You have my number. Thank you."

Ben listened to the message again, trying to remember her. Before calling her, he called the clinic to review the records.

He had met with Denise Harbin twice before she relocated to Colorado. Denise had made the appointments in hopes of resolving marital issues. Her husband refused to attend. With that information, Ben returned the call.

"Thank you for calling me, Dr. Raymond. I'm wondering if you remember me."

"Yes, I do, Denise. We met twice before you moved. How can I be of help? I might tell you that I am on a sabbatical and not presently working at the clinic."

"Oh, I am sorry to hear that, because my plans are to return to Minneapolis. I was hoping to be able to see you again in June. Any chance you will be returning to your practice this summer?"

"Sorry, Denise, I am at least a full year from my practice, but the clinic has several excellent therapists once you are back in town. You could schedule an appointment with the administrator to discuss the options."

"That make sense. I am in therapy here and want to stay on track. Not sure you know, but we left Minnesota abruptly when Gary insisted. We relocated to his hometown, near to his parents. I agreed to come, but everything deteriorated once we were in Colorado.

"We separated, and Gary moved in with his parents for a time and continued drinking and using drugs. He became paranoid and delusional. His parents hospitalized him for his safety. When he was released, he moved into the foothills on family land and lived like a hermit until moving in with a woman and her brother. Didn't sound good.

"He would call me every few days, asking for money and begging me to get back together, but his drinking and drug use became worse. He blamed me, his parents, even you for our divorce.

"The last time we talked, he was so angry, it scared me, and I called the police. They couldn't find him. He disappeared several weeks ago. We all just hope he is OK."

"How long has he been missing, Denise?"

"I spoke with him on December 20, and his mother talked to him on the twenty-first. No one has heard from him since. He had plans to go to Idaho, but who knows. Since I have no reason to stay in Colorado, I am planning to return to Minnesota. Sorry, but I must go to work now. I appreciate you calling me back. I will reconnect with the clinic and try to get something scheduled. Thank you again. Goodbye, Dr. Raymond."

"Goodbye, Denise. I wish you the best."

Ben's mind raced. *Could this be the missing link to the puzzle?* He didn't want to overlook any possibility and called the Minneapolis Police Department. He was transferred to a Sgt. Adams. He shared the information, including Denise's number.

Near the end of the call, Sgt. Adams said, "We found an abandoned car in your neighborhood. The car was from Denver, the plates from Iowa. Both the car and plates were stolen. I will follow up and be in touch."

During the second week, Ben continued writing, pleased with his progress but questioning the quality. *February in Minnesota could make anyone an author if they had a pen and paper.* The weather was brutally cold. The ice on the road kept him home, inside, and on task. He plodded forward toward the end of chapter 3.

As he wrote, his thoughts of Dahlia were never far at hand. Sometime a simple refill of coffee or a gaze out the window would result in thoughts of her.

He wrote steadily, often for eight to ten hours a day, but he didn't have a clue if his writing was worth a damn.

Sunday morning was slow and quiet, and he chose to have some coffee alone. There was a voice mail from Sgt. Adams that was brief and to the point: "I have an update for you. Call me."

Ben called immediately and was connected to Sgt. Adams.

"Do you have a few minutes, Mr. Raymond? We are making progress in the investigation. I have spoken to Gary Harbin's ex-wife and parents. They tell me he has been delusional and violent for some time.

"Police in Colorado have detained Mr. Harbin at a cabin owned by a woman and her brother. It's somewhere outside of Durango. I understand Gary had been living there a while. She said her brother and Gary had gone to Minneapolis to collect money on a drug deal gone bad. The police in Durango are interrogating Mr. Harbin. That's what I know. I will be in touch as soon as there is any definitive answer. Do you have any questions, Mr. Raymond?"

Ben didn't have any questions. He sat down, blindsided.

Leah interrupted his thoughts. "Ben, can I come down? Is this too early?"

"Of course, Leah, come down."

Leah was a fresh-faced young woman with a sparkle in her eyes and a smile guaranteed to impact. "Good morning, Ben. Did you have fun last night? Mom and Dad have been laughing all morning. They woke me up. Hate to bug you about this, but I have a project for my AP Psych class and was wondering if I could interview you. If you can't, that's cool. I know you are writing a book. Bet it'll be a good one!"

Bet it won't, Ben thought. "I'd be honored, Leah. You are so busy; I've hardly seen you, and it's been over two weeks. You let me know when, and I am ready and willing."

"Great! How about the day after tomorrow?"

"Perfect. Can't wait."

That afternoon, he did the unimaginable to anyone south of the Mason-Dixon Line by going for a run in fifteen-degree weather. Years ago, Alison, a more avid runner, taught him that it's always about the clothes.

His grandfather used to say, "There isn't any bad weather, only bad clothes." He remembered another Grandpa Ben quote: "You know there are no mental institutions in Norway; we send them to Sweden to teach school." He was funny.

Ben often joked about "running from something all his life," though halfheartedly, he believed that was true. Running had always been a mind-expanding experience. He frequently returned from a run to grab his laptop and jot down notes. Ideas flowed when he was running, and the adrenaline rush never failed him.

Midafternoon, Russ and Twila invited him for a glass of wine by the cozy stone fireplace.

"Time is flying. Three weeks already. I want to thank you. Living with you is an experience I won't forget. When I was desperate, you guys stepped up. This wine is great, by the way. What is it?"

"Zinfandel. Napa Black Goose," Twila said, looking at the bottle.

"Mmm, delicious. A toast to the only family I would let adopt me. Don't answer now, think about it, talk it over—just know I'm available."

Russ took a phone call and briefly left the room. "I have to run to the club. Shouldn't be long."

"Want company, Russ?"

"Temp is fifteen, you're in the company of my beautiful wife, sitting by the fire, enjoying fine wine. Even I know better. Stay, Ben. I will be back soon."

"So, Ben, how are you really? Are you doing OK?" Twila asked almost immediately.

Ben thought about brushing off the question, but after seeing her expression, he was embarrassed. "It's been tough, some parts tougher. The divorce was by far the worst. I expected Afghanistan and Iraq to be difficult, and I was somewhat prepared, although in hindsight, there isn't really a way to mentally prepare for war.

"When I was overseas, Alison was my lifeline to sanity. Coming home and having our marriage disintegrate was overwhelming. The divorce crushed me and put me in a tailspin. I tried everything; nothing worked. I've always known the blame was mostly mine. I never put in the work, just thinking everything would happen."

Realizing he had been staring at the floor for a few seconds, Ben stood up and looked to escape. A second wave of emotion hit him. He walked to Twila and put his arms around her. He held her close in silence. Time stopped. Neither knew how long.

Finally, they both sat down looking at each other until Ben said, "I guess I needed that question to be asked. You sure got a response. One I wasn't prepared to give. Living alone kept me from getting in touch with myself. There hasn't been anyone to ask those questions."

Twila said, "Listening to you is a reminder of how few real conversations exist in my and Russ's world. We are so busy being busy, we never have talks like this. Life is so interesting. Sometimes I think about how young Russ and I were when we met. My life is settled, complacent . . . I wonder what I've missed."

"Your life represents all that is good. My life has been chaotic. I used to think that people who said they were happy had learned a way to accept mediocrity. I was wrong. I crave what you have. Stability, love, family, contentment."

"Well, there are pluses and minuses. I have devoted my life to Russ and our kids. What might I have done if I could have followed my dreams? It is impossible not to think *what if*. You and I have time to right the ship, change course, or jump ship. We are in control of our own destiny, right?"

Pouring more wine, they regressed to safer topics, talking about their kids, traveling, their business, Leah going to college, Lily graduating in June, and them becoming empty nesters. The uncomfortable box of worms was on hold.

When the wine was gone and Russ hadn't returned, they called it a night, both feeling a little exposed. Their friendship had reached a higher plane. The conversation had forced them to rethink their chosen paths. For tonight, that was enough. They hugged and said good night. Ben went downstairs feeling unfinished.

He saw a text from Alison. "Please call me when you can. We must talk."

Not up for it, he responded, "Will call you tomorrow."

The next day, there was another text from Alison. "Please call ASAP."

"We must talk about something important," she said when he finally returned her call. "Could you meet with my therapist and me this morning at eleven? She and I agreed that this meeting was the best way to handle this. Can you?"

"Give me a hint, Alison. Is it medical, Lily, or something else?"

"Please, Ben, just do this. Don't make me beg. It's important."

"OK, OK, I will. Give me the address . . . 420 Park Lane, Suite 4, Wayzata. Got it. I'll be there."

Arriving at 420 Park Lane, he saw Alison's car. He put his hand on the hood. Cold. She had been there for a while. Ben surmised that her therapist must have wanted to plan for his arrival.

Entering Suite 4, he was greeted by an assistant, who took his coat and offered coffee, tea, or water. He declined.

Sixty seconds later, a woman introduced herself. "Mr. Raymond, I am Dr. Irene Schwartz. Thank you for coming. Please join Alison and me."

Alison was obviously upset, her eyes red and her face flushed. Ben put his hand on her shoulder and sat down next to her.

Dr. Schwartz spoke first. "This is a difficult meeting for many reasons. Because Alison and I have talked about this previously, she has convinced me you will be cooperative and able to handle this new information. This was counter to my judgment, and I wanted to have security standing by. However, I have agreed to do this Alison's way. I have instructed my assistant to call 911 if I request. I want to be completely up front. Do you have any questions?"

"No. Let's get to it. Alison, what is this about? Security? Really, you can't be afraid of me."

Dr. Schwartz said, "Alison and I have talked this through, and she wants to take the lead. I will intervene only if necessary. Alison, are you ready?"

Trembling, Alison began, "Ben, I will never expect you to forgive me or even understand what I am about to tell you. This story goes back over twenty years to when you were in Iraq."

Alison's voice was cracking, and she was trembling.

"When I was admitted to the hospital, you were granted an emergency leave to come home. You understood the reasons were because of the stress and fears of you being in a war zone. Those facts are true. I was a nervous wreck for months, hardly sleeping, having nightmares of you being killed. However, there is a larger piece that you never knew."

Alison began sobbing uncontrollably, and Dr. Schwartz asked her if she wanted to continue. She did.

"The last straw was . . . the last straw was me cheating on you. I-I-I slept with a coworker and was so overwhelmed with guilt, I wanted to kill myself. You were the one in danger, and I was so weak. When I didn't come to work, my boss sent the police to do a welfare check, and I was hospitalized."

Ben was shell-shocked. He could count his pulse in his forehead.

Alison continued, "It was one time, only once, totally unplanned, and the coworker quit and moved away. I never saw him again."

Unable to contain himself, Ben said, "Why are you telling me this now, years after the divorce? Why didn't you keep this secret? Relieving your guilt at my expense!"

"It gets worse. There is more. After being released from the hospital, you and I resumed our marriage. Soon after, we found out I was pregnant. It was bittersweet news because we both wanted children, but the timing wasn't the best."

Ben felt nauseous hearing Alison's next words.

"I didn't know who the father was. That's why I was so unstable and talked about having an abortion. You felt strongly that we should have the baby. After Lily was born, I requested a DNA test. You are not Lily's biological father."

Of all the possibilities that had consumed his mind, never in his wildest imagination could he have guessed this one. He was overtaken with emotion and shock.

Needing to escape the madness, he got up, walked out of the office, and went to his car. Sitting there, he begged to be awakened from this nightmare. He sat for several minutes until his phone rang.

"This is Dr. Schwartz, Ben. Can you come back to the office?"

He responded, "Not sure. Less sure I want to."

"As difficult as it may be to understand, there is more to the story, and if you are unwilling, I will be forced to call the police. There is information you must hear. Out of respect for you and Alison, I am hoping you will return, but I need an answer."

Fighting all his instincts, Ben said, "I'll come back."

Alison looked like death warmed over, and for the first time in his life, he ignored her pain.

He was a bundle of confusion, hurt, and anger. Grasping at words, he said, "Isn't this enough for one day?"

Dr. Schwartz began by saying, "I fully understand the trauma of this news, Mr. Raymond. There is another fact you must know. Lily's biological father was killed in a car crash in California six months after she was born. He never knew about the pregnancy."

He was done. He needed to be alone. Never in his life had he been more discombobulated. He wanted out and said so. "I am leaving. Anything else? Do not communicate this information to Lily under any circumstances. She deserves better." He got up to leave.

Dr. Schwartz said, "I need to know you are safe and won't harm—"

Ben interjected before she could finish. "I am safe, and so is everyone else. I don't need your advice about how to deal with this, OK?"

To Alison, Ben said, "You were right. This is unforgivable. This is beyond betrayal. Living with your lies and deceit is your punishment. I feel sorry for you."

He left. His emotions rotated from pain to rage every few seconds. He sat in his car for a time before driving away. His heart raced; his hands were shaking. Deciding there was no way to return to the Curtis home, he drove to a nearby hotel and checked in for the night.

The next morning after two shots of double espresso, his concern was for Lily. He needed Alison's reassurance. He returned to the Curtises' empty house and went to his room to call Alison. *After deceiving me for twenty years, who knows what she is capable of. I can't leave anything to chance.*

She answered, saying, "I understand how you must feel, and I accept that you must hate me. It's what I deserve—"

Ben interrupted, "You have no idea how I feel. I am concerned about Lily. This information must not be shared with her. I don't know what to think. She is a victim of your lie. Do not promise unless you can keep it. Can you make this promise?"

"I can. I have lived with guilt, destroyed our marriage, and have carried this burden for over twenty years. I will never share this information with anyone. I will die first."

"I have nothing more to say. Goodbye."

He heard an upstairs door slam. His life was forced into another transition as he heard Leah's voice.

"Are you ready for me?"

Almost incapacitated, Ben was hardly ready for anyone. He had totally forgotten about his appointment with Leah. Options escaped him, so he put on his game face.

"Sure enough, Leah. Come on down."

They sat on the couch facing each other. Preferring to listen, not having to think, Ben said, "We've hardly had a chance to talk. I don't want to ask you all those boring questions like what you are going to study in college. Just tell me two good things about your life today."

"Wow, Ben, that might have been harder some days, but not today. I've been dating this guy, he has kind of a weird name, Gunnar. He is so kind and considerate. We love hanging out. Second thing, dance. After school, I have dance. I flat-out love, love, love it. That's my two today. What are your two today?"

He wished the question had come on any other day. "Today, I appreciate your family for welcoming me during a difficult time. Second, as you know, I am attempting to write a novel and love being able to do something I enjoy. That's mine. Thanks for asking, Leah. Now, what about that interview?"

Leah interviewed; Ben answered in a trance. It was a brief escape from reality. Then he was relieved to, once again, be alone.

The last week passed quickly. Everyone in the Curtis household was busy. Ben took relief in solitude. He was anxious to leave. His mind was cluttered with painful memories, and the only peace he found was thinking about Dahlia. Knowing that was a dead end didn't matter. Dahlia was a precious memory, of which he had too few. Writing was impossible. He was catatonic.

He would be transitioning the next day. The plan was to leave early, at 5:00 a.m., so he could be in Kansas City by early afternoon. Ben said goodbye the night before. He smiled, doing what he was good at, camouflaging his pain. Then he disappeared.

MITIGATION

Driving south, his mind was blank. He was fatigued. Outside Mason City, unable to keep his eyes open any longer, Ben pulled into a Days Inn. He took three Advil from the packets he bought in the lobby and collapsed, not rousing again until a knock on his door announced that it was 2:00 p.m., past time to check out.

The home he'd be staying at in Kansas City belonged to a military friend who had served with him in Afghanistan. Retired Sgt. Major José Rivera was living in Kansas City with his wife, Barbara. The last time Ben had seen José, José was being medevaced from a firefight. Ben cranked the volume of Tom Waits's "Cold Water," stared at the highway, and mumbled along to the song.

The reservation on his February rental car had expired. He traded it in for a BMW 435. His first stop was 10 Water Street. Parking in front of his lot, he looked at the hole where his house used to stand. That house had been 115 years old, historic, and full of character. He'd put an offer in five minutes after passing through the front door.

Now, there were foundation walls and a poured concrete floor where that home used to be. Winter had slowed the progress. Driving away, Ben was ambivalent about the status of the construction. Before Belize, he was energized to build a home with desirable comforts and idiosyncrasies. He was installing sliding metal barn doors that would allow for openness and privacy. He ordered a Viking cooktop and oven, a claw-foot porcelain soaking tub, and a large hammered-bronze farmhouse-style kitchen sink. He insisted on a third-floor loft with a glass bubble ceiling surrounded by a balcony view of the city skyline behind Bde Maka Ska. He thought of watching weather, particularly snowflakes, from his new loft next Christmas. Ben loved wind, rain, and active weather. He was having two fireplaces installed. He appreciated an eye-level fire during Minnesota's cooler seasons.

Now, the construction hardly provided a speck of relief for him. He had lost interest in the project and felt relieved to be leaving town. *Nothing matters much today.*

Heading south on I-35, he was reminded of the training trips he had made to San Antonio. Ben was a psychological officer assigned to the army's elite Fifth Special Forces Group. He was cross trained as a medic. Fort Sam Houston near San Antonio was where medical staff received training. He wasn't keen on this type of training, but it was the army's way. The Pentagon never asked for his opinion.

Music was his companion on road trips. He used an eclectic mix of tunes as coping devices. Music got him through stretches of boring geography and night drives when it was too dark to see the scenery. On his way to Kansas City, he hoped music would bring back positive memories. He remembered the *Steel Wheels* CD was perfect to get through Oklahoma. Because Ben had lost all his music in the fire, Russ gave him downloads instead.

He listened to the Traveling Wilburys, Bob Dylan's *Oh Mercy*, Neil Young's *Freedom*, Los Lobos's *How Will the Wolf Survive?*, ZZ Top's *Eliminator*, Steve Earle's *Guitar Town*, Prince's *1999*, and Patsy Cline's greatest hits.

He thought about how he and José had hardly spent any time together stateside. He looked forward to being with someone who understood the value of keeping secrets. Not talking was a strength, not a weakness. José understood the concept of bare-bones soldiers. Pertinacity disappears. Bullshit disappears. Real dominates. That environment was José's domain. *He was better at war than I was.*

A pheasant flying across the freeway brought Ben back to the present. He was beginning to view his life as an outsider. He was realizing that his loneliness was a result of his own decisions. Blaming others or bad luck wasn't working. He knew that he needed to change his behavior. The question was *how*.

He was listening to Patsy Cline as he passed a *Kansas City 82 miles* road sign. In the bright Missouri sunshine, Patsy was "Walking After Midnight." He tried to sing along.

This would be his first trip to the Rivera home. José had recently retired from the army. Barbara was an anesthesiology RN. José Jr. was a freshman at Mizzou. They were a one-and-done family. For the first time, Ben and José would be wearing civilian clothes together. In honor of José, Ben switched from Patsy to Los Lobos. *Music is my medication.*

Twenty minutes later, with Siri's help, he saw 227 Lilac Lane. As he slid into their driveway, he felt proud for José and his family. The Riveras had spent many years living in military housing. Now they were living the American dream. José and Barbara had built a new house.

José's parents had always been employed, but never retired and never owned their own home. They didn't live long enough to see their son's new home.

Talk about a welcome. He felt as if he were returning on VE or VJ Day. There was a familiar message over the garage: *De Oppresso Liber.* The front door opened before he could get out of the car. "Free the Oppressed," the Fifth SFG's motto, brought an unexpected smile to his face.

Barbara and José were standing in the garage with a drum and bugle playing an unrecognizable marching song that would make John Philip Sousa spin in his grave. José in shorts, muscle shirt, and his Fifth Special Forces beret, Barbara in a Hawaiian grass skirt and two coconuts. José looked like "Mr. KC," bronze and toned. Barbara looked happy and Hawaiian.

Their welcome was a shot of adrenaline to Ben's state of mind. Ben, Barbara, and José all hugged and kissed each other simultaneously.

After moving his luggage inside, the trio moved to the backyard gazebo. José had fired up his grill. Large comfy chairs, a wood-burning fireplace, and room-temperature Guinness awaited José and Ben. The room was a soldier's heaven.

"God, it's good to see your ugly mug again. Last night, Barbara and I were so excited we could hardly sleep. You look great, Ben. Well, honestly, you look fair, and prettier than I remember. Where the hell have you been the past few years? I expected more of you."

I let you down.

They were laughing. José had a charm that allowed people to feel good about anything, complimentary or not. He had a disarming demeanor that was on the right side of everything. He exemplified honor, justice, and compassion. Ben witnessed José's overflow of affection and emotion. José was laughing, singing, dancing. He was a self-contained party. Ben was reminded why he loved this guy.

I haven't been a good friend to this good friend.

Both hid tears when they hugged. It was too early into their reunion for that display.

Ben, José, and Barbara shared a festival of food, music, and conversation. Ben thought José and Barbara were like canned ham, always ready. José and Barbara danced and forced him to join them on the gazebo floor.

The three moved, swayed, and hotfooted to Santana's "Oye Cómo Va" and "Soul Sacrifice." They did a slow circle dance to "Black Magic Woman."

Ah, Ben thought, *panacea for my soul.* He kissed Barbara's hand and planted a second kiss on the top of José's head.

Discussions on family updates, Ben's writing, Barbara's job at the VA, and their house-building projects in Kansas City and Minneapolis consumed the next few hours. The conversation was enhanced by margaritas, barbecued ribs, sweet corn, and key lime pie.

It was 2100 before anyone noticed.

"Please allow me to clean up. We can do this again tomorrow, but if it continues for the next thirty days, we might need new livers," Ben said.

José offered to help him with KP after a bathroom break.

When José left the room, Barbara said, "I am so pleased you are here, Ben. José talks about you all the time. Your time together will be good for him. Don't get me wrong, José is happy. I just know there are conversations you and he can have that *only* you and he can have. We love you, Ben. Thank you for connecting with us. It's been a while. José often wondered why you didn't call more."

I haven't been a good friend.

The next morning, he checked his emails, had coffee, and talked with José about the upcoming days.

Coffee with José was a privilege. Ben pondered growing up with a brother. Maybe with a brother, he would have navigated his family stuff better.

They talked about the upcoming days. José planned to visit José Jr. at college for a couple of days and invited Ben. The offer was genuine; however, he needed to write; his deadline was only eight months away. José planned to leave the day after tomorrow and return in three days, after spending some time with his freshman son.

Ben found secluding, researching, writing, and dealing with details of his home construction slightly rejuvenating. He was also communicating by email with Lily. He hoped that when she returned to Minneapolis, they could live together for the month of June. There were a few irons in the fire, but he was pursuing the idea.

After a day in Kansas City, the Rivera residence seemed like home.

That evening, José and Barbara had to attend a birthday party for a friend. They invited Ben, but he knew he needed to be alone. The bombshell that he wasn't Lily's biological father was weighing on him.

Tired of writing, he watched the movie *Stockholm*, a true account of a bank robbery and hostage situation that resulted in Stockholm syndrome.

The next morning, he went to the kitchen. Barbara was sitting at the table having breakfast.

"Good morning, Ben. Coffee, some breakfast? José left early, will call you later, didn't see any reason to wake you."

"Was hoping to catch him before he left. Junior sounds like an impressive young man. Good parenting, I'd say. Never happens by accident. Listen, I know you have a job, don't want to hold you up. I can find something to eat later."

"I am working ten to six today, so I will be here for a while. Why not join me?"

He agreed and sat down with a Belgian waffle topped with bananas and blueberries. "This is delicious. My compliments to the chef."

"I love waffles but haven't made them in weeks. Thought I would be a good hostess this morning. Glad you like them. It is comforting to hear that you have a good life going, Ben. Your transition to an author is amazing. José and I are in a book club. We'd love to pick yours up someday. José showed the book club some pictures of the two of you. They were surprised; José never talks about the army. I love the one picture of the two of you standing next to a sign reading 'Mazar-i-Sharif.' You probably remember that, right?"

Ben felt a shiver down his back and a bead of perspiration running from his temple. True to form, he hid what was happening as his stomach churned and body tingled. He was skilled at concealing, and conceal he did. But he knew concealing was unhealthy. That was a change. *How can I change this sick behavior?*

He said, "Yes, I remember; that was an interesting place. Would like to see the picture after José gets home. We could talk about it then."

"José never really talks about being in Afghanistan. I know there must have been some traumatic times for you guys. To be honest, I've chosen to leave it alone."

"I think most soldiers separate war from life at home because there isn't any common thread." He took a small risk. "I have my demons too. An occasional nightmare. From what I see, you and José have a wonderful marriage. José adores you. He is such a solid person. But if there are issues, I would get professional help. I'm sure there are good options at the VA."

Barbara said, "On occasion, José has nightmares too. They have decreased over the years. He says, 'Old tapes.' Going fishing is therapeutic for him. He goes for two to three days along the Mississippi and always comes back relaxed. He'd like to take you. Be prepared. José always laughs about you not being a fan of nature. He quotes you as saying you'd 'rather have pink eye than go camping.'

"Listen, I have a job to do. Must hustle or will be late. You should visit the VA sometime while you are here."

Barbara jumped up, blew Ben a kiss, and disappeared.

He was writing when José and José Jr. wanted to FaceTime. Junior reminded Ben of José when he'd met José decades ago. Ben experienced something uniquely special about seeing his friend's son. The joy of watching José's genes in the face of a young man was delightful. The three talked about their desire to get together with Lily sometime.

For the next few days, he continued to write and was closing in on the end of chapter 4. He was preoccupied with writing, which he thought was a miracle. He was determined to finish by the December deadline, whether good, bad, or ugly. His last sentence for the day was, "Do I ever cross your mind? You seem to reside in mine."

He witnessed how spending time with his son was like nutrition for José. He was an engaged father, committed to making a difference. His relationship with his son inspired Ben, now more than ever. He vowed to keep the truth from Lily. The truth seemed evil. However, Ben was beginning to challenge that concept. *I have been my daughter's only father. Is the truth that bad? Am I making it about me again?*

Over the next couple of weeks, he continued writing. When he needed a break, the Riveras showed him the hot spots, such as the Negro Leagues Baseball Museum where he watched films of Satchel Paige and Jackie Robinson, "The Wettest Block in the USA" distillery tours, the East Bottoms district, art galleries, the National World War I Museum and Memorial, and restaurants showcasing unique local cuisine. Ben joked about staying another month.

Approaching the final week in March, José asked him to go on a three-day fishing expedition along the Mississippi. He set Ben up by saying, "I know you'd rather have pink eye, but come on, man, you and me, three days. Remember when we used to talk about doing this when we were in 'Stan?"

"If you promise I only have to do this once and you will never ask me to do it again or tell anyone I did it! Promise? Let me see your hands, no fingers crossed. OK. Deal—once!"

They loaded up the Chevy with gear, food, beer, Cuban cigars, a generator, and items Ben could not identify and scurried down a river road. The destination was one of José's hidden campsites. The three-hour ride was a lazy Huck Finn trek. They stopped for lunch, a red-eye beer, and snacks. Soon after, they set up camp within ten feet of the mighty Mississippi. They were isolated from the real world, evidenced by a single bar of cell phone service.

Determined to make the best of his onetime experience, Ben admitted that if he had to camp and fish, José was the man with whom to do it. He had knowledge and stuff that Ben would never own or understand. Other than the tent and sleeping bag, he was at his friend's mercy. José was the brains of the operation.

Following a tasty dinner of fingerling potatoes, grilled chicken, and naan, they relaxed by the fire, watching the river flow by until they were talked out. They doused the fire, got into the heated tent, and settled in for the night.

Ben said, "This is the finest tent and most comfortable bed I have ever slept on in the wild. It's soft, José. But understand, I will never do this again."

Both laughed and fell asleep mesmerized by the sound of the river.

The air was cool, about forty degrees. The heater kept the tent temperature around fifty, perfect for sleeping.

The next morning, José started a crackling fire and had a pot of coffee waiting as Ben came out of the tent. *Will a crackling fire always remind me?*

"Fishing will be good today. We will have a royal Mississippi dinner of catfish, black-eyed peas, and roasted carrots. All we need is catfish."

They fished all day, talking about life, liberty, and the pursuit of women, sometimes combined with happiness, sometimes not. Ben watched with an admiration tinted with envy whenever José talked about Barbara.

José caught fifteen catfish to Ben's four. They released many and returned with a few for the evening feast. Ben was reminded of his dad's words: "If you kill something, be prepared to eat it." He was starving, and José's cooking was marvelous. Seasonings and olive oil produced results mirroring that of a five-star restaurant. José was the master chef the Mississippi riverbank.

After dinner, relaxing by the river, the two soldiers talked philosophically. Sipping an IPA, José said, "Ever wonder how the war changed you, amigo? I mean, had you and I never seen what we saw, would we be different than we are? Know what I mean, Ben? Can you have thoughts like this, or are officers' brains wired differently?"

"Heavy question, mi amigo. Officers need some time to think to give the answer your question deserves."

The only sounds for two to three minutes were those of the fire and the river. Ben was uncomfortable, unsure of what to say and what not to say. He had zero experience talking about the war, even with himself. However, with Dahlia, he'd shared tidbits about his family, and she hadn't run away. Or had she?

Finally, Ben said, "My problems existed before the army, but I am different. I am more afraid and less afraid. More afraid because I have seen what people can do. Less afraid because I survived and somehow lost some fear along the way. War is a disease given to the young. We were young.

"When I was a kid, I shot a bird, and my mother read me the riot act. She said, 'What did that bird do that gave you the right to kill it?' I stopped shooting birds. Two years later, I shot a rabbit and proudly showed my dad. He said, 'If you want to hunt, hunt, but be prepared to eat anything you kill,' adding, 'Never kill for fun.' Minus alcohol, Dad was a kind man.

"A rabbit was the last creature I ever killed, and that was when I was ten. I started target shooting instead. In basic training, I was an M4 sharpshooter in my company and earned a plaque labeling me 'Lethal.' Odd, for a man who had killed one bird and one rabbit and regretted both."

Ben continued, "In Afghanistan, you and I saw shit that scars the soul. We were there to do a job, and we protected each other. In my naive mind, my intentions were honorable. Thousands of Americans died on 9/11. There were threats of more attacks. Right or wrong, I was motivated to prevent those from happening."

"You couldn't have said it better, Ben. You and I lived parallel lives in 'Stan. I feel similarly about war. Is it OK to have this talk?"

"You are the only person on this planet that knows what we did. I couldn't have this talk with anyone else, nor would I. I have never talked about combat with anyone."

José said, "So much is cloudy, my wandering mind hasn't done me much good. Being wounded, morphed up, so much is fuzzy. After all this time, I still don't know what was real and what I imagined. Dreams come and go; some are not what I remember. It's fucked up. What do you remember about Mazar-i-Sharif? Tell me, my friend. Tell me like I wasn't there."

"I'll try. After landing at the airfield, we were hustled into a hangar. First Sgt. Juan Carlos Luna walked in and said, 'Buenos dias, chicos y chicas, for you illiterates, that's 'Good morning, boys and girls.' And if any of you are thinking I am politically incorrect, I couldn't care less what you think. This mission isn't about correctness.'

"Sgt. Luna laid it on the line: 'We are here to kill Bin Laden's friends who planned 9/11, attacked my hometown, and killed 2,753 people in the WTC, 265 passengers on planes, and 125 in the Pentagon. That'd be enough for me, but it's more personal because they killed my brother too. He was an electrician in the South Tower. The murders of innocent people will always motivate Americans to right a wrong. You are here because Americans want you here. Don't disappoint them.'

"'We are going to honor the people who died on September 11 by showing those low-life bastards how America responds to our citizens being murdered. When the Taliban meet this group of American warriors, they'll stop worrying about little girls going to school and they won't be beheading people for flying kites.

"'Make no mistake, gentlemen, our mission is clear, anyone carrying a weapon is our enemy. Kill 'em all, let God sort it out. You were sent here because you are the baddest motherfuckers on this planet. I expect you to show the world what happens to those who murder Americans. We have a score to settle, and settle it we will. I pity those bastards. Hooah!'

"Then he handed out playing cards with pictures of the towers in flames. He added, 'Leave one card on every dead enemy. That's an order. I want the world to understand why we came here. I hope you run out of cards. Get ready to rock and roll. Be brave. I know you are prepared.'

"Then he turned and walked away."

He couldn't believe he recalled the words verbatim. Those memories were vivid, yet unvisited.

"At 0300, we were aboard our choppers. Our first mission was to capture a Taliban leader, and my responsibility was to interrogate him for intel. We got him just before daybreak, snatched him from his bed, not a shot fired, and moved to a secure area to be airlifted. The mission was like clockwork. The intel was perfect. Arriving at our dust-off zone, we were ambushed by a force of seventy to one hundred people. All hell broke loose.

"There was a three-pronged attack from pickups with large-caliber machine guns coming at us and other units attempting to outflank us. Because our position was difficult to defend, the main force moved a couple of hundred yards to the rear to engage the enemy from higher ground. Our three-man team was ordered to stay put and secure the prisoner. Cobras were on their way.

"The enemy was raking us with machine gun and following the main force. A small unit attacked our perimeter with grenade launchers and small arms. They were after our prisoner. PFC Stevens was hit in the upper leg and bled profusely. After applying a tourniquet, I morphed him up. Two more RPGs landed in our area. You and I took cover behind large rocks with shrapnel flying. The noise was deafening." His entire body was sweating.

"You and I were pinned down with a prisoner and a seriously wounded buddy. We were outgunned and outmanned, about to be overrun, and the Cobras were twelve minutes out. We had our M4s, grenades, and bayonets. The enemy was coming straight at us. Sweat was running down my face into my eyes. I could barely see. I was paralyzed with fear. Wiping my brow, I saw a hole in my fatigue pant leg and a growing bloodstain. A piece of shrapnel had lodged somewhere, but I had no pain.

"Should I continue?"

José said nothing, just nodded. Ben started again.

"You said, 'They've almost got us surrounded, the poor bastards.' Your confidence was riveting. I didn't understand, but, man, I was grateful for you. Then you said, 'We're separating and circling behind them.' The look on your face, followed by your voice. 'Or we are dead.' You gave orders. 'Stay low, and on three, roll to your left twenty yards. I am going right twenty and look for cover behind those assholes. Our only chance is to outfox these fuckers. One, two, three!'

"Without thought, I rolled left for who-knows-how-many yards. The noise was incredible. Suddenly, I was free from rounds ricocheting off the ground. Low crawling with my face in the dirt, dragging my M4, I moved ahead for what seemed like an hour but was probably forty-five seconds. I could hear AK-47 fire behind me."

Ben looked at José. The look said, *Keep talking.*

"Looking up, I saw the best face of my life—you, grinning and saying, 'It's payback time. We are going to hit 'em fast to keep 'em from getting to Stevens. There are six to eight targets. Doesn't matter. Kill 'em all.'"

Ben stopped talking, took a deep breath, and looked at José.

"You can't stop, not now. Tell it all. I need to know."

Ben started again. "You were running the show. I just listened and followed orders. You said, 'Your kill zone is from twelve to three o'clock, mine is nine to twelve. This isn't what you signed up for, sir, but we've gotta move. Shoot to kill. Don't miss. Every round finds a target.' The sergeant was commanding the officer.

"We zigzagged for about twenty yards. The Taliban were still firing at our old location. You said, 'Remember once we open up, the secret's out. In the words of Cher, "It's all or nothing." If we don't zap 'em in thirty seconds, Stevens is dead, and we are too. Move until you see a target. Get ready to rock and roll. Put your M4 on auto, pick a target, squeeze off short bursts once you hear me engaging. Check your magazines. You're going to need to reload. Let's go! Follow me. Hooah!'

"I charged behind you on the right, seeing two enemy troops. Sweat was running out of every one of my pores. Running, I wiped my brow. My fingers were red with blood from my leg, and the two enemy turned toward me. You started to rock and roll. I fired eight to ten rounds. You were leading, and I followed. Two more enemy soldiers popped up on my right. I dropped to the ground and fired two bursts, emptying my magazine. I slammed a full magazine, jumped up, and followed you again.

"Two enemy retreated toward our former position close to where PFC Stevens and our prisoner were located. You gave chase, disappearing over a hill in pursuit. I heard rapid shooting and silence. When I got over the side of the hill, I saw you on the ground bleeding. You looked up and said, 'Got 'em, sir, but one winged me.' You had taken a round in the chest. The prisoner was unhurt. Stevens was unconscious. The main recon force returned and secured our perimeter. In less than ten minutes, two choppers were on the scene, and we were out of harm's way. Stevens survived, the prisoner was turned over to intel, and you were in surgery. I had a few stitches on my leg and a scratch on my cheek. Story over." Ben took a deep breath, sighed, and said, "This was way too real. Never again."

José looked serious. "I never need to hear that story again. You must have a camera in your brain. If you do, erase it. It's over and done, Ben. You cleared my head. Holy shit. Did I really make the Cher comment?"

"Yes, José, you did. Unbelievable."

José shook his head in disbelief.

Ben felt a sense of something and hoped it was relief. Maybe their two damaged souls would have a chance to heal. He had never relived that story. *Never again!*

He had something more to say. "PFC Stevens and I owe you our lives. We would have been KIA. You saved our lives. I called Stevens last week to share we were getting together. We had never talked since 'Stan."

"He said, 'Tell José that my wife, son, and daughter are forever grateful. Share our love with José and his family. Because of him, I had a second chance.'"

He looked at José. Neither spoke. José looked at Ben and then down. He reached over and took Ben's hand, looking him in the eye.

As Ben crawled into his sleeping bag, he was aware of what he had not shared with José. He had taken steps forward but still held back. His left knee ached, reminding him of the piece of shrapnel that was behind his patella. He moved his hand to his right cheek and felt the scar from the flesh wound of an AK-47 round that grazed his face. One inch to the left would have been curtains.

He resisted the second memory that was so horrific, he denied its existence. Bits and pieces were exposed unpredictably, but the nightmare had been pushed deep, never completely surfacing. He closed his eyes, seeking peace.

"Wake up! Wake up! Ben! Ben!" José was screaming, shaking Ben by the shoulders.

Ben was shaking and perspiring, as if in a trance. José was on top of him, holding him down, trying to control him. Again, he said, "Wake up, Ben. Wake up!"

José turned on the lantern and saw blood running down Ben's chin. He had bitten his tongue. Grabbing a towel, he put it on Ben's face while continuing to hold him in place. Thirty seconds later, Ben calmed and opened his eyes.

A minute passed in silence before José said, "You're scaring the hell out of me. I'm guessing a nightmare. Am I right? Are you OK, Ben? Talk to me."

Ben muttered, "Yeah, a nightmare. I'm OK. Have had the same one a couple of hundred times."

He sat up, looked at José, and wiped the mixture of blood and sweat from his face. "I'm a basket case, José, and I'm about to tell you why, if you want to hear it."

"I want to know. Tell me."

"When deployed to Iraq, I was interrogating a prisoner in Fallujah. The temp was over one hundred, and my unit had been in firefights for over twenty-four hours. Everyone was exhausted. I asked a new guy to guard the prisoner so I could grab some water. I heard commotion and ran back. The prisoner had jumped our guy and was trying to get his weapon. Another soldier shot him. If only I would have asked the new guy to get me water, it wouldn't have happened.

I caused his death. He didn't need to die. His face, his eyes remain with me. I accept the nightmares as a punishment for taking his life."

José said, "Forgiveness is essential for all of us. You know all the words I could say. War is one big mistake. I have one wish: forgive yourself, Ben. It's the only way out."

After José fell asleep, Ben got up, sat by the river, and watched the sunrise. He had relived the nightmare, once asleep, once awake. He couldn't tell the difference.

Ben and José never revisited their last night on the river. Driving back, Ben admitted that sleeping on the ground reminded him of combat. He cranked some Led Zeppelin, leaned back, and fell asleep. *I have let someone else in. Did either of us benefit?*

José said, "We're home. You must not have slept much last night. I slept like a baby."

Ben only had a couple of days more in Kansas City. He wanted to finish chapter 4 before heading north. He isolated himself and finished the task. That night, he shared his last dinner with Barbara and José before he'd leave in the morning.

As he was packing, he heard a soft knock on the door and Barbara's voice say, "Ben, excuse me, can I come in?"

"Of course, Barbara, just finishing up. About to head north."

Barbara said, "Last night, José told me that some demons were buried by the river. A few months ago, José said he never doubted you in war but was beginning to doubt you in peace. It bothered him. He wondered why you didn't answer his calls. I hope you reconnected."

"Barbara, I learned from my time with José. He is a quality human being. I have work to do. If I can become half the person he is, I will be satisfied. My life has included some bumps, but no more than many people's. I hope to God our time on the river was healing for us. You and José have my respect and admiration. You and José have set a high bar that challenges me to do better."

Ben and José spoke few words on the driveway. They'd said much during the month of March. They gave each other silent hugs, kissed each other's cheeks, and looked into each other's souls with misty eyes. Ben backed out of the driveway and headed west until he reached 35 North. The first sign said *Minneapolis 398 miles.*

5

PEARLS OF WISDOM

Ben didn't welcome the time to think as he headed north. Issues bubbled up as soon as his tires were on the interstate.

He thought about the enemy soldiers who were killed that day. He considered what had happened when their lives ended. They were human beings. They had families. There were parents who lost sons, wives who lost husbands, and children who lost fathers. The man's face flashed across his eyes, and he pulled over and stopped. Ben was nauseous. He opened the window for some fresh air and was mesmerized by the sounds of the speeding traffic.

Did I join the military out of anger? Was it an escape from my family? I own the consequences of war. I chose the army. It didn't choose me.

He surmised that war was the most unnatural experience for a human being: joining the military, heading to war, pretending to have nothing to lose, yet having everything to lose . . . It wasn't normal. He'd been prepared to take everything from another human being who'd been defined as the enemy. For that, he felt self-loathing. His muscles were tight, mouth dry, and jaw clenched. He continued driving.

Ben forced his mind to the month of April and to Julia and Arthur Carlson. Julia was a ninety-eight-year-old woman; Arthur was a ninety-nine-year-old man. They had been married for seventy-five years and were neighbors of Ben's family when he was in the first grade. Because his parents worked, he would go to the Carlsons' house after school.

He had tried to stay in touch with them over the years, sometimes successfully, often not. *There was no excuse for not seeing them more. I need to stop pretending and start being a better person.* Ben had seen them at his mother's funeral three years earlier. Julia and Arthur were in good health, living independently in the same house in Mankato, an hour south of Minneapolis.

When he'd called them after the fire, they'd had a three-way conversation on their landline. Arthur was in the kitchen, and Julia was in the bedroom. "We have four bedrooms and only use two. You are always welcome," they said.

Ben remembered how kind Julia and Arthur were to him as a child. They smiled at him, gave him cookies and milk, and always made him feel welcome. It was always better to go to their home than to his empty one. *I want to do some payback. Years later, I need their support again. Strange how life comes around, some things change, and some things stay the same.*

He decided to stay with them and do this the right way. The last time he'd stopped at their home, he'd had a coffee and left after an hour. Now, he had time and could do the right thing. When he'd asked in January, their words were, "That would be so wonderful, Ben. Please do. And stay as long as you want."

He decided he would move into the Carlsons' home until either he, Arthur, or Julia thought the time was up. January, February, and March were somewhat predictable visits for Ben. He was a little apprehensive about April, but he wasn't about to disappoint them by backing out. He thought he would stay as long as he should.

Julia was a US Army nurse and had met Arthur, a sailor, in 1944 when she was stationed in Pearl Harbor. Arthur was wounded and evacuated from Midway Island after his ship was hit by a torpedo. Recovering, he became head over heels with his nurse, Julia, who wanted no part of his advances. She had received plenty of them from lonely, wounded men.

Arthur was discharged from the hospital and stationed in Hawaii for the remainder of the war. His advances, pursuit, and persistence eventually wore Julia down, and out of sympathy, she agreed to see a movie with him. No one will ever know if it was the movie, *For Whom the Bell Tolls*, or Arthur's charm, but the spark flickered into a flame. Whatever the reason, their world continued to light up for seventy-five years.

They were married in 1945 at the navy chapel on Pearl Harbor. Because Julia was from Minnesota and Arthur was from South Dakota, they moved back to the Midwest and settled in Mankato, where Arthur went to college. GI Bill money paid for college and bought their home. Julia worked as a nurse at the local hospital for decades. Arthur designed snowmobiles for Polaris before retiring. They never had children or found a reason to leave Mankato.

Ben's plan was to drive to Minneapolis, spend the night at Louie's, reconnect with Junior, and head to Mankato the next day. The drive north was more tiring than expected. He was fatigued and hungry. He stopped once for gas and once to grab a burrito supreme at a Taco Bell outside Des Moines. Crossing the Minnesota border, he found solace listening to Smokey Robinson's "The Tears of a Clown."

Entering Minnesota was uplifting. He was home. However, he didn't have a strategy to deal with his excess baggage. He was living minute to minute and committing to change.

His cell rang.

"Hi, Dad. Where are you? I can tell you are on the road."

"Just passing Albert Lea, about ninety miles from touchdown, Lily. How about you?"

"Closing in on midnight, tired, just wanted to hear your voice. Been thinking about June and wanted you to know that I want to live with you. Hope we can swing it. Gotta sleep now. Love you."

"Love you, Lily. Thanks for calling."

It was their first conversation since he'd learned Alison's secret. *Lily must never know.*

Pulling into Louie's driveway was like déjà vu. Junior Walker was on the front step, looking like the Lion King. His ears perked up when he saw the white Beemer. He sprinted toward the car. Junior recognized Ben. Ben got out, and Junior leaped into his arms and licked his ear.

Louie heard the car door and came out. "Hey, Ben, don't think you are getting Junior back. He and I have agreed this is his permanent dwelling. In my will, you get him back if something happens to me."

Ben and Louie greeted each other with bear hugs. "How have you been, my friend?"

"Good. Junior and I have been busy. Lots happening here, will bring you up to speed. You missed some good snowstorms in March. Real doozies. Let's get your luggage."

The weather was typically unpredictable in April. It was close to seventy when Ben crossed the border from Iowa, and snowflakes were falling walking into Louie's house. Every day, every hour could be a different season.

Louie had created enticing aromas. Ben recognized the scent. *Ah, curry, my favorite.* He recalled Louie's Thai green curry with scallops.

Louie brought two Singhas, and they sat down on the couch. Junior came into the room looking confused, jumping between them. In the background was Sade's "Your Love Is King."

"Skol," Louie toasted. "Someone is joining us for dinner soon; hopefully, that's OK. I met this woman—so far, no runs, no hits, no errors. I like her a lot, Ben. Her name is Sheri."

"Great, Louie, am looking forward to meeting her almost as much as enjoying your green curry."

Dinner was an awakening of taste buds accompanied by an abundance of wine. By ten that night, Ben was struggling to stay alert. His mind kept wandering. Concentrating on the moment, he watched Louie and Sheri banter, tease, and laugh. Sheri owned an art gallery in Edina. Louie appreciated art. They were a compatible, tight fit. *They are happy. I've underestimated happiness. Tonight, I'd donate a kidney for some.*

After Ben enjoyed some pineapple ice cream, he and Junior excused themselves and entered the mannequin room. *Dahlia is my most pleasant memory since the fire. How sad, spending my time thinking about a woman who is planning her wedding.*

He woke up with Alice and Junior staring at him. *Another day, another home, quite a life. I wonder what Sheri thinks of Alice. How many men own a mannequin? Is this a pink or red flag? Sheri is an artist, probably loves the creativity. I'm jealous of Louie, but happy for him.*

Seeing his two suitcases by the door, he thought, *At least there's no packing.*

He called Julia and Arthur, estimating a midafternoon ETA. Both were on the phone in different rooms, cracking jokes about going to bed at seven and getting up at four, hoping those times would work for him. "Breakfast is at five, lunch at ten, dinner at three." They were in stitches. Ben hoped they were kidding.

He showered and had coffee with Louie. Sheri hadn't stayed. Louie said, "We're trying to do this slow; we might have something pretty special going here." With the clock ticking, he hugged Louie and Junior goodbye and headed south on 169. A beautiful April morning was unfolding.

Feeling better about being in Minnesota, he wanted to focus on what he could control: writing, building his new home, and most importantly, becoming a healthier person. He thought of Dahlia often, hoping those memories would diminish with time. Compared to the trek from KC to Minneapolis, the drive to Arthur and Julia's was a cakewalk. Only an hour and change. His cell rang, but it was an unknown caller. He didn't answer. Soon after, his phone beeped with a voice mail.

"Mr. Raymond, this is Sgt. Adams, Minneapolis Police Department. I have new information. As I shared with you, Gary Harbin was arrested in Durango regarding the stolen car. The short version is that Mr. Harbin has confessed to starting the fire. In his confession, he stated he picked your home because he remembered your name, was high, and looked your address up online. There was no further motive than that. Normally, I wouldn't leave a voice mail, but I wanted you to have this information as soon as it was available. Please call me and confirm you have received this message."

Ben took the message in stride. A conclusion was a small consolation. So many issues were a higher priority. He took a deep breath and kept driving, turning up the volume to *Step Inside This House*, focusing on Lyle Lovett's soothing voice.

Passing into the Mankato city limits, he left a message for Sgt. Adams, thanking him for the information. He didn't need any further discussion. The Carlsons were his priority. They mattered; the arsonist didn't.

Hickory Avenue was nostalgic, since he'd last lived there when he was ten. Parking in the driveway at 618 Hickory Avenue and seeing his family home next door seemed surreal. He thought it looked worn out, then realized the house was built over a hundred years ago. It was old, small, and sad.

The Carlson home looked cared for. The lawn and trees were manicured with window boxes awaiting spring flowers. The siding had a fresh coat of caramel paint with burnt-orange trim. Ben thought their home was inviting and happy. He left his suitcase in the trunk, rang the doorbell, and waited. He heard a dog bark, and the door opened.

Two smiling faces emerged.

"Little Benny, you look so handsome!" Julia shrieked.

"Welcome, Ben. Julia's right. You look great, almost handsome, but let me tell you up front, don't mess with my girlfriend or there will be hell to pay."

Julia hugged Ben, and at the same time, Arthur shook his left hand. Affection was important to Arthur. Walking into the house, Ben saw a bulldog. The dog growled.

"Don't worry about Ike. His growl is worse than his bite. Arthur and I laugh about Ike being older than we are. We figure he's 102 in dog years. Ike's determined to outlast us."

"Yeah, when we got him, I wanted to name him Halsey after a navy admiral, but Julia pulled rank and named him after Eisenhower. The army and Ike won out. I learned to pick my battles."

Following a few pleasantries, they caught up over coffee and bagels with lingonberry jam. Ben retrieved his luggage.

"Let me get that for you. You're our guest." Ben watched this ninety-nine-year-old snatch two suitcases out of his hands and carry them inside the house. Julia led Ben to his living quarters. He unpacked, committing to a few days, maybe longer.

Hanging his clothes in the closet, he shook his head in amazement at Arthur and Julia. None of his relatives lived this long. His previous visits in Belize, rural Minnesota, and Kansas City were unique in their own way. But this experience—*Well*, Ben thought, *what a gift!*

Ike was waiting in the hallway, growling as he passed.

Ben, Julia, and Arthur took a slow afternoon stroll through the neighborhood. They talked about the changes over the years and the number of families that had lived in Ben's family home. The conversation covered demolished homes, replacement cookie-cutter styles, and the loss of almost all their friends who had passed.

Returning home, Julia said, "This is when Arthur and I nap for an hour or two."

"This is the only time we sleep together." Arthur winked.

As Arthur and Julia went into a bedroom, Ben decided to reconnect at the neighborhood park and make some calls. He had a need to touch base with Russ, Twila, José, and Barbara. Mostly, Ben needed to talk to Alison. He perspired at what he had been avoiding.

The conversations with the Curtis and Rivera families were defining reminders of lifelong friendships and commitment. The calls were pleasant and reassuring. Then, he called Alison.

Luckily, she answered, "Hello, Ben. I am surprised you called. I wouldn't blame you if you never spoke to me again."

Ben said, "If it weren't for Lily, I wouldn't, but we have a complicated situation and there are extenuating circumstances. For now, I want to emphasize that there is no reason for Lily to have to deal with this. Do you still agree not to tell her? And that goes for anyone else too. Have you told Ted?"

"I will never tell another soul, including Ted. This is a promise I will keep. Lily's telling me when she comes back, she may live with you. I think Lily would be better off with you than with Ted and me."

Ben heard what he wanted and was done with the conversation. "I will do whatever is necessary to protect Lily. I will only be in contact whenever necessary. I must take this call," he said, lying.

He couldn't hide his hostile behavior and jabbed the end call button down hard. *Why do I talk to Alison this way? God knows, I'm at fault too.*

Returning to the Carlson household, he decided to organize some of his writing. Seeing a photo of Arthur and Julia in the Canadian Rockies, his mind went to Toronto. He thought of Dahlia. She continued to impact him in unexpected ways. Of all the issues facing him, Dahlia the engaged bride-to-be was the most preposterous.

Deep inside, he knew he was unworthy of a relationship with a woman of her quality. He had messed up most every relationship in his forty-nine years. *Dahlia saved lives, I . . .*

The first dinner at the Carlsons' included baked torsk, mashed potatoes, and glazed carrots, followed by blueberry cobbler. It was comfort food at its best.

Ben used the opportunity to ask his burning questions. "To what do you attribute your amazing longevity? You probably get asked this all the time. Also, did I stay at your house as a kid? Last night, I had the strangest thought looking at the ceiling light. Seemed like I had been there before. And did Anne ever stay here?"

Arthur said, "It's embarrassing to admit that light has never been changed. Yes, on occasion, you and your sister would stay over when your parents needed some space. Good memory."

You knew!

Julia added, "That is the past. Long ago, Ben. Your dad would go on a bender sometimes. Your mom wanted to protect you. Don't be too hard on your parents. All families have bumps in the road."

Arthur jumped in, "Longevity, huh? Growing up, we had a neighbor who went bankrupt and committed suicide. He went into a walk-in freezer. When he was found dead with a note to his family, the police were stunned because the freezer wasn't running. It never got below fifty degrees. Yet he died. He thought he was freezing to death and died.

"This had a big effect on me as a kid. I was amazed at what the man's thoughts had done to him. I thought, what if I could get my brain to think the other way, that I could be healthy and live a long time? Over the years, I have seen a lot of evidence that what goes on in your head matters. Once I read that the number one factor in longevity is how long a person thinks they will live. Who knows for sure? But Julia and I have practiced being positive thinkers for about three-quarters of a century. Even when we feel like we're getting a cold, we will tell our brains to rally our immune system and knock the virus out. Some might say we're crazy, but they can't prove us wrong. It works for us. If there is one thing I know, it's that there's a lot we don't know about the mind."

"When I met Arthur, I thought he was a little loony. During the war, we both saw horrible sights. Arthur was badly wounded, and I didn't think he would live. But every day, he would smile at me and say, 'I'm going to make it. And when I do, I'm going to have a date with you.' Like I said, I thought he was a few bricks short of a load. In my mind, neither were going to happen. Yet here I am sitting across the table from that crazy man, married to him for seventy-five years. If we make it to eighty, I might have to admit he's right."

Both Arthur and Julia burst into laughter and proposed a toast. "To a long, happy life! Skol!"

They talked for a couple of hours more. Ben was astonished at their knowledge. They had not allowed life to pass them by. Ben was a sponge, soaking up every word of wisdom.

Surprisingly, Julia said, "We have to watch *The Voice*. You can join us or not. We never miss it. We even turn our chairs and pretend to be judges."

Ben excused himself after they reluctantly agreed to let him do dishes. He cleaned up the kitchen, went to his bedroom, and lay down on the bed. He looked at the ceiling, filled with thoughts about Arthur and Julia. He started writing them down. Obviously, Arthur and Julia had decades of stories and lessons for him. He wasn't leaving until he had heard every one of them.

In the morning, Julia was having coffee on the porch with a neighbor. Arthur pulled up and asked Ben if he wanted to ride along to the hardware store. Incredibly, Arthur still drove. Julia handed him his Buddy Holly glasses. Arthur had a twenty-year-old red Ford pickup with eighteen thousand miles on it. It looked almost new. Carefully and slowly, Arthur drove a few blocks to the True Value.

After picking up a garden hose and plant fertilizer, they headed back toward Hickory Avenue.

"How long have you been retired, Arthur?"

"Thirty-nine years. I retired at sixty—as soon as I could. Hard to believe, I worked forty and have almost been retired as long. Retirement came easy, was like graduating from high school with an income. Julia and I had an interesting life while working yet had more things to do than time allowed. Julia could retire at the same time, and neither of us could think of a good reason to keep working.

"Julia had a working list of goals. We decided to try to do all the things we hadn't had time for while working. She started painting, I took guitar lessons, we took a ceramics class together, learned a little Spanish, I started jogging, she biked, we fixed up the house a bit and started traveling. You know, Ben, I have never been bored with that woman. I have loved being with her every second of my seventy-five years. Even before that, when I was lying in that hospital bed, Julia gave me a reason to live. God only knows what might have happened to me if she hadn't gone to that movie.

"I still love sleeping with her, and it pains me that we are in different rooms now. That just started about a year ago, when we bought a single adjustable bed that raised and lowered because of her back pain at night. That's when I agreed to separate rooms if she would agree to napping with me in my room. Sometimes at night, I just go into her room and sleep in a chair to be close to my dear Julia. I am usually pretty tired the next day because sleeping in a chair isn't so great, but it still feels better than being away from her."

As they pulled into the garage, Ben thought, *If there is a luckier couple in the world, they would have to prove it. If I could have watched them when I was young, my life could have been different.*

On the garage wall in front of his pickup was a large picture of Arthur in his navy uniform. On the right in front of their car was a poster-size picture of Julia in her army uniform. Ben had to ask.

"Years ago, I had this three-by-five picture of Julia framed, and I put it on the garage wall in front of her car. Teasing her, I said she would always know where to park now. Well, a couple of weeks later, there was one of me on the other side. She was not to be outdone. Quite a woman, that Julia."

Ben concentrated on writing during the next couple of weeks. His mind was like a bubbling fountain of creativity. He'd learned from experience to take advantage of those days because they didn't happen often. He was certain that being around Julia and Arthur was the catalyst for his creativity. They were incredible role models for living. In their nineties, they were still reaching for every possible morsel. There was no giving up and no settling. *If only I were as committed to living as Arthur and Julia.*

He wrote, "Thinking of you gives me peace. Dreaming of you makes me want to sleep. Living with you keeps me alive."

Most days were routine. He was up early, went for a run, wrote for three or four hours, had lunch, walked with Julia and Arthur, made phone calls, emails, and dinner, and had a relaxing evening. Conversations with Julia and Arthur became more enlightening each day. Ben was impressed with their sharp minds and frequently asked them about their lifestyles, which were hardly routine.

Every day they played a game of gin. Sometimes they played at seven in the morning, sometimes nine at night, but neither gave an inch. Win or lose, it was a battle from beginning to end. Their language was astonishing too. Both swore like drunken sailors.

Arthur began taking vitamins as a teenager and continued to religiously. He said, "I never felt like my diet was perfect, and vitamins gave me confidence that I was taking care of myself. Over the years, I heard doctors go back and forth on the benefits. It's common sense to me. What do you have to lose except a few bucks? The affirming upside seems worth it. Julia takes them too. I lay out her vitamins every morning."

Neither Julia nor Arthur drank much alcohol. They enjoyed beer and wine but mainly as a social pleasure. Julia said, "Hangovers are enough evidence that drinking too much isn't good for me. On occasion, for fun, drinking is a necessary evil, worth a little pain. I have learned to be selective."

One day, Arthur was doing yard work while Julia and Ben were talking. Ben asked about the life goals list that Arthur had mentioned.

"When I was young," she began, "there were so damn many rules for girls. Way too many limits on the way to act, dress, behave, and do just about everything. I know you know all this stuff. As a young woman, I was mad. When I looked at my brother's life compared to mine, it was so unfair. He had choices. I had limitations. I wasn't going to take that sitting down.

"I read a book called *Life Dreams*. It was not the kind of dreams when you are sleeping but rather the kind you wish would happen. The author suggested that if you write down your dreams and goals, you have a much better chance of making them happen. So, I started writing down my dreams as a teenager and kept the list, changing it as I saw fit over the years. Believe it or not, I still have my original list. I could show you if you want. You'd be the second person I have shown it to, after Arthur."

"I'd be honored."

Julia and Ben went into her bedroom, and she opened a small chest. She took out a yellowed piece of paper and unfolded it. The paper had been written on both sides, some items crossed off, many added over the years. Her original list at age fifteen, included:

1. Fall in love

2. Get married to a good man

3. Be a mother

4. Make my parents proud

5. Help others

6. Earn my own money

7. Be brave

8. Serve my country

9. Vote

10. Graduate from HS

11. Travel somewhere outside the USA

12. Have fun sometimes

13. Learn to sing a little

14. Stay well

15. Have a dog

Ben thought, *What gems from a fifteen-year-old over eighty years ago. These are still applicable today. Coming here, I'd hoped to repay some kindness and love to this couple that were so good to me. Instead, I am gaining wisdom and learning about living from them.*

Julia looked at Ben. "So far, I met all my original goals except be a mother. And God knows Arthur and I tried, almost every day, sometimes more than once a day. Just didn't happen, but it wasn't for lack of trying. Arthur and I have never worried about the cards in our hand. We make the best out of whatever hand we've been dealt. We're not whiners. Never liked to hang out with whiners. Who does? Arthur and I have always figured that things turn out best for the people who make the best out of the way things turn out."

Ben knew at that moment that he was not looking forward to leaving the Carlson household. Being with them had been an escape from his troubles and a rejuvenating relook into his own life. Staying with them had been a treasure. They reminded him that age is strictly a case of mind over matter. If you don't mind, it doesn't matter.

During his last week with them, he attempted to do a few home projects with Arthur and Julia. They didn't need his help, but he enjoyed giving them a hand with some of the physical labor like digging holes for flowers, repairing a window box, sawing some replacement boards for their deck, and carrying loads of wood chips and fertilizer for their landscaping.

Their yard was already beautiful, and he could only imagine how much nicer it would look in June and July. Physical work, being close to nature, having beautiful flowers, and making your home your favorite place were other lessons for how to live from Arthur and Julia.

The last few days with the Carlsons were bittersweet. Wishing they lived closer to Minneapolis, Ben caught himself slipping into the trap of looking for the easy way out. He was reminded of an often-used quote: "People will always do what they want to do." Ben believed in that statement. If he wanted to spend time with these wonderful human beings, he could commit to doing so and sacrifice an hour and a half to drive to them. He knew it's what Arthur and Julia would do.

Ben was leaving the next day, so he decided to take Arthur and Julia out for lunch at their favorite seafood restaurant, the Lobster Shack. They ordered the Sailor Special, a combination of seafoods that included scallops, lobster, shrimp, clams, grilled grouper, and blackened halibut. Ben, Julia, and Arthur laughed about no one touching the fries or hush puppies. All the seafood was gone when the hot fudge sundaes were served.

Julia and Arthur looked at Ben, and Julia said, "We want to ask you something and probably should have brought it up before today."

Arthur said, "I remember telling Julia when I turned seventy that we had to make every day count because I only had thirty years left. And now, approaching three digits, even I know there is an end in sight. Without children, Julia and I need some advice."

Julia said, "This may surprise you, Ben, but Arthur and I have been talking about this since hearing of your fire. You may think we are being foolish, but we are serious. We want to leave our assets to you after we move on to heaven. We have drawn up the will and made it all official but thought you should know."

"I don't know what to say. This is a total shock. I don't feel the least bit deserving. It's uncomfortable even thinking about it. Especially since you two have time to blow some money and let your last check bounce. Let's think about it."

"Good idea, Ben. We don't have to beat a dead horse here, no pun intended. Let's enjoy this ice cream," Arthur said, licking his spoon.

Once back on Hickory, Ben said, "I have a little surprise. You've been so good to me; I love you like family. I thought over and over about what I could give you as a little token of my appreciation. Follow me, please, hold on to each other's hands, and close your eyes." He led them down the hallway, passed growling Ike, into the bedroom.

"OK, open your eyes!"

In front of Julia and Arthur was a king-size split adjustable bed. No more sleeping in different rooms. Julia and Arthur laughed, hugged each other, and sandwiched Ben.

Julia said, "Simply wonderful, Ben. This is the greatest gift we have ever had in our whole life. Thank you, thank you, thank you."

As Ben packed, he savored the month of April. He had reconnected with exceptional people who had protected him as a young boy. He loved Arthur and Julia. He had learned about a higher level of love from them. He had finished chapter 5 thanks to pearls of wisdom from Arthur and Julia.

Following a precious goodbye, he got in his car, smiled at the four waving hands, looked down at the plate of cookies riding shotgun, and backed out of the driveway. Every block tempted him to go back. He had the sadness of leaving someone he loved. Arthur and Julia had stood by each other through hell and high water. He had learned a hard lesson. *They showed me what true love looks like.* He imagined Ike going from room to room, making sure Ben was really gone.

Deeds, not words, he thought. Ben took the first exit and headed back. Soon, he was knocking on their door. Julia answered the door followed by Arthur, "Did you forget something, Ben?"

"No, I didn't forget anything. I have an idea to run past you. I want to start a Julia and Arthur Carlson Foundation. Your remarkable lives should be honored. Any inheritance could be the base for a perpetual charitable fund you two want to support. I am willing to do the legwork after we work out the details. What do you think?"

Julia said, "What a fine idea, Ben."

Arthur said, "Does it have to be named after us?"

Ben said, "Absolutely!"

For the second time that day, Ben sped toward Minneapolis.

6

METAMORPHOSIS

It had been a week since Ben had talked with Nathan about moving in for the month of May. Nathan was a high school counselor in a large metro suburb of Minneapolis. Ben and Nathan met in a book club about fifteen years prior. Nathan, now in his mid-fifties, had lost his wife to cancer five years earlier. Since Joan's death, Ben had tried to invite Nathan to any event that could get him out of the house.

He found Nathan to be one of the kindest, most upbeat people, despite Joan's illness and eventual death. When the fire became public, Nathan was quick to contact Ben. Nathan was young at heart, and Ben was certain that high school kids could relate to him. Nathan had one married son and one single daughter, both in the metro area.

Ben thought that living in St. Louis Park would be a practical setting from which to monitor his home's progress, while continuing to write since Nathan would be working and coaching most daytimes. Since leaving Minneapolis, he didn't feel like he had pulled his share of responsibilities in his friends' homes. With Nathan's busy schedule, Ben wanted to contribute more. He was trying to be a better friend, and this would be different from the previous months.

He hoped to put his life on track and become more together than he had been before the fire. Mentally, he was neutral—not bad, not good. He was like a paratrooper standing in the door about to make his first jump—ready, willing, and anxious, but determined. He needed to change.

Even at midday, Nathan's house looked gloomy. Ben found the key in the fake rock on the deck. Inside, there was only emptiness. No welcoming hugs or even a growl.

This was my life before the fire. Alone.

Once inside, he texted Nathan, "Found key, in house. Thanks, C U soon."

Seconds later: "Relax, make yourself at home. BB game tonight, be home about seven."

The quietness at Nathan's was as startling as the noise had been at other homes. After hanging some clothes, Ben decided to go for a run. He walked down the hallway, seeing Nathan and Joan's anniversary picture on the wall. They were in Maui, wearing leis amid a tropical paradise. They looked happy. They had a loving marriage that had ended far too soon.

Needing a pre-run drink, Ben opened the refrigerator. His favorite beverages were stocked inside: Guinness, Steel Toe Size 7, San Pellegrino pomegranate and black currant sparkling water, and Reed's Jamaican Ginger Beer were a reminder of Nathan's personality. He paid attention to details and remembered the little things. There wasn't another person on planet Earth that would remember Ben's favorite drinks. Even though Ben was amazed at his thoughtfulness, he knew Nathan would and could do the same for all his friends. A special man, indeed. *When's the last time I did something thoughtful for a friend?*

Ben's run was like an Utepils moment; it reminded him of the Norwegian tradition of enjoying a first beer outside in the spring. This was his first run outside in normal clothes with no face mask, gloves, or arctic wear; just shorts, a shirt, and a twenty-year-old *Late Night* David Letterman hat.

As his sneakers met the road, he thought of Julia and Arthur sharing a life of honesty, integrity, and devotion. This was new modeling to him. He had never witnessed this before and certainly never experienced it. He passed a women's health clinic and thought of Dahlia. Their interaction had been brief, but wonderful.

His mind moved to Russ and Twila, his reunion with high school friends, José, the Carlsons, and now Nathan. Each were high-impact months. Fire, Dahlia, Alison's disclosure, Lily, José, and the Carlsons comprised a myriad of emotions. He wanted to be a different person from before the fire. His solitary existence was no longer acceptable.

What contributions have I made to my friends? What would they say about their time with me?

Following his run, he decided to plan dinner. "Dinner will be waiting at seven," he texted. "Looking forward to breaking bread and beers with you." He ordered his favorite Thai food, Roat Osha's pad thai, for delivery at seven. *Why don't I know Nathan's favorite food? He knows mine.* "What's your favorite dinner?" Ben texted again.

"I love food; you decide."

At seven thirty, Nathan came home, and within a minute, they were sitting on the deck sipping a Size 7, toasting their friendship and health. Nathan's team had just lost a game 3–2 in the bottom of the ninth. Tough loss, but Nathan said the team had left it all on the field. "Great game against a good team. We didn't beat ourselves. They beat us."

Nathan was grateful for the pad thai and suggested eating outside. Ben decided a Guinness was his next choice. Nathan had a second Size 7 as they devoured the pad thai.

"So, how's the house building, Ben?"

"Slowly but surely, looks like a December move-in, just in time for the holidays. Until then, my book and monthly moving are taking most of my time."

"You know you can stay here until December. Seriously, I would enjoy the company. Living alone sucks. I hate to think how long it's been since someone made me dinner."

"Thanks, I really appreciate the offer. I have Lily coming back into town next month, and I hope to be living with her. At her age, this might be the last time. She's a woman now."

"In the teachers' lounge, I mentioned you were working on your book, and an English teacher overheard and asked if you'd like to speak to his creative writing class. Of course, you don't have to unless you want to."

"No big deal to me, Nathan. If you want me to do it, I'll do it."

They finished dinner and decided their next beer would be their last. Nathan had an early morning. Ben had a second Guinness, and Nathan had a third Size 7. Their conversation turned serious.

"Are you seeing anyone, Nathan? Dating?"

"Nothing serious, a few casual setups. I am sure you are familiar with being single. You know, dinner with friends and someone they think you might like. Honestly, it's been a struggle. Doesn't seem fair to date anyone until I am ready. You're a psychologist. What do you think? On another topic, I would be interested in hearing about some of the psychology used in military interrogations."

Caught a bit off guard, Ben felt the hair on his neck move and his face flush. He considered diverting the conversation but chose otherwise. Arthur and Julia had taught him a lesson about openness in conversations. Instead of adding a brick to the wall around him, he began talking.

"I'm not proud of my interrogations in the military. I have never talked about it with anyone. War is an insane proposition that demands that humans carry out inhumane behavior. No one wants to admit it, but *war* is a glamorized word for *killing*. Maybe talking would be good for me. Up to now, I have refused to even think about it."

"In all the time I have known you, this is the first personal disclosure you have made. You know that is healthy, Ben. I know you know that. Keep going, somehow, if not tonight, then some other time. Just don't stop."

"You'd think after forty-nine years I would have figured more out. I haven't. But I'm learning. Maybe an old dog can learn new tricks. I'm learning from you too." Nathan's eyes drooped. "My wish for you is rest. There will be a few hundred teenagers needing you tomorrow, right?"

"Yeah, I'm bushed, had a twelve-hour day, need some shut-eye. But, man, it was great coming home tonight knowing you were here."

Ben remembered his mood change after Dahlia had come to Belize. *Even a stranger made life better. Maybe we don't know what we're missing until we have it.*

The next day, Ben started writing. Still lacking confidence, he pushed forward, finishing ten pages without stopping. The quality of his book was less important today; December was the goal.

The next day, he focused on his new home, picking stone for the fireplace, flooring, lighting, and cabinets. He was impressed with the architect's 3D images. Losing his house was sad, but the new creation was slowly becoming a dim light at the end of a dark tunnel. He thought about being in his new home for the holidays. *A chance for a better life.*

That evening, Nathan asked Ben if he would be willing to speak to a group of seniors. Two teachers wanted Ben to combine writing with psychology. Ben agreed, but admitted, "I haven't been in a high school since graduating. Might put some to sleep."

The next couple of days fell into a halfway normal range. Writing, dinners with Nathan, working out, decisions on the house, and connecting with people filled his time. The following week, Ben would give his presentation. He was reminded that incessant talking was a military interrogation technique. Laughing to himself, he committed to avoiding it.

He believed writing was simply the recording of thoughts, so his presentation would emphasize creative positive thinking. In therapy, he found that struggling people were like a rudderless sailboat—out at sea, in the wind, without direction. Giving yourself time to think provides direction. This is the message he wanted to deliver.

When the day arrived, he had given zero thought to what he would wear, and his wardrobe was hilariously limited. Looking in the closet, he viewed the lack of rhyme or reason. Since Nathan had already gone, Ben was on his own and didn't have time to shop. He went to Nathan's closet and looked for an appropriate shirt. This was the first time in months he had given any thought to clothes.

Showing up at school was stressful. He couldn't believe the size of the parking lot and how difficult it was to find a space. The building was huge, and security was tight. He had to show a driver's license and wear an ID. The school had close to four thousand students, an incredible sight for someone who had rarely been in a high school for over thirty years. Eventually, he found Nathan and was relieved but nervous.

"Cool. I have the same shirt," said Nathan.

Ben just smiled. He'd confess at dinner. Nathan led him to an auditorium, where he met the two teachers of AP Psych and Creative Writing. He didn't remember the last time he had spoken to a group.

He was struck by the students' appearance. They looked older, maturer than he'd expected. He was surprised at how healthy they appeared. There was none of the acne or bad haircuts that had plagued his high school days.

Introduced as an author, psychologist, and veteran, he walked to the podium. "I am honored to be here as a guest of my friend Mr. Wilski.

"Socrates said an unexamined life is not worth living. I would propose that a thinking life can make life worth living. Each of us must answer the question, *What kind of person am I, and what factors led me to be who I am?* To date, most of your choices have been out of your control. Your parents, family, where you live, your classes, your classmates, and many other aspects of your life have been predetermined by others.

"Next year, all that changes. You have a marvelous opportunity to design and chart your course. You are 100 percent responsible for your journey, which includes being happy, and only you can control your happiness. If you are happy, the rest tends to fall into place.

"You will live approximately ninety years, and you'll spend one-third of that sleeping, so invest in a good bed, and be careful who you let in it. You'll spend one-third of your time working, so find a way to make money that doesn't seem like work. This is America—pick something! Finally, you will have one-third of your life to do as you please. For that, you must develop interests and passions. There's music, art, cooking, astronomy, nature, traveling, and thousands more choices. Interesting people live interesting lives. Be one, have one!"

Regarding grades, Ben said, "The number of people who get good grades without studying is equal to the number of people who are in great physical condition without exercising. Zero. If you want to learn, put in the time. If you want to be in better condition, work out. The number of people who drink or do drugs daily and are happy is zero too. Sometimes life isn't as complicated as we think."

Ben closed by encouraging people to dream about the life they want. "Dreams energize us and give us direction. Your brain is like a muscle. Use it and it will get stronger. Know this—you are so much more than you think you are.

"Over the years, I have learned ten principles for a meaningful, healthy life. Practice forgiveness. Do what you say or explain why you didn't. Never lie. Embrace kindness. Take care of your body. Help others. Seek justice and resist injustice. Know more than yesterday. Seek a higher power. Discover reasons to be grateful."

Stepping back from the podium, Ben acknowledged that, unlike Julia, he was a hypocrite. He believed in the ten principles; hell, he had written them. But he wasn't living them. Ben was a fraud and knew it. Making eye contact with Nathan, Ben accepted that he knew too. *I must change.*

That night at dinner, Nathan and Ben talked about the presentation.

"We know how important it is to support young people," began Nathan. "Yet as adults, we often face challenges alone. Losing Joan, my life companion, the love of my life, was devastating. There is more to the story too."

Nathan stared down for a few seconds, tapping his foot and fingers. "Eight years ago, Joan and I were struggling, growing apart, taking care of the kids but not ourselves. Joan had an affair with a coworker. One Saturday afternoon, I got an anonymous phone call telling me they were together at his house, leaving me an address. I thought it was a prank but couldn't let it go.

"I drove over there and saw her car across the street. I panicked and sat for two hours, waiting. Watching him walk her to the car and kiss her was as close to wanting to die as I have ever imagined. The pain turned into anger and hate during the following weeks. She had violated our marriage in the worst possible way. I hated her. I wanted her to leave but was afraid of losing her.

"For reasons I will never understand, I never told her. I didn't have the courage. I kept waiting for the bombshell that never came. Two months later, she was diagnosed with cancer. The disease consumed our lives after that. Watching her deal with cancer was painful enough. She didn't need any more. Joan died without ever knowing that I knew. Even though she had hurt me in a way I could never forget, I still loved her. I didn't want her to feel any more pain. As strange as it sounds, I have no regrets. I have never shared that story. I hope this wasn't a mistake. This wasn't planned."

Ben was dumbfounded. He walked over and sat next to Nathan. "You made an honorable sacrifice protecting Joan. Tonight, you did the right thing by beginning to take care of yourself. You have held on to this for over eight years. I don't know why, but tonight was the right time to let it go."

"I feel like a huge weight just left my shoulders. Please don't think badly of Joan. She was a good human being but, like all of us, imperfect."

"Divorce is like a death without any closure. Sometimes, I think death would be easier than my divorce."

Nathan snapped, "I don't think you understand what real love is. So much of what you say reverts to you. I sacrificed for Joan because of my love for her. I'm not sure you get it. Your choice has been to walk away. I need to be alone. Good night, Ben."

Ben sat alone pondering Nathan's words. They were spot-on.

The next day, Ben was motivated to make dinner. Around noon, he got a text saying, "Thanks for last night, I have no regrets. Hope that is a good sign. Nathan."

He never mentioned the evening's final words. *No need. He made his point.*

Ben chose his favorite childhood dinner—breaded pork chops, mashed potatoes, and sweet corn. For dessert, he bought Cherry Garcia ice cream. *I wish I knew Nathan's favorite childhood dinner.*

Nathan came home, and in classic male form, the two sat down at dinner without a reference to the previous night. The mood seemed lighter, and the food was almost as Ben remembered, only not as good.

Nathan said, "Being a psychologist, you probably think I am a mental case, but I'm not, or at least don't think so. Sharing that story last night was big for me. I may ask you down the road for a referral to someone who can help put it to rest. But for now, I would rather leave it alone."

"You get to decide when and with whom you talk."

"I really want to get out of this rut. It's been five long years. If there is a game plan for my recovery, I haven't found it. I'm stuck and lonely, and no one knows. Who wants to spend time with a fifty-five-year-old whose wife died? Sounds depressing just saying it. You're single, Ben. How are you managing? Seeing anyone?"

"I'm not. Often, I wonder what my deal is because it seems there are always more reasons not to pursue a relationship. Everyone, including me, has baggage. Used to think it was easier to not have a relationship than to have a bad one. Not sure anymore. But you said it well, it's lonely."

Offering some levity, he said, "You and I are too good of men to be alone forever. I do wonder whether someone our age can fall madly in love. Maybe we have had our turn."

"I work with many women, always have. But I was always married, and most of them knew Joan. It's awkward. There is one woman I work with that interests me. I get uptight around her. It's flat-out weird. I feel like an insecure fifteen-year-old. After being married for years, I find the single life so empty. I would never choose this, but I don't know how to change it. The most exciting thing lately is that I have you living in my house. No offense, Ben, but that's pathetic."

"So, why not have a little social gathering here? A happy hour of sorts. You invite whoever you want, but make sure you invite that special woman. It would be good for both of us to socialize. I'm single too. Maybe it will put a little spark in our lives. Whatcha think?"

"Not much to lose. I could invite a few people over Friday afternoon. Can I ask for some help with the house? It looks like two bears live here." Nathan laughed. Ben noticed a sparkle in Nathan's eye for the first time.

Ben decided to pull out all the stops, thinking, *Why not? Do something altruistic. Become a better person. Like José.*

Friday morning, he skipped running and bought four potted flowers for the deck and two vases of fresh flowers for the kitchen and living room. He vacuumed and shined the house up. He looked at the pictures of Joan and wondered. Keeping them on display would be a sensitive subject. Maybe for another day.

He ordered barbecued chicken and ribs with all the fixings of baked beans, tater tots, and johnnycake from Famous Dave's. He had a brainstorm. He knew a friend of Lily's who worked at France 44 Liquor. Once before, she was able to set up a little portable bar and bartend for a party Ben attended. It was worth a call.

Lady Luck was on his side; Mandy, Lily's friend, agreed to do it. She would bring the liquor, a bartender friend, and a host. He texted Nathan. "Party is set, all you must do is get that woman here, even if it's just the three of us."

Nathan texted back, "You're my hero, man, I talked to her this morning before my nerves woke up. She is stopping by. Thank you, Ben. C U @ 3:30."

Nathan came home with a skip in his jump, looking like the man Ben had met years ago.

Not knowing whether to mention Joan's pictures, Ben asked Nathan. "How's the house look?"

"It hasn't looked like this since Joan." He stopped and took a deep breath. "The food, bartender, flowers. Just wonderful, wonderful, Ben."

"You're alive, Nathan, and Joan wants you to continue living. Life is precious, my friend. You know it better than I do. I was going to mention moving a couple of Joan's pictures, but—"

"I know, I know, it has crossed my mind. Mainly because they are a sad reminder every day. Doesn't feel right today, but I appreciate you mentioning. You are a good friend, Ben. Those are difficult conversations to start. I need to have more of them. I'm sorry for my reaction to you the other night."

You made a valid point. I get it. I should be thanking you. And yet, Ben never got around to actually saying the words.

At 0400, the high school troops started arriving. The people were aged from right out of college to seasoned thirty-year veterans.

All of them seemed young, as though working in a high school kept their hearts young.

Natalie. Ben took a guess, bull's-eye. She was five feet, nine inches tall and in her late forties. She had short black hair with Caribbean-blue eyes. Her style was funky. Ben figured she had to be an art teacher.

Soon after Ben spotted her, Nathan brought her over. "Ben, I would like you to meet Natalie Isbelli, a colleague. Natalie, this is my friend, Ben Raymond."

Natalie shook his hand. "I remember reading your article in the *Tribune* a couple of months back. I haven't read your first book but promise to read the next one. How exciting!"

"Thank you, Natalie. It's a pleasure to meet you. What do you teach?"

"This term, I am teaching Ceramics and Sculpture, Drawing and Painting, and AP Art. Most of my students are juniors and seniors with an interest in art. I think I learn as much from them as I teach."

"Congratulations to you for the lives you have touched. Education is the game changer. You, Nathan, and the others are in the trenches making a difference. I commend you. Teaching is the only profession that teaches all the other professions. I am fortunate to have a friend like Nathan who offered me his home so I could continue writing this month. I can hardly believe there is only one more week here."

Wanting to leave Natalie and Nathan alone, Ben went outside to the deck, where Mandy and the beefy bartender, Jeff, were pouring drinks and delivering beer and wine with style and charm. Ben told Mandy that Lily would be back next month. Ben had always liked Mandy. He'd known her since Lily and she were fourth-grade classmates.

The party was smashing fun, and people seemed to linger. People started saying goodbye around eight, with a half dozen diehards dancing like they planned on spending the night. Ben was gratified to see Natalie and Nathan spending time together, sometimes alone and often in a group.

He had noticed that Jeff, the testosterone-emitting buffed bartender, was enjoying his own scent and seemed to be paying more-
than-normal attention to Natalie. Harmless as it seemed, Ben didn't
want any interference with his friend's progress. Jeff delivered a few
beverages across the room and moseyed through the dancing women.
Ben saw Jeff inconspicuously pat Natalie on the butt. She ignored him.

When Etta James's hit "At Last" played, Nathan walked toward
Natalie.

Perfect, Ben thought.

Then Jeff hurried toward her too. Ben was Johnny-on-the-spot.
He stepped between Natalie and the oncoming bartender. "How
about fetching me a manhattan, partner?" In his peripheral vision,
Ben saw Nathan and Natalie slow dance.

Jeff returned a few minutes later with the drink.

"I put a lot of time into this party so those two could spend some
time together. I can't let you get in the way, my friend."

With a sarcastic smirk, Jeff said, "Everything's fair in love and
war. A guy's gotta try, right?"

"First of all, you're misinformed. Very little is fair in love or war.
I saw you pat Natalie's butt. Is that how your dad taught you to treat
women?"

"Older women appreciate when a young guy still finds her attractive. What's the big deal, man?"

"I don't think you meant any harm, but it's still wrong. I'm going
to tip you now and let you take off. The party is winding down. I will
tell Mandy. Take care, buddy. Thanks for your help tonight."

Ben turned and saw that Natalie and Nathan were still dancing. *All is well that ends well.* From Ben's observation post, the party
worked. He recalled conversations with smart, gregarious people. *If
you can teach, you can do anything. Teachers are special.*

By ten, everyone felt obligated to leave. A few millennials were
talking about where to go next. Ah, to be young. Ben appreciated
their tenacity, although he wasn't waving any white flags. He found
Mandy and gave her a tip. "Jeff had to leave a few minutes ago."

Natalie was last to leave. Ben watched Nathan walk her to the
car. A hug, a kiss on the cheek, a second hug. A baby step.

When Nathan came back inside, he said, "I can't thank you enough. All I did was show up. This is the most fun I have had in, I am embarrassed to say, but years. Tell me the cost, and I will reimburse you, full amount. Tell me in the morning. I'm going to bed."

"Sleep well, we'll talk tomorrow."

The next morning, Ben was watching CNN when Nathan came into the living room. "Let me get you a coffee. Last night was on me, a small contribution to you for your lessons in life, and for putting me up, my good friend. Natalie is impressive. How'd it go?"

"I was amazed at what I didn't know. Natalie came to the district about four years ago, I met her, but over time, we just had professional conversations. Last night was the first time I got to know her a little. She's forty-eight, was married once, has no children, has been single ten years, has moved around and taught internationally in Italy, Japan, and Turkey, and her ex-husband is a school principal in Vienna. We had a good conversation, a comfortable time. Felt good that she stayed until the end. Time will tell. I am interested in her. Who knows what she thinks? We shall see next week when I ask her out. To do what, I haven't a clue. I haven't had a date for twenty-five years."

The serious comment made both men laugh.

The last week at Nathan's house, Ben was task oriented. He finalized the apartment agreement for June, anxiously looking forward to his time with Lily. It had been years since they had shared the same roof. He still struggled with the secret.

On Wednesday, Nathan texted that he was going over to Natalie's after work. A budding romance was in the works. Nathan was reentering the world. He came home at about ten o'clock, and they talked briefly. Nathan was smiling. "If we hadn't thrown the party, this wouldn't have happened. You made it happen."

"No, you and Natalie made it happen."

The last night in St. Louis Park, Ben suggested dinner together. Nathan had plans with Natalie. Every man knows when a friend chooses a woman over him, something special is happening.

As Ben carried his suitcase out to the car, he noticed the picture missing from Nathan's wall. He backed his car out of the driveway, satisfied that chapter 5 was done. The last sentence read, "An irresistible desire is to be irresistibly desired." Looking back at Nathan's home, Ben smiled and could have sworn the house smiled back.

DNA

Thanks to Louie's girlfriend, Ben was able to sublet a condo at the Towers for June. It was a stroke of luck. Sheri worked with a woman who was going to Europe in June and wanted someone to live in her condo. Her place was a tenth-floor, two-bedroom flat overlooking Cedar Lake.

Lily was flying from Madrid to New York to Minneapolis. She was scheduled to arrive on June 2, leaving Ben less than a day to move. Lily had texted him to let him know the flight was on time.

The condo was one year old. Sheri's coworker was an interior designer who made the flat beautifully idiosyncratic. The interior was encased with steel frames. There were floor-to-ceiling windows, and the walls had been painted in rich, vibrant shades of red and purple. The space was warm and inviting but quirky.

Ben decided odd might be the new normal. He checked each room and surveyed the views from every direction. *Lily will enjoy living here. I am Lily's father. I've been the only one she's ever known.*

Lily's KLM flight to JFK landed a few minutes early. Customs went smoothly, and her Delta flight was on time. Her ETA at MSP was 7:49 p.m. She would be jet-lagged, so he thought better of taking her out for dinner. He'd bought fruits, vegetables, and healthy snacks. He would make her dinner the next evening. He constantly wrestled with the secret, wishing Alison had kept silent for another twenty years. He continued to push the negative topic aside, focusing on Lily's return.

She would be graduating from the University of Minnesota, his alma mater. They were both rabid Gopher fans and regularly went to games. Lily had been a solid high school volleyball player. She made the Gopher squad but rarely played. The Women Gophers VB team was nationally ranked all four years she was in school. She was grateful to be part of the program but knew that part of her life was over. She was motivated to find a job.

She'd gone abroad to widen her cultural experiences and improve her Spanish. The curriculum in Seville was culture based, and she'd lived with a Spanish family. Her major was biomed engineering. She had been fascinated by the intersection of biology and engineering ever since eighth grade when her maternal grandfather had to have three stents placed in his arteries. She had been at the hospital during the crisis and had listened to the doctors, mesmerized.

In college, she shadowed a Boston Scientific rep, and late in her freshman year of college, she decided biomed would be her major.

Ben tried to think of other things, but he couldn't kick the shock of not being her biological father. He wanted to trust Alison. *Is Alison the problem, or is it me?*

He wondered if she carried enormous guilt for having watched Ben strive to be a good father to another man's baby. They had tried marriage counseling, and Ben never understood why their marriage couldn't survive.

He wanted to forgive but couldn't. He knew he was in direct opposition to his tenets of life; he was denying his own culpability. He had left Alison for months at a time. He was emotionally unavailable, afraid she'd find out who he really was and stop loving him. *Alison never liked my family. Could someone love me if they didn't like my family?*

Ben's army unit was activated and sent to Iraq. His deployment to a second war was traumatic for everyone. Lily and her mom's relationship flourished. Alison was more at peace away from their dysfunctional marriage, and she had her mother's help.

He wondered if seeing him back then made Alison feel guilty. When he and Lily would FaceTime, Alison would never join in. Her behavior was hurtful and confusing until now.

When he returned from Iraq, he no longer wanted to practice therapy, having used his skills in interrogations. After a couple of weeks back in America, he took Lily to Belize for a month. *Before living with Nathan, I never thought of forgiving Alison. Now I do and hope I can.*

He wanted to make the most of his time with Lily now. He was committed to doing whatever was best for their relationship.

He put orange lilies on the living room coffee table and a purple, red, and yellow flower arrangement in Lily's bedroom. His stomach quivered. *What would happen if she knew?*

Lily left the country following a Hanukkah dinner at her mother's home in Golden Valley. Ben had brought her to the airport. This time, he wanted to go inside the airport instead of a curbside pickup.

"Landed" and a heart emoji appeared on his phone. *This is right up there with coming home from Iraq.* Twenty minutes later, Lily came through the swinging doors. At first, Ben didn't recognize her. She was wearing shoes that made her look four inches taller, and she had cut her hair very short.

She'd left as a college student and returned as a young woman. At least at this moment, it seemed so to Ben. He ran toward her, she to him, and they hugged for a long time before looking at each other.

"You're as tall as I am. I missed you. Life is better now that you are back," Ben said.

"Dad, it is so good to see you. I am so glad you came to meet me. I was hoping you would."

Conversation in the car was lively. They jumped topics from Spain and living with the Ortiz family in Seville to her visits to Morocco and Istanbul, new friends, food, music, and weather.

Lily giggled. "I can't believe I am going to live with you. It will be so fun, even at twenty-one." Ben was working hard to ignore the secret. He had learned the harm of secrets over the past year, yet he felt that, sadly, this one had to remain.

Quickly up the twenty-story elevator and into the condo, he gave Lily a tour of every room, ending on the balcony. The night skyline was sparkling. In the west, the remnants of a passing sunset glistened on Cedar Lake.

"I think we should buy this place," Lily whispered. On Ben's insistence, Lily picked the bedroom with the view of downtown. "OK, but only if you let me do all the cooking," she joked. She had meager kitchen skills and had inherited her mother's talent for creating strange cuisine.

She had been awake for over twenty-four hours. She took a hot bath and got into pajamas before hugging Ben good night. She excused herself about midnight.

"I love you to the moon . . ."

"I love you to Pluto, Lily. See you in the morning. I'll close the drapes. The sunrise over the city is pretty, but it starts at about five o'clock. You can enjoy it on other days. Sleep in tomorrow. We have a whole month together. Who knows, maybe longer, if we buy this place."

Ben was exhausted but decided to review the first pages of chapter 6. The first sentence read, "Love often, trust few, be tender, damage no one." His writing had flowed more easily lately. Productive writing days continued to be a mystery. He thought there was a chance this novel could be finished early.

Having Lily home put Ben in a state of wonderment. Her birth seemed like a lifetime ago; now the speed of her life seemed supersonic. He knew this was probably the last time they'd ever live together.

The next morning, as he was dressing for his sunrise run, he noticed a missed call. The number was Canadian. A wrong number, though he wished it weren't.

It was a typical June morning, crisp air, brilliant blue sky, and warming sunshine. Ben's mind and body felt in sync, and ideas were coming to him rapidly.

He ran the path around Cedar Lake to Lake of the Isles. He tried not to look at Lily differently, to analyze her nuances—the way she wrinkled her nose reminded him of his mother; her walk and wave goodbye looked familiar. Or was that his hopeful imagination? Now, he wasn't sure.

His love was the same, but he was fighting the idea that Lily had another man's genes. His anger grew toward Alison. He knew that revenge was sick, yet he considered telling Ted. Alison had unloaded her guilt. He was the one hurting now.

He wondered about her giggle, which had always been entirely her own. And she loved biology more than he or her mother had. *None of this should matter. Will this ever go away? Will I be a good fake father? Will she notice any difference in how I am?*

His legs began cramping. His breathing was difficult. Running faster than normal, he had to stop. His heart was pounding. He bent over, sweat dripped from his brow onto his shoes. He chose to walk.

Reaching the east side of Isles, he decided to take a detour to Isles Bun and Coffee to pick up puppy dog tails. Lily and Ben had a long history of enjoying them. Ben ran faster on the way home to ensure their warmth.

Seeing Lily on the balcony was grounding, yet unsettling. He hated the demons in his mind. He quickly made a latte, plated the baked treats, and joined her.

"Good morning! Hope you slept well."

Lily was deep in thought, staring at the water. She looked at her dad. "Being in Seville was really humbling." She stopped and looked out over the lake. "When I woke up this morning, came out here, and saw you running with that white bag, I just got emotional. I even knew what was in the bag. In Spain, I met people." She stopped again and looked over the lake a second time. "In Spain, I guess—I guess what I'm trying to say is I feel lucky. I've been given a lot. Things I took for granted until I was on my own somewhere else. I learned so much yet feel more unsure of what I want than ever before. A job, money, a future. It all seems so superficial. Guess I'm admitting there's a lot to figure out, more than I thought before Spain."

"Benjamin Disraeli once said, 'Most people die with their music still in them.' Sounds to me like you're deciding how to let your music out." Ben picked up his coffee, took a sip, and saw an eagle circling the lake. "I'm proud of you thinking this way."

Lily turned the conversation practical.

"Well, what do you want to do next, Lily?"

"Number one, I want a job. Boston Scientific and Medtronic are my dream jobs. Plus, I just heard there is an upstart company called Bio-Med Solutions. That looks interesting. Even though I have graduated, my advisor told me to take this one class in genetics that will give me a double minor. I plan to take that first summer session."

"This is exciting! I am here for you if ever you want to bounce an idea off me."

"Thanks! Right now, I think exercise is what I need. I am going to run off these puppy dog tails," Lily said with her mysterious giggle.

Ben sipped a second latte sprinkled with cinnamon and watched Lily head off. "Thank you," he said to the sky.

The next few days flew by. Lily caught up with friends. Ben wrote and stopped by Louie's. Junior and Louie were flourishing, and Louie's relationship with Sheri was blossoming. That, too, was gratifying for Ben. He was relieved to be back in Minneapolis. Then Lily told him she was going to see her mother, and all his anxiety flooded back.

Time was passing fast, and Ben began thinking about his sister, Anne, and her husband, Andrew, with whom he would be living in July.

Anne was ten years older than Ben, and they had gotten to know each other mainly as adults. Before retiring, Anne had been a public defender for Ramsey County, and Andrew had been an English teacher and coach for St. Paul Public Schools. Ben always enjoyed time with them and looked forward to reconnecting.

Pulling into the underground parking at the Towers, his phone vibrated. His hands were full of groceries, and he ignored the text until he got into the condo. Glancing at his phone, he saw Dahlia's name next to a text. He walked onto the balcony.

He updated his publisher about his progress and called Anne. Both calls were short because his head was in the clouds. Like an adolescent boy, he retreated to his private bedroom, shut the door, and opened his phone.

"Major Raymond—whoops, I mean *Ben*—four months is a long time, huh? I hope you are well, happy, and readjusted to Minneapolis.

I would guess June is a beautiful time of year for you. Flowers, warm sun, and budding trees are a nice change from snow and cold. I thought of calling you but decided a text might be the more respectful route. I will get right to it. I am going to be in Minneapolis from June 20–23 for a Mayo Clinic Conference. I will be staying at the airport Hilton; the conference is on-site. If you want, I would love to see you, have dinner, and catch up. If you are unavailable, I understand. Just couldn't imagine being in your city without trying. Dahlia."

Ben put down his phone and walked into the living room. He paced, then sat down on the balcony. *What to do? How to respond? I don't know what to do.*

"Hi, Dahlia," he wrote promptly. "Thanks for reaching out. Hope all is good in 'Karlsen-World.' Have to check out some complications with those dates. Will be in touch ASAP . . . B."

Classic Raymondism, Ben thought after sending the text. No committal, no details, just friendly communication buying time. Being the perceptive woman she was, Ben was certain that Dahlia would read between the lines, knowing exactly what he was doing.

She had probably written a half dozen texts, deleted all of them, and second-guessed her decision until she pulled the trigger. If Ben was sure of anything, they were both fully aware of the dangers of a rendezvous. *Is she married and just wanting to reconnect, or what? I don't have a clue.*

When Lily walked in, Ben considered telling her the story but chickened out.

"How's your day, Lily?"

"So far, so good. Registered for my class this morning. Just had lunch with Mom at Tilia's. Did you know they might be selling the place in Belize?" Then, with the enthusiasm of youth, Lily added, "Boy, if I had some dough, I would buy it. I have some great memories there. I wish I could make some more." Laughing, she said, "Guess I should work on getting a job and my first home before worrying about a second."

Ben said, "If you want something you have never had, you have to do something you have never done. You'll figure it out. Just like the rest of us did."

"I contacted Boston Scientific, Medtronic, and Bio-Med Solutions, got access to the online applications, requested letters of recommendation, and hope to, at least, get interviews."

Ben called Louie and invited him for a beer at either the Towers or Lowry Café. Louie picked the Lowry because he wanted some poutine. Ben wanted Louie's straight talk.

At the Lowry, Ben ordered a Steel Toe Size 7 for himself and a Surly Furious for Louie. They had two orders of poutine.

"What's up, partner?" Louie said between mouthfuls.

"I never talked about this before because I never thought she would be an issue."

"She? Does she have a name?"

"Yeah, yeah. Sorry, Louie. I sure have a hard time sharing stuff, no secret to you. I met this woman, Dahlia, in Belize. She's from Toronto, and she's engaged. All we did was hang out, talk, and have a few drinks, but we connected. No sex, nothing physical, nothing like that, but her leaving was an unexpected bummer. Now she is coming to Minneapolis and suggested we get together. I am not sure whether to see her. Thought if I bounced it off you, it might help. Am I making any sense, Louie?"

Louie took a swig of Furious. "Makes all the sense in the world, amigo."

"OK, knowing what you know, should I see her or not? How do I make this decision? Crazy as it sounds, I am afraid of seeing her. I sound like a twelve-year-old."

"You are making complete sense. Let me be the devil's advocate. Why wouldn't you see Dahlia?"

"Because when she left Belize, I was a basket case."

"A pessimist sees difficulty in every opportunity. Maybe you need to change the way you see things, and the things you see will change. Plus, you've always been a basket case. A physical specimen, yes, but an emotional basket case."

"First of all, she is or was engaged to be married. She is ten years younger than I am, and she lives in Toronto. Listen to me, Louie. Why the hell does she want to see me?"

Louie said, "Beats me, man, maybe she's farsighted. Look, we've all got shit to work on. I love ya, man, but face it, relationships have not been your strength. You're about to be fifty, and you've been alone a long time. If you don't want to be alone forever, well, you get the picture. Do some work. Take a risk. Stop being just another pretty face."

Ben took a big gulp of Size 7 and stared at Louie. "Tough love, Louie. People like me, but almost no one loves me. Because I haven't let anyone know me well enough to love me. And to be saying that at middle age . . . it's pathetic." Ben took a bigger gulp of Size 7. "I don't want to get burned. I'm scared. If I don't let anyone in, I can't get hurt. I was crazy about her when she was engaged. Red flag. I don't need another train wreck."

The next morning, Ben wondered whether his brain had worked through the decision all night. He woke up, took out his phone, and texted, "Dahlia, I am available the days you are in town, would love to see you. Let me know your schedule so we can finalize a time."

He didn't want any information. He just wanted to see her before he lost his mind.

During the next few days, Lily started her class and worked on job applications. Her adult life was taking shape.

He received another text from Dahlia saying the schedule was structured and wondering if they could have dinner at the hotel restaurant Friday evening. That way, they could have time together catching up rather than driving around the city. Ben had no objection and said he would make a reservation for seven o'clock.

He was struggling with his writing again. His preoccupation with Dahlia was having a negative effect. He called Anne and Andrew and asked them to have dinner at W. A. Frost. He hadn't seen them for a while, and neither had Lily.

The night was cool, and they were seated outside next to a rustic stone fireplace filled with huge, warm, glowing logs. Ben was quieter than normal. He loved seeing Anne and Lily interact as two adult women. Anne had protected him and cared for him when he was young. Watching her with Lily, oblivious to genetics and having a beautiful exchange was teaching Ben another lesson. He could learn to take the higher road. The crackling fire brought back memories.

The next morning, Ben's phone was vibrating at 6:00 a.m. Dahlia texted, "Ben, do you have a minute to talk this morning? OMG, just noticed the time, am so sorry, just left hospital, worked last night. Again, sorry if I woke you. Give me a time, if you can, I will call."

Ben sat up, took a deep breath, and his heart began racing.

She's not coming, change of plans, has cold feet.

He caught himself and stopped exploring the unknown. He texted back, "No problem, flexible morning, how about 9 EST in Toronto, 8 CST, Minneapolis."

She responded instantly. "I will call, thank you."

He had about two hours to kill. He regretted not saying, "Call now." Lily had gone to her class. He was pacing like a caged animal, asking himself whether she was going to cancel. He decided a short run made sense and was out the door in five minutes, his pace faster than normal. He had always run as fast as his body suggested. Never timing himself, he would run slowly if the weather was beautiful and he wanted to enjoy nature and faster if he just wanted to get the job done. he had raced many unwitting runners around the lakes; they never knew.

At home, he showered, ate a banana, and paced again. The clock showed 7:45 CST, 8:45 EST. He looked at the lake for a few minutes, then back at the clock. It read 7:47. He sighed and did fifty push-ups in the living room. The clock read 7:51.

How time flies when you are having fun.

Nervously laughing to himself, he returned to the balcony with his phone gripped in his sweaty hand. It vibrated, and he heard the familiar cosmic ringtone. Her voice had never left him.

"Hi, Ben. So sorry for doing this but felt I had to talk with you."

He anticipated disappointment. His stomach ached, and the muscles in his neck tightened. "Not a problem, Dahlia." He wanted to delay any possible bad news. "How are you? What's new in your life? We haven't talked for so long. Is everything OK?"

"Yes, I am fine, Ben. Listen, I just must talk to you about our meeting."

He prepared for the inevitable.

"I got to thinking that my suggestion of us getting together was all about me, and I had never even considered what was happening in your life. Or whether you wanted to get together. Texting you just didn't seem fair. I had to ask you whether you want to see me. Are you OK with this, Ben, or is it a bad idea? I want to know your opinion."

"Dahlia, I agreed to have dinner with you because I want to see you. I don't know what to expect. I enjoyed being with you before, and maybe it's that simple. I am planning on seeing you unless you have changed your mind or have reservations. If you do, talk to me."

"No, I appreciate your words, Ben. I don't want to be an obligation. After texting you, I just wanted to ask in person."

"Yes, Dahlia, I want to see you and have dinner. I am looking forward to it." "Wonderful. I will see you in a few days. Friday night, 7:00 p.m. Goodbye, Ben."

"Goodbye, Dahlia."

Ben spent his next few hours trying to write, acutely aware of having not asked her the hard question. *Is she married? I don't want to know.*

Rainstorms moved into Minneapolis for the next couple of days, cementing his plans to continue writing. But his head was chaotic. *If I remained married to Alison, would she have cheated anyhow? Would there have been a fire? Am I cursed? Tomorrow, I'm having dinner with a woman from Toronto because of a fire. What will I think when she describes her happy marriage? I can't even remember my last date.*

On Friday, he woke up relieved, knowing soon he would not have to worry about seeing her. By the next morning, the dinner would be over.

Lily had plans with friends, so Ben was unable to talk with her. Driving to the hotel restaurant, he was reminded again of what Dahlia hadn't talked about during the phone call. Was she engaged or married? There would be time for those topics at dinner. He let the valet park his car, feeling uncharacteristically relaxed and eager to see Dahlia.

He walked into the Akvavit restaurant at 6:55. The name was Norwegian for a potato-based alcohol that meant "water of life." He was seated and asked about a beverage, which he declined. He glanced down at his phone, read 7:00, and took three deep breaths. *God, am I nervous.*

Dahlia was being escorted to the table by a hostess. Her graceful movements and short, black dress attracted attention. Eyes at the bar followed her. She had a commanding presence. Ben smiled, thinking of her as an officer in the Canadian army. In his eyes, Dahlia epitomized grace and strength.

He stood up to greet her. "Hello, Dahlia." He kissed her hand.

"So good to see your face, Ben."

Looking at each other, both knew immediately that this was the absolute correct decision. For a moment or two, these two verbal people just smiled and investigated each other's eyes. Dahlia spoke first as the hostess pulled out her chair.

"Thank you for coming. I still feel a little sheepish about invading your territory, but selfishly, I am not sorry. I needed to see you, at least one more time."

"I wanted to see you and would have been very disappointed had you canceled. You have been on my mind often, and now I know why. Being with you feels natural. It did in Belize. It does here. Would you prefer wine or something else?"

Dahlia selected a Malbec. She sampled a taste and gave the waiter a thumbs-up.

Small talk was minimal. Briefly, she spoke of the conference and then said, "I want you to know that Ben and I are no longer together. He wanted to be close to his family and took the job in Boston. We had many long discussions about our future together and decided to go our own ways. Our individual circumstances felt more important than being together. We split on good terms, though, wishing each other happiness. I want you to know the decision had nothing to do with San Pedro. Ben and I were together out of convenience, and once other issues surfaced, that became clear."

"I am not sure how to react, Dahlia." He lifted his glass. "How about a toast to happiness?"

"To happiness, Ben."

Dahlia smiled, and each time, Ben's face flushed. Something about her pulled forth his physical reactions. His breathing and pulse quickened. He sipped water as his mouth dried. He'd felt it in Belize, but the reactions grew worse over time.

For the next two hours, Ben and Dahlia shared their lives and dinners. They had broiled scallops, linguine, and blackened halibut with jasmine rice. Ben watched Dahlia's precise handling of her knife and fork.

His heart rate doubled from sitting across from her. He was enthralled with her.

"Oh, my. Taste this, Ben." She slid her fork between his lips. He returned the favor.

The emotional intimacy that had connected them in San Pedro returned. More likely, it had never left. *No wonder I have had her on my mind for months. She is magical. This is magical.*

He felt sadness creeping in, unsure of how the dinner would end, even unsure of how he wanted it to end. As in San Pedro, he was beginning to feel regret for ever having met Dahlia. They were quiet for a couple of minutes before she spoke.

"Ben, I must ask you a question. Do you think that if a relationship couldn't be long term, it would be wise not to have it at all?"

Ben responded as a therapist, "Can you say more? I'm not sure I understand."

"I spent two days with you and have thought about you often since. There is a connection between us that scares me a little. I wanted more with you in Belize but knew that was not the right time. I know we might be on different paths. My family and I live in Toronto. Your roots are here. I do understand that long-distance relationships are often sad and painful. I want to avoid regrets."

Ben tried to speak, but Dahlia said, "Let me finish. I want to spend the night with you, even if tonight will be our only night together, but I don't want to talk you into it. Follow your heart." She slid her room key across the table. "If I don't see you again, at least I had the chance to speak from my heart."

She squeezed his shoulder and walked away.

Ben got up, circled aimlessly in the lobby, then took the elevator to the eleventh floor. He stood outside her door, hesitating. He knew what he knew. If he struggled to erase her memory after two days of talking in San Pedro, what would spending the night with her do?

He inserted the card and walked into the room. Dahlia was standing with her back to him, looking out the window. Ben walked to her. She turned and put her arms around his neck. Their lips met for the first time.

Their physical connection was intense, gentle, and loving. Every moment seemed to bring them closer. They caressed each other's minds and bodies simultaneously, giving of themselves like never before.

Months of pent-up thoughts and feelings flowed from him. They found undiscovered heights. She held his face, peering into his soul. Ben accepted that he would love her forever, no matter what tomorrow would bring.

Holding Dahlia in his arms, Ben couldn't stop looking at her. It was 3:47 a.m. He pulled her close and whispered in her ear, "I will always cherish tonight. This moment will always be a part of me."

Dahlia slid against the contours of his body. He was in ecstasy, wanting to become part of her.

"I feel like water with you, limitless, flowing together," she said.

"I have to stay with you until the last moment." Ben held her in his arms, resisting sleep, fearing the passing of time. He stayed awake, holding her close, cherishing every second.

Startled by a room-service call, they faced their dreaded parting. Her flight was in a couple of hours. They made love again, slowly, tenderly, seizing every second together.

Dahlia told him she did not want to say goodbye at the airport. San Pedro was difficult. Minneapolis would be cruel. Ben understood. He hoped for the impossible. He put his arms around her, holding her until the last heartbreaking moment. He let go. There was no other choice.

Ben said, "If you cannot hold me, hold our memory."

The time had come to leave. Their lips met one last time, sealing their souls. Ben smiled at Dahlia, backed out of the room, and walked away. He stepped into the elevator. *Behavior is controllable, emotions are not.* He merged onto 494, the airport in his rearview.

Dahlia looked down at the Minneapolis skyline and wondered if once was enough.

When Ben returned to the Towers, Lily had left for class. He wondered if she'd noticed that he hadn't come home. He was relieved to be alone. He went into his bedroom and pulled a pillow over his head. He could feel his heartbeat.

The next morning, Lily never mentioned his absence. Ben assumed she had come home late, gone to bed, got up early, and never noticed. He collapsed with exhaustion. Five hours later, physically rested but emotionally drained, he went for a long run around all three lakes.

Ben broke his own rules by texting her. "Had to do this. How are you, dear Dahlia? Ben."

Her reply was instantaneous. "Ben, without question, I would make the same decision again. Love, Dahlia."

After the text with Dahlia, Ben burrowed his face in a pillow. He had a glimmer of hope to move forward. He cherished the authenticity of their relationship. Neither of them would ever forget their night together. He had gone from lost to found to lost again.

He called the builder and met him at his skeleton home. The frame was up, and the outline against the sky allowed him to visualize his new home. Knowing his home was being built provided him a fraction of stability. Afterward, he decided to swing by Louie's and say hello to him and Junior. Louie sensed Ben's fragile state of mind and gave him a hug. Junior jumped on Ben's lap and licked his ear. Ben wasn't ready to talk, but he lingered in their company.

When Ben came home, Lily was having lunch and offered to make him a salad. Ben realized he hadn't eaten all day. He felt strange to be on an emotional roller coaster without Lily knowing.

"I met this woman yesterday who I connected with in San Pedro. We had dinner and spent some time together. She is from Toronto, here for a conference, and now back in Canada."

"Good for you, Dad. Do you like her? Actually, I know you like her. You'd never have dinner with a woman you didn't like. So, what's the scoop? Tell me about her."

"Well, her name is Dahlia Karlsen. She's a vascular surgeon from Toronto. She was deployed to Iraq with a medical team—oh yes, and she's half-Norwegian. So, we had that in common, we had a great time, and I have to say, a platonic relationship in Belize. She was alone, and so we hung out. But as I said, she lives in Toronto and is very connected to her family. You would think one of us could move, but both of our ties and roots are deep. So, end of story."

"Wish I could meet her. Maybe sometime down the road. Who knows? Funny you should mention Norwegian—my genetics class all took DNA tests, and mine came back wrong. There must have been a mix-up at the lab. I was only a fraction Norwegian. I resubmitted it. Will get the results in about a week."

Lily left for class, and Ben walked to his bedroom window and made a call. "We have to talk."

Alison said, "What about?"

"Lily took a DNA test. The results will be back in about a week." The phone was silent.

Seconds later, Ben heard, "I'm speechless. Can we meet now?"

"Yes, Caribou in Glen Lake?"

Fifteen minutes later, Ben and Alison were looking at each other in the coffee shop.

"Tell me what you know."

"Lily is taking a genetics class to complete her double minor. She told me over lunch that the class took DNA tests and there was a mix-up. She assumed a lab mistake and resubmitted a new one, which will be back next week. That's what I know."

"Oh my God, I am in shock. I never thought this would happen. What can we do? What should we do? I feel paralyzed." Alison started to cry.

"Let's get out of here and go for a walk in the park. There's one a block down the street."

Soon after, they were sitting on a bench by a duck pond, still speechless.

"Let's talk about our options," Ben said.

Staring at the pond, Alison did not seem ready or able to talk.

"We could do nothing and see what Lily says about the second result, and then we can decide, or we could talk with Lily and tell her the truth. The last choice—not one I'm suggesting—we can make up a lie."

"We could plead ignorance and see what happens."

"Yes, we could do that too. Despite this turn of events, we are not in a desperate situation. We have a week. There is a slim chance that Lily will never bring it up."

"I am so sorry, Ben, but my mind is blank. I am in shock. I must be part of the solution, but at this moment, I'm not capable. Let's talk in the morning. I will call you about nine. Will Lily be gone by then?"

"Yes, she leaves for class about quarter after eight."

They walked back to the Caribou parking lot.

"What does Ted know?" Ben asked.

"Nothing."

They both got in their cars and drove away.

Ben hoped there was an option they hadn't thought of. The ones on the table were painful.

The following day, Alison called promptly at 9:00 a.m. "I wished there were a clear answer in my head, but there isn't. I am beside myself looking for a solution, but there doesn't seem to be one. All I can say is I want to do whatever is best for Lily."

"I have gone over and over what we might do, and it seems inevitable to me that Lily will ask for answers. We just must be prepared and have a plan when that happens."

"If and when Lily asks those questions, do you think we should both talk with her?"

"Yes, I believe it would be best if both of us talked with her."

"It's tempting to say I don't want to be part of that conversation, but I own this nightmare."

"Because Lily is living here, the topic will probably arise when she's with me. Should that happen unexpectedly, I just ask you to be available. Can I count on you, Alison?"

"Yes, I could be at your place in fifteen minutes."

The following Monday, Lily went to class early. Ben began putting the finishing touches on chapter 6, writing, "I've tried to stop thinking about you, but now I realize thoughts of you help me to survive."

After running some afternoon errands, Ben came home and found Lily reading on the balcony. He sat down near her and asked about her day.

"My class was emotional today. My lab partner told me and the class she found out she was adopted. Until yesterday, she had always thought she and her brother were biological siblings. Last night, with her DNA results, her parents confessed she was adopted and that her brother was their only biological child. This poor girl is having some serious personal turmoil. I feel bad for her.

"My DNA results came back. Again, they say the same genetic composition—25 percent Iberian Peninsula, 25 percent Norwegian, 25 percent French, and 25 percent European Jewish. I don't get it." Clearly, her classmate's experience had shaken Lily. "Do you have any idea why they'd come back this way again?"

The day of reckoning was here. Ben went in the bedroom and called Alison. "Come now."

Sitting down next to Lily, he put his arms around her. "There is information that your mother and I want to share with you. She will be here in a couple of minutes."

Lily looked shocked, then angry. "What are you talking about? What information? Is this a bad joke? What the hell is going on? Talk to me now!"

"I promised your mother I would wait for her, and I am keeping my word. You have a right to the truth and will know everything as soon as she gets here. What I can tell you is that you are the light of my life. I love you as only a father can love a daughter."

Alison got there quickly and hugged Lily, her eyes red. Lily and Alison sat down next to each other.

Ben looked at the two of them, one he had loved and married, the other he had been a father to and loved from the second she was born. Both were in pain, one in search of the truth and the other afraid of the truth.

Ben said, "This is difficult. But each of us has a responsibility to make sure that, no matter what, our care for each other will prevail."

Hearing himself disgusted Ben. He sounded like a therapist, not a father, but he couldn't stop.

"Lily, after your mother and I were married, we were very happy. Then 9/11 interrupted a wonderful time for us. I was deployed, and it was a challenge for two newly married young people. Leaving your mother was painful, and she didn't want me to go. She had the added burden of worrying about whether I would come back alive."

"I have to do this, Ben," Alison interrupted. "I look back on those days with such sadness. Your dad was in a war, facing life and death each day, and I was a wreck. I couldn't sleep or eat. My health suffered. I started therapy and at times felt better. But every month, I deteriorated mentally and physically. I kept having dreams of your dad being killed."

Alison took a deep breath and continued, "My supervisor at work was sympathetic and supportive. He let me come in late, leave early . . . whatever I needed. One night, after work—" Alison started to cry uncontrollably and stopped talking.

Ben said, "I can explain, Alison."

Alison said loudly, "No! This is my responsibility. One day after work, I had a car issue, and my boss, Terry, offered me a ride home. I broke down in the car, and he wasn't comfortable leaving me alone. He came in the house. Short story, simple answer, we drank too much, he spent the night. Disgusted and humiliated, I never returned to work or spoke to him again. Soon after, a friend at work told me that he had transferred to Los Angeles. There is more, Lily. Soon after, Ben came home, and I found out that I was pregnant. I didn't know who the father was. I am not looking for forgiveness, but I contemplated suicide and planned to have an abortion. Your father, the man you know as your father, stopped me. He was confused about why I was so distraught because he never knew the truth until recently." Alison was exhausted.

Angrily, Lily lashed out, "I can't believe what you are saying to me. I am twenty-one years old, and you kept this from me my whole life. The words I want to say are so awful I can't even say them. You are telling me I have a different father, now, after twenty-one years? This is so sick."

"Lily, your mother has told you the truth. I would be lying if I said this wasn't as shocking to me. It's painful and continues to be, but you and I must deal with it. How I feel about you is the same. I love you, and you are my daughter."

Lily sat between the only two parents she had known and sobbed, her face in hands.

"Lily, you are my daughter and have been my daughter since the second you were born. I was the first to hold you, and I will hold you until I die."

Lily ignored Ben and looked to her mother, shaking and almost yelling, "You said *was* my father. What did you mean?"

"After he moved to LA, he died in a car accident, before you were born."

Lily stood up. "This is more than I can handle. I need to be alone. I don't want to be in the same room with either of you." She went to her room.

Alison and Ben sat in silence. Fifteen minutes later, Lily returned.

"I'm leaving. I just made a reservation at a hotel. I don't want to be around either of you."

Alison left soon after Lily. Ben sat in silence. He texted Lily. "I need to know where you are."

An hour later, Lily texted back, "University Radisson. Leave me alone."

Ben drove to the University Radisson and texted her again. "I am here and need 5 minutes, please."

Lily texted back, "No, I need to be alone."

Ben went to the desk, saying he needed to see his daughter. The clerk said he needed to ask her permission and called her. "I will respect your privacy. It's your decision."

Reluctantly, Lily agreed to see her dad.

"Give me two minutes, and I will respect your wish to be alone. Twenty-one years ago, your mother had a choice of aborting you or keeping you. We talked at length, and she chose to protect you. I am sorry for the hurt you have now. I know what hurt and anger can do to a person. We must resolve what has happened. I came here tonight because you are my only daughter, and I am your only father. That doesn't change. There. I've had my say."

He turned to walk away when Lily said, "You must understand I am in shock. I need to be alone to sort this out."

"I do." Ben left with a pounding headache.

The next day was June 30, and he would move to St. Paul to live with Anne and Andrew. Lily was moving to Uptown. He'd completed another chapter in his book, and in living with Lily for the last time, he felt like he'd lost a chapter of his life.

REMEMBRANCE

Lily returned from class, and she and Ben spent their last hour at the Towers quietly. The shock had dissolved, but the pain had soaked in. Lily faced several new issues. She was somber, knowing there was a biological father whom she would never meet. Lily said there may be a time that she would explore who he was and learn about her heritage. But not now.

There were pressing realities of applying for a job, moving into an apartment, finishing her degree, and putting her life back on track. Ben asked Lily to communicate with him. They had been connected for twenty-one years, and he hoped the bridge could be rebuilt. They pulled out of the Towers and drove in different directions.

Like Lily, Ben wanted solitude. He was depressed. His closest family connection was in limbo, and he was moving to his sister and brother-in-law's home. In all directions of his life, he saw failure.

Arriving at Pierce Street, his seventh bedroom of 2023, Ben was shown to his living quarters. He unpacked, hung his sparse wardrobe in the closet, and laid on the bed looking at the ceiling.

Anne and Andrew had lived at 448 Pierce Street for twenty years. The house was built by a Civil War general after returning to Minnesota in 1866. Many famous people were said to have dined there, including Sinclair Lewis, the "red-haired tornado" and first American to be awarded a Nobel Prize in Literature. Ben wished some of Harry's creativity and talent would inspire him. He needed all the help he could get. Writing was impossible. He stayed in his room a long time.

The only positive was that he was alone. Most of the year, he had been questioning why he was lonely. Now, he found peace in not having to communicate. His living area was probably twenty yards from Anne and Andrew's bedroom. Anne and Andrew had spent years restoring the home to its original charm. When they had bought the home, it was divided into six apartments. They lived in one and began researching the original design. The restoration took five years.

The house was glorious. Anne and Andrew were retired and had the time and energy to fine-tune the house. It was impossible to drive by without wanting to stop and look. The character of the house conveyed that it had stories to tell.

On Ben's first night, Anne made dinner. Breaded pork chops, caramelized brussels sprouts, garlic mashed potatoes, and strawberry rhubarb pie. Anne had a knack for thoughtful gestures. She was familiar with the sadness in his eyes and hoped to elevate his mood with a sweet memory.

The evening was as close to a classic Raymond dinner as Ben could remember. Afterward, they sat in the formal living room and chatted about life, liberty, and the pursuit of happiness. Feeling like a train wreck, Ben was quieter than usual and confessed to being tired. He hoped he'd successfully hidden his sadness. Anne and Andrew gave him space and privacy.

Alone, Ben was ambivalent, almost catatonic, uncertain of most everything. He heard a creaking sound and wondered if Sinclair's ghost was visiting. He hoped so. He had many questions, no answers, and would welcome help from anywhere. His thoughts went to Lily. *I miss her already.*

Then there was Ted and Alison. Although his anger toward her was real, he understood the inner turmoil she would feel, keeping this secret from Ted.

"Dahlia, Dahlia, Dahlia." Ben surprised himself, saying her name out loud and praying, "Please, God, Mom, and Dad, please keep Dahlia safe from harm." The thought of having their help comforted him.

Three loud pops pierced the night. Ben was on the floor, grasping for his M4 before realizing he was in St. Paul. Getting up and sitting on the bed, he felt a drip of sweat running down the side of his face. He listened again. Firecrackers.

His phone read 2:02 a.m. He had never been never a fan of firecrackers, but after being deployed, he despised their sound. He heard someone in the kitchen and decided to get a drink of water.

Andrew was sitting at the table. "I guess you heard the firecrackers too."

"Sure did. I know the Fourth is close, but two in the morning?"

"I flew out of bed. It's been many years since 'Nam, for you in Iraq a much shorter time. We come back to the world, but from time to time, the war visits us. For me, it happens maybe a few times a year. Usually from a sound. Helicopters get me sometimes. You?"

"Not bad, occasional dreams, rare situations trigger me. I'm going to try to get some sleep."

"Good idea."

The morning offered a tranquil beginning. Ben woke to the aroma of bacon and remembered his friend saying, "I'm a vegetarian except for bacon."

Soon after, he heard Anne holler, "Breakfast time!"

Anne had outdone herself. Blueberry pancakes, scrambled eggs with tomato and onions, thick smoked, crispy bacon, croissants, and black raspberry jam.

A Valhalla breakfast. Andrew and Anne laughed about never having made as good a breakfast in all their years of marriage.

"Enjoy it. There won't be another one like this for the rest of July," Andrew and Anne teased as they left to meet their crew club on the Mississippi River. Anne and Andrew were easy to be around. Ben appreciated the calm environment. He decided to start writing chapter 7.

He had a resurgence of energy. He wrote for hours without stopping. His creativity flourished. *This is my best so far.* He wrote all afternoon. "Who knows why love began? It just did. Will the inevitable end be as sudden? Or sadly, no end, just pangs of hurt."

He took a break on the rooftop balcony.

He studied the separate skylines of Minneapolis and St. Paul. The golden horses on the capitol, the Basilica, the Mississippi River, the Space Tower at the state fairgrounds, and the Viking and Wild stadiums. This was Ben's home. *Dahlia must cherish Toronto too.*

Anne and Andrew brought home Cossetta's pizza for dinner. Anne brought out the Raymond family photo album. "This will be fun to look at later."

The album opened with Grandfather Ben, who'd emigrated from Bergen as a sixteen-year-old to take a job working on the railroad in St. Paul. On June 6, 1944, Grandpa Ben returned to Europe on D-day as a Screaming Eagle of the 101st Airborne Division. He enlisted the day after Germany invaded Norway.

The pictures of Grandpa Ben and Grandma Anne were precious. Anne worked at the Ford factory making military vehicles during the war. They married a few months before he left. After the war, they had six children and remained in St. Paul all their lives. They were buried together at the Fort Snelling National Cemetery.

Anne looked at Ben. "We should be so damn proud to be named after those two."

Next, they looked at pictures of their mother and father, Ellen and Oliver Raymond. They retold stories. A favorite one revolved around Oliver and Ellen's secret elopement to California. However, they ended up making their vows in North Platte, Nebraska. For years, no one knew why.

One of her last days on earth, Ben asked her why they got married in Nebraska.

She'd said, "You might as well know; I wouldn't check into a hotel with your dad until we were married."

"Dad was always so protective of Mom. Once when I said something to Mom that he didn't like, Dad grabbed my arm and said, 'That's my girlfriend you're talking to.' The message was clear, and I never did it again. Boy, did he teach me a lesson that day."

Andrew excused himself to go play pickleball.

"Have you and Andrew ever talked about Vietnam?"

"Not really, just bits and pieces."

"I just heard this story from Andrew a couple of months ago. I kept asking him questions. Finally, he handed me this citation from a box, the Bronze Star for Valor."

"He risked his life to save two wounded soldiers," Ben said. "I didn't have a choice. I was a medic; they were bleeding to death, and it was my job."

"That's the Andrew I fell in love with, and he has never changed. Let's take a drive to the cemetery to see our grandparents' grave site."

After viewing their grave, Anne asked, "Ben, do you think our grandparents and parents are in heaven?"

"If there is a heaven, they're there. Interesting you should ask because I was just thinking about how I try to communicate with Mom and Dad. I can't really explain why, but it gives me comfort. I think my problems would be trivial to a higher power, so I ask Mom and Dad for help. What do you think of your little brother now?"

"I love hearing that. I am proud to have you as my brother."

Back on Pierce Street, Lily accepted Anne's invitation to join them for coffee following the Fourth of July parade.

The military parade was important to Andrew and Ben. They spoke little. Words weren't necessary. Each knew what the other knew, and that was enough.

The fireworks cast noisy, spectacular colors against the black sky, yet they felt anticlimactic after the real-life stories of the day.

Ben walked Lily to her car. "Thank you for coming today. This meant so much to me. I love you, Lily. Stay connected."

"I'll try."

They said goodbye, and she drove away.

Sometimes, on the Fourth of July, Ben found himself frustrated with Americans. They didn't seem to appreciate their privileged lives. In his younger days, Ben looked to Merle Haggard's fighting side when people bad-mouthed his country. Now, he was wiser. He knew firsthand that violence never changed anyone's mind.

The next few days, everyone was back into their normal routines, and Ben returned to writing. The historic house on Pierce Street continued to be stimulating. Whether it was the spirit of Grandpa Ben,

Grandma Anne, or Sinclair Lewis, the source of his inspiration didn't matter; he was grateful.

Stories about Ben and Anne's dad surfaced too. Oliver was a passive man, but he was passionate. He had coal-black hair and olive skin and was often questioned about his ethnicity. Usually, he would say, "Why would my ethnicity matter to you?" He resisted saying his parents were from Norway because he said the answer "capitulated to prejudicial thinking." He was a kind, gentle man when he wasn't drinking.

Lily's own line of thinking, lately, had landed on rejecting her biology. *We came from ordinary people who lived extraordinary lives. These are my people. I am Lily Raymond.*

With Ben having a couple of days remaining in St. Paul, Louie invited Ben to join him, Sheri, and a friend for dinner at the Khyber Pass, an Afghan restaurant. Ben had never visited a restaurant during his entire year in Afghanistan. He made Louie promise it was not a blind date. Louie conceded the dinner was a setup and told Ben to make the best of it. Somehow, that made it OK.

Ben noticed a colorfully dressed woman standing at the counter. She had long, curly black hair, black eyes, and olive skin. She wore a mustard-colored dress, a purple-and-orange scarf, and dangling gold earrings. She was striking. Sheri and Louie were already seated when Ben joined them.

"Maddie!" Sheri called. The woman came over and sat down next to Ben. She shook his hand. Ben considered how life is filled with surprises. He felt overdue for something good.

Dinner was a carnival of flavor. The conversation was sublime. The night felt like a welcome breath of fresh air. Maddie was a buyer of women's attire and traveled internationally frequently. Ben enjoyed her energy. She had an admirable zest for life, and her worldly travels, intelligence, and quick wit were unique.

Louie looked at Ben with an expression suggesting Maddie was a keeper. Ben felt weird because of his recent time with Dahlia. He tried unsuccessfully to let go of the feeling. At the end of the evening, Maddie and Ben exchanged cell numbers. By the time he was driving home, he decided he would like to know Maddie better.

The next morning, Anne sat on the bed while he packed. "You seemed sad when you moved in. I wanted to give you time and respect your privacy. Where did the time go? Now you're leaving, and I wonder how you are, I mean *really* are. You seem more at peace now, but I still wanted to ask if you're all right before you leave."

"Anne, the past few months have been a roller coaster. What I've learned is that I am my worst enemy. I've made so many mistakes. Now, all I can do is try to forgive myself by being a better person."

Anne didn't seem surprised. "Our family has always been good at store fronting. You and I were taught that skill by Mom and Dad. We learned how to look happy. I was thinking the other night about how much we talk about our grandparents and how little about our parents."

"We never talk about the other stuff," Ben said. "It's painful. I never want to bring up bad memories. Not once did we ever talk about Dad's drinking or Mom's brothers. We've never even talked about Dad dying or driving drunk. I was younger. You probably saw the worst of it."

Anne stared at Ben. "I learned so much when Andrew went through treatment. You and I lived in a classic alcoholic family. There was a hard-core no-talk rule. My God, Ben, we're still living it. I tried to protect you. You were little. I never knew what you remembered, so I never brought it up. The times the police had to come to the house because Dad was violent. Once, you tried to protect Mom from Dad. You were probably four or five. I hated leaving you alone after graduating. Even then, you were only nine."

"I have always been afraid of becoming Dad. The past few months have shown me that not everyone lives like this. I've only been talking to myself. I have to let some of this out. I don't remember much of Mom and Dad fighting."

Ben was determined to change. He started spilling part of his guts with Anne. He talked about the wars, fire, the divorce, and Dahlia, but never mentioned Lily's biological father. That story was owned by Lily.

Anne teared up listening to her little brother.

"I am so very sorry for you. You deserve better. Don't give up; you are a strong person, and life is unpredictable. Just as you met Dahlia, you can meet someone new."

The time had come to leave.

"Goodbye, my favorite brother."

"Goodbye, my favorite sister."

He drove to 10 Water Street looking for a little hope. Four more months, he thought, and for once, four months felt soon.

ZWEI FRAUEN

The house at 10 Water Street was only a ten-minute drive to La Rive. Moving downriver to St. Anthony Main was effortless. Although Ben had communicated with Caroline many times, he hadn't called her to confirm his move-in date. She and Rachel were out of the country, so he didn't feel any urgency. They were returning on August 10 from Buenos Aires and had given him the lockbox combination, expecting him to be there.

Caroline and Ben had been friends since enrolling at the University of Minnesota. They had met during the fall semester of their freshman year. Caroline and Rachel had been married over ten years and lived in La Rive, a twenty-nine-floor high-rise in the St. Anthony Main area of Minneapolis.

Caroline and Rachel were businesswomen who arranged, rented, and sold housing for Minnesota corporations. If a company employee needed housing, internationally or stateside, their business made the arrangement. Caroline started the company. She'd met Rachel while traveling in Europe. Rachel was an Austrian national whose home was Salzburg. Since marriage, their primary home had been in Minneapolis. They had no children.

Ben pulled into the underground parking space, relieved to be moving into an empty condo.

The condo was like an art gallery surrounded by skyscrapers. Caroline and Rachel had paintings and drawings everywhere. He'd met Caroline in an art class. She had been instrumental in helping him survive his most challenging class. Ben experienced some pride in his recognition of *Flaming June, Dance at Bougival, Portrait of Edith Schiele,* and *Nude Sitting on a Divan.*

Their home was a direct contrast to the historic house on Pierce. Metal beams, floor-to-ceiling glass, and soft white walls coupled with the Mississippi River and the Minneapolis skyline made for a stimulating, yet calming, vista. Ben sat on the balcony with a glass of wine.

Caroline and Rachel had a collection of fine wines. Ben chose a pinot noir. On the counter was a note. "Welcome to La Rive, my good friend! Rachel and I want you to feel at home. We will reconnect soon. Shalom, Caroline and Rachel."

Ben poured the pinot into a rose chalice and retreated to a balcony chaise. The sun was directly behind the skyline shooting arrows of light into the glistening river. He breathed deeply and welcomed a surge of gratitude. The trials and tribulations since the fire encouraged him to be grateful. During this fleeting moment of his rollercoaster year, Ben's soul was at peace.

He questioned the meaning and value of a solitary life. He was beginning to comprehend the qualities of a long-term relationship. Russ, José, Arthur, Louie, Nathan, Andrew, and Caroline had relationships with a committed companion. He wanted to figure out why he'd prioritized being alone. The answer was elusive. However, he had a sound hypothesis. *I am the problem and need to change.*

Construction was progressing, and he was ready to start choosing design elements for his home. He hoped his new home could be the catalyst for a genesis of sorts, a new beginning for the second half of his life. Finishing the pinot, he watched the sun disappear.

That night was quiet. No firecrackers, no alarms, no sounds penetrated the concrete walls. Awaking, he cherished the silence. The quiet generated peacefulness, and he stayed in bed for several minutes, almost in a meditative state. He went to the balcony and contrasted the view from the night. The morning skyline sparkled with diamonds of sunlight. Everything was the same except for the position of a star ninety-three-million miles away. An ordinary star delivering an extraordinary service to planet Earth.

After making a latte and adding a smiling cinnamon face, Ben returned to the chaise and began evaluating his past, searching for an answer to the question of why he was alone. He'd had serious relationships since his divorce twenty years before. He knew the reasons those had failed. *The walls around me are red flags to anyone, so I always ended relationships before they could leave me.*

He continued writing during his first week and devoted time each day to self-analysis. Eight months after the fire, he was learning about himself. Each month, he had watched different approaches to life. At times, he accepted that being alone could be his lifestyle of choice.

I am learning to be honest with myself.

His novel was developing in parallel lines with the nonfiction that was his life. At times, he challenged the blurred lines between fiction and nonfiction. All his fiction was inspired by reality. *What if there is no truth and there are no lies?*

Living at La Rive was stimulating. The elevation offered magnificent views of the city. Ben observed the hustle and bustle of urban life. He was entertained by the changing light and rhythms of a day, and his sleep patterns became unpredictable. Sometimes, he would write on the balcony from midnight until three in the morning, watching the city fall asleep. Other times, he would rise at four to watch the city wake up.

He loved the view from heights and looked forward to the third-story tower on his home. As a young man, he'd watched the NASA channel late at night. Seeing continents sliding over oceans in a minute was fascinating. He recalled that the *Mayflower* needed sixty-six days to cross the Atlantic in 1620, while the space shuttle traveled the same distance in less than thirty minutes.

He considered calling Maddie. He couldn't think of a reason not to call her, but in lieu of his powerful emotions with Dahlia, he decided to wait another day. He was cautious with relationships. *If I can't deal with my own issues, how can I deal with another's?*

The following day, he called Maddie because he had said he would. They agreed they'd walk across the Stone Arch Bridge and have dinner somewhere yet undetermined. It all felt so normal to him, although this was only the second real date of the year for him. The first was meeting Dahlia. It was already August. He realized his life was slipping away, and there was no reason to wait.

Maddie suggested meeting in front of the Aster Café. After a short walk, Ben waited on a bench facing the Mississippi. The evening was warm, but a cool breeze slid off the river. He dressed for his date, realizing again that since the fire, he owned a clown wardrobe. It was only his second time seeing Maddie, though, and he could get three dates out of his wardrobe before he had to repeat items.

As Maddie crossed Main Street in her black slacks and silky white blouse, Ben saw her turn toward him and smile. His apprehension partially dissolved. Maddie's smile alone could make the evening enjoyable.

He remembered the conversation they had shared at the restaurant and considered the coincidence that a woman from Afghanistan was having dinner in Minneapolis with him, a soldier who'd been in her country.

Their greeting was polite. Ben kissed her hand, and Maddie smiled again. Her sparkling eyes and quiet soul hinted of a peaceful mind. After small talk about their day and comments about the beautiful evening, they strolled toward Stone Arch. Turning toward downtown Minneapolis and onto the bridge, Ben asked Maddie about her family.

Her family fled Afghanistan after the Russian invasion in 1979. Her grandparents worked for the deposed government in Kabul. Several former government officials were arrested or assassinated. No one knew who was ordering the killings or why they were happening. When an entire family in their neighborhood was murdered, her grandfather planned to move the family to England.

Her grandparents, parents, and extended family left Afghanistan and traveled to Mumbai, then to England where relatives resided. The family lived in London for a year before her father was offered a job in Minneapolis. Her parents moved, hoping her grandparents would follow. Five years later, they did, and her extended family was reunited in Golden Valley.

Maddie had lived in the States since she was a little girl. After graduating from high school, she attended DePaul University in Chicago. After graduation, Maddie's cousin offered her a job in London. Maddie moved and remained there for eight years until the pull of family brought her back to Minnesota.

In London, she gained experience importing goods from Asia. She started her own company in the States. With a small staff, she built a thriving business. Her work and lifestyle never entertained marriage or children. She lived alone on Nicollet Island across the river. Her home was probably visible from the balcony at La Rive.

Ben and Maddie ended up at the Sample Room after a short Uber. She was inquisitive and probed for character evidence. Ben understood that being single in one's forties encouraged a person to get to the point.

By the end of dinner, Maddie knew more about Ben than many people who had known him longer. He had learned little about her personal life, though. She was smart and knew which questions to ask and which answers she wanted to hear.

When Maddie asked what brought Ben joy and made him happy, he knew it would not be a boring dinner.

"To live a life that makes a difference. I'm still working on identifying what I need to be happy."

After dinner, they walked along the river toward St. Anthony Main. Watching the sun set, Maddie took Ben's hand in hers. "I have always longed to see another sunset in my motherland."

Ben put his arm around her shoulders. She leaned into his chest, and they stood in silence for a couple of minutes. "I have an early Zoom meeting at seven with a buyer in New York. Maybe the wise choice would be to go home and get some sleep. It's been a long day."

Ben called an Uber, and they were dropped in front of the Aster Café in two minutes. He walked Maddie to her car. They joked about his short walk and her quarter-mile drive home.

He felt as if he were back in high school as they stood next to Maddie's red Audi, neither one sure of how to end the evening. Maddie took the lead, leaned forward, kissed Ben on the cheek, and said,

"I like you, Ben Raymond. Our dinner and conversation were more than I expected."

She smiled again, and Ben embraced the pleasant impact of this woman. He leaned forward, put his arms around her, and kissed the top of her head.

Looking up at La Rive, he said, "Call me when you are home safely. I will be on the balcony waving good night." He opened the door, and Maddie got in and drove away. By the time Ben walked out on the balcony, his phone rang.

"I'm home, Ben. Safe. Thank you for your protective thoughts. I appreciate that quality. Good night, Ben."

"Thank you for a delightful evening, Maddie. Good night."

Looking down on Nicollet Island, he wondered which home lights belonged to her.

Caroline and Rachel were returning from Buenos Aires the next day. The first days of August passed quickly. Although Ben had enjoyed the solitude and made progress on his book, he looked forward to seeing Caroline again. She was a friend in the same realm as Louie. Over the years, Ben had met Caroline for a drink, lunch, or dinner, but had only met Rachel a couple of times.

In the morning, he and the builder had a promising meeting on Water Street. The final drawing of his third-floor tower was complete. The combination of windows, stone walls, and conical wooden ceiling were unique. He relished the thought of being in the tower during inclement weather. He could see the moment when he would once again have a home.

He sat on the balcony watching the sunset as he waited for Caroline and Rachel to arrive. He had offered to pick them up, but Caroline assured him that they had already arranged for a van to come get them.

His eyes drifted to Nicollet Island and Maddie. She was a mysterious woman. Ben had shared more information than usual on a first date. *I'm trying.* Although sensing no red flags, he knew he didn't know her well. His feelings for Maddie were in infancy. He wasn't drawn to her as he had been to Dahlia. The emotional sharing with

Dahlia made their first evening breathtaking. Maddie's sharing was more objective. She was interesting, yet cautious.

Caroline and Rachel called from downstairs to give Ben a heads-up. He had three minutes of privacy remaining. One hundred and eighty seconds later, the married couple were in the door, looking tired and relieved to be home after hours of flying. After brief hugs and greetings, both said, "We need a shower and then a glass of wine." Ben understood, and they disappeared.

Fifteen minutes later, Caroline and Rachel emerged with wet hair and robes, and they poured themselves a glass of wine. The trio moved to the balcony. Caroline said, "God, I missed this view. Minneapolis looks beautiful. How good our bed will feel. Let's never leave home again."

Conversation quickly turned to the house fire, new home building, updates on Ben's past seven months, and their travels in Patagonia. However, serious talk had to wait. Caroline and Rachel were exhausted. They disappeared, and Ben was on the balcony asking the same redundant questions.

He called Lily.

"Hi." There was little enthusiasm in her voice. He tried not to make too much of it.

"Have you spoken to your mother?" Ben asked.

"We talked once. Ted is having a difficult time with the news. Guess he was pretty upset. Duh. He's not alone."

The conversation was cool, and Lily had regressed a bit from their time on the Fourth.

The next morning, the trio at La Rive shared breakfast. Ben was just becoming acquainted with Rachel when out of the blue, she asked, "Have you ever considered being a sperm donor?"

"No, I guess I never had a reason to think about it."

Rachel said, "Caroline and I have been talking about having a child. She is forty-nine, and I am thirty-eight, the clock is running. We haven't made any decision, but it is a hot topic these days. I'm curious about how men feel about being a donor."

"I like you and Caroline too much to donate my genes to your child. Trust me, you can do better."

Caroline joined them, made a cappuccino, and sat down by Ben. "Good morning. God, it's good to be home. I never moved for nine hours. How's everybody else?"

"Well, we are going to need a different donor."

"What? You asked him?" Suddenly, the *zwei frauen* were speaking German.

"No, she didn't ask me! We just had a brief conversation about my perspective of male donors."

"I hope that is all it was! If anyone were to ask you, it would be me. But I will admit that when we talked about a child and a donor in Argentina, I thought of you. So, what was your response?"

"As I said to Rachel, I have never considered being a donor. You can do better. There are some great resources available. They do all the genetic testing too. How exciting."

Conversation over.

Every day, Caroline and Rachel left early and came home late. Although Ben admired their success, their lifestyle was so demanding that he wondered about how they'd manage a child. He recalled Alison struggling with motherhood and work. Rachel and Caroline loved their work, the challenges, the independence, and the rewards. Their lives were a reminder of how many times women must choose between a career or being a mother. Rarely, and unfairly, did men ever face the same choice. *Any child would be fortunate to have Rachel and Caroline for parents.*

Ben called Maddie after a few days and asked her to meet for a drink at the Nicollet Island Inn. The location was somewhat of a midpoint, walking distance for each. They met at five o'clock and shared a bottle of Chablis accompanied by artichoke tapenade.

He wanted to know more about Maddie. "Did you ever come close to marrying? From the little I know of you, there'd have been plenty of interested men."

Maddie flashed the wonderful smile that Ben had seen a few times. The captivating smile. However, this time, he saw the smile differently, even secretive.

He tried to use his skill to understand Maddie.

"Of course, every woman my age has had serious relationships, Ben. You know that."

Maddie knew her attempt to defuse the question by being vague had failed when Ben said, "How long have you been truly single? When did your last relationship end?"

Maddie's expression changed from playful to serious, perhaps slightly offended. "Couldn't we just enjoy the wine and each other's company?"

"Of course. Sorry. The other night I did a lot of talking, and so I wanted to know more about you. Didn't mean to overstep."

"I just got out of a five-year relationship last month. This is a major readjustment for me. I still care for him but know the relationship cannot work. I haven't had a date with another man in over seven years. That is what you are seeing, Ben."

Ben's intuition was correct. He saw a woman in a transition. "Thank you for telling me. That kind of thing isn't easy to say. I like you, Maddie. Being with you has made me want to know you. Maybe this is too soon or rushed for you. I don't want to be a burden while you sort your life out. You and I are not an emergency. I am in Minneapolis for the long haul."

They talked for another hour and came to an agreement about the direction of their relationship. Maddie wanted to continue to see Ben. "I just need to get more distance between him and you."

He agreed.

Darkness had fallen when they left the Nicollet Island Inn. Although she lived only a few blocks away, he insisted on walking her home. He was seeing another side of her.

She was present, more relaxed, having shared her personal life with him. Ben felt closer to Maddie and took her hand to reassure her that his interest had not waned. He was interested and wanted her to know.

"Oh no, please go."

Ben looked up and saw a man standing on Maddie's front porch, his hands on his hips.

"Of course. I'll leave when I know the situation is OK," Ben said.

The man on the porch walked toward them angrily. "So, you are already seeing someone. Guess you are really having a hard time over this, huh? Who the hell are you? You sleeping with my woman?" he said, turning his attention to Ben.

"First of all, Maddie is not property. Secondly, we only met at a dinner party with friends a week ago. I live in the neighborhood and was walking her home."

"Bullshit. I know what you're all about, you lying lowlife." He stepped in Ben's direction. Ben remained calm.

Maddie kept saying, "Stop it, Chad, stop it. He was just making sure I got home safely. We just met. Come in the house, and we can talk."

Chad continued to glare at Ben, never responding to Maddie's suggestion.

"Chad, you have no issue with me, but I am not leaving Maddie alone here until you are talking normally."

"Listen, asshole, you aren't telling me anything. I would suggest you leave while you still can."

"Chad, I am not leaving until you calm down."

Chad calmed down slightly.

Hoping to defuse the situation for Maddie, Ben said, "Maddie, do you think Chad and I can talk alone? If you have another idea, I'm an open book."

"Sure, I'll be back in a few minutes."

Maddie couldn't believe what was happening but agreed to go inside. Ben asked Chad to sit on the porch with him. Surprisingly, Chad agreed.

Angry men were not new to Ben. He had experienced plenty of male anger in the military and as a therapist.

"What's going on with you, man? I might understand what you are going through; I've been there. I'm divorced. But for the record, I just met Maddie."

Chad shook his head a couple of times. "I don't believe this." Then he looked up and said, "Who the fuck are you, some kind of Gandhi?"

"No, man, I'm just another guy who's been around the block a few times."

They continued talking. Chad was becoming human. Ben asked him who was his best friend, and Chad named Jim.

Ben said, "I want you to call Jim now and tell him you are having a hard night. Then I want to talk to Jim. OK?" Chad took out his phone, called Jim, and told him he was hurting from the breakup and handed the phone to Ben.

Ben asked Jim a few questions about their friendship, and when he determined it was legit, he asked Jim to check in with Chad later that night and try to connect him with a therapist the next day. With Chad listening, Ben said that if he had any concerns about Chad's safety, to call the police.

With that, Ben said, "I think we have done all we can here tonight. Are you OK to drive? Will you promise you won't do anything to harm yourself or anyone else tonight?"

"Yeah, man."

"You need a therapist. Promise me you will find one."

Chad looked at Ben and again said, "I'll try." Ben shook his hand and reminded him that Jim would be calling him later. "I will bring Maddie up to speed and head home. I am tired and have a book to write. Maybe I'll put you in it."

Chad chuckled and walked to his car.

Ben went to Maddie's door and gave her the scoop. "If Chad shows up here, call 911."

He continued, "I like you, Maddie. Neither of us expected this. But all is well that ends well. I hope we can still see each other. What you think matters the most. I'm not sure whether to exit or remain. You'll have to help me with that."

"It's late, Ben. I'm feeling a little unsure myself. I'll be in touch."

Ben took her hand. "Good night, Maddie. I look forward to hearing from you." Then he turned and walked away.

Rachel and Caroline were having a croissant and coffee when Ben entered the kitchen the following morning. "How'd the date go, Ben?"

"Long story! Certainly was interesting. Time will tell."

He had zero interest in running through the previous night. *Live in the present. Some secrets are better kept secret.*

The trio agreed to have dinner together that night. Ben said he would make dinner or cater one. Caroline and Rachel had to leave for the office, and Ben's phone was ringing. Living in the present just returned to last night.

"Good morning, Maddie. How are you?"

"I am probably the last person you want to talk to this morning. I want to thank you for your handling of a very uncomfortable situation. You deescalated a nightmare. I just wanted you to know that Jim called me and said he and Chad were having breakfast together. Most importantly, Chad has agreed to start therapy. Jim said that Chad understands the relationship is over. He is embarrassed and knows he needs help. Jim said whatever happened last night produced a great result. That was you, Ben. That's all I wanted to say. I need some time to sort issues out. I may contact you down the line. I'm not sure. We'll talk then. Goodbye."

Hearing a click, the call ended. Maddie was gone. She wasn't interested in listening to Ben. The answer was simple. She wasn't sure.

Ben had numerous issues to resolve before dinner. Louie, Lily, Alison, José, Arthur, Nathan, Russ, Anne, and Andrew, and maybe Eva were getting a phone call today. September was closing in, and he had a decision to make. As of now, Clayton and Sarah's home looked like the best option.

Clayton and Sarah had moved to Minneapolis from Georgia twenty years earlier. They offered Ben lodging for as long as it took to rebuild. Being on Water Street, their home would offer him a bird's-eye view of his own construction project. It would be a comfortable transition back into the neighborhood.

He spent his last day at Caroline's reconnecting with everyone he'd spent the last eight months with. He called Louie, José, Arthur, Nathan, and Russ. Those calls were typical of his male conversations: friendly, to the point, and short. He had come to see how special these people were, and his life was improving because of them. It was up to him to return the favor. Lily didn't answer, so he left a message.

Ben wanted his friends to know how much he valued them. He insisted they share his message with Sheri, Barbara, Julia, Natalie, and Twila. The men in his life were better human beings because of their partners. Ben had been privileged to have witnessed their impact. In a sense, they had changed him. *They are blessed with life partners. If I deserve one, it can happen. It's on me.*

Then he called Alison. He wanted an update about her state of mind. She and Ted had a very difficult week. Ted was shocked. They had started seeing a marriage counselor, but their progress was slow.

Alison was concerned about her relationship with Lily. She said they hadn't been talking and that Lily was struggling. She had offered to see her therapist with Lily to no avail. Alison was committed to staying connected and texted Lily daily. Alison was sad but hopeful. Despite his anger, Ben was learning. He tried to be reassuring and suggested that over time, Lily would heal.

He called Lily again. There was still no answer. "Hi, Lily, just checking in and letting you know I will be living back in the 'hood tomorrow. That means we are only a few blocks apart. Looking forward to running Bde Maka Ska with you."

He called Anne and Andrew too. "Hi, favorite sister and brother-in-law. Just updating you. My address has changed again for September. Go army . . . Love from your favorite brother."

He also had a burning desire to call Dahlia. He wasn't sure whether that made sense. After all this time apart, his thoughts turned to her every day. He decided not to call. *I miss her more than ever.*

He ordered dinner from the Monte Carlo to thank Caroline and Rachel on their last night together. They dined on Szechuan green beans, seafood fettuccine with clams, shrimp, and scallops, and pasta primavera with sautéed chicken breast.

Dinner was delicious. They had no wine because of early-morning commitments. Ben and Rachel had developed a friendship. Because Caroline had been a friend for so long, Ben had hoped Rachel wouldn't feel excluded. The dinner was evidence that the three of them were on solid ground. They discussed Mozart, the Roman

Empire, living in Minneapolis, and Rachel's journey to marry an American woman.

During dinner, Caroline said, "Rachel and I are going to have a baby. We've decided we want a family, and so no wine for a while. We have an appointment tomorrow to begin the process."

"How wonderful. Congratulations! I am delighted, and that baby will be very lucky to have the two of you for parents. I'm throwing my hat in the ring for godparenting."

The evening was a culmination of love, commitment, and friendship.

Chapter 8 ended, "Life will be difficult until change is less painful than stagnation."

10

SPIRITUAL MONTAGE

September was one of Ben's favorite months. Warm sunny days, cool evenings, and brilliant red, gold, and orange leaves contributed to an exquisite life in Minnesota. He was especially looking forward to being back in his neighborhood, close to the shores of Bde Maka Ska.

Clayton and Sarah Jones epitomized neighborliness. They were thoughtful, spiritual, compassionate people. Being philosophical, Clayton and Sarah tended to delve into big questions. Every time Ben left a conversation with them, something had happened. He didn't always know what, but something shifted.

After eight months, he had become a master at temporary living, packing, and moving. Leaving La Rive was simple, except for the goodbye. He had found a deeper sense of gratitude for his hosts as the months progressed. He had learned that inviting a guest for a month was an exceptional act of kindness. Not only had they offered him their home but also a glimpse into their lives.

Saying goodbye to Caroline and Rachel was less than sad, but far from happy. He was committed to doing more for others over himself. His personality had softened because of other people's kindness. *I must become a more compassionate person. Not just for my benefit but for those I care about.*

Driving to the Joneses' was like driving home. He parked in front of their house and saw Clayton and Sarah on the front porch. Their presence was calming and reassuring. Ben asked if they would be willing to walk two doors south so he could peek at the infancy of his home. The three strolled through the sunlit warmth to 10 Water Street.

"Ben, we need you back on the block. Since you left, Sarah and I have known that something is missing. Now, we know what it is. It's you. We want you back."

"Out of the ashes comes a new beginning. This is going to be a special home, and we can't wait for you to invite us for dinner," Sarah agreed.

"You will be my first guests." *This time, I mean it. My promises are my word.*

The home was a skeleton and a roof without much to admire. However, the frame was a symbol of hope, a glimmer of optimism. He looked forward to watching the daily progress.

Clayton, Sarah, and Ben ambled back toward the Joneses' home, the most charming on the block. Their home always looked inviting. He had frequently told Clayton and Sarah that theirs was the happiest house in the 'hood. It was not the biggest, but the house always had a smile.

Clayton and Sarah were gracious people. "Ben, we will feel bad if you don't make this your home. Please take, use, and ask for whatever you need. You will make us happy by being at home here," Sarah said.

Although Ben expected hospitality from Clayton and Sarah, listening to them was a testimony to who they were. They didn't have to think about how to treat others. If anyone was evidence of a God, Clayton and Sarah were. They were people of faith. Baptist pastors. But their demeanor had something else to it—something enigmatic and true that Ben wanted.

They were in their sixties and had been married forty years. They met in Chicago at a Baptist convention as newly ordained pastors. They'd both grown up in rural Georgia, twenty miles apart. Surprisingly, both left Georgia and attended Ohio State University. Clayton had grown up as a member of a conservative Southern Baptist congregation and was a little taken aback by a woman pastor. Sarah was one of the first women pastors in a more liberal sect of the church.

They found their way to Minneapolis in the 1990s. They were living on Water Street when Ben bought his house. On his first night, Sarah brought a plate of warm chocolate chip cookies as a welcoming gesture. From that day forward, their friendship flourished. Ben learned a life lesson, the power of a small gesture. On several occasions since, he had brought a loaf of bread to a new neighbor.

Sarah and Clayton never had children. They wanted a family, but it never happened. They accepted their fate and chose to parent foster children instead. Furthermore, as pastors, they did a fair share of parenting to all the people in their congregation.

Once settled in, Ben decided to ask Lily to run Bde Maka Ska with him. She declined, saying she was busy. He was disappointed and concerned that their relationship was changing. Although they had shared this run hundreds of times, it never got old. He told himself that her adult life was busy, there were bound to be changes.

While running, he considered ways he could be more grateful. Ben didn't know who or what higher power he was talking to, but he looked to the sky, compelled to express the feeling.

That evening, he acknowledged his ninth bed of the year. Counting the beds was humorous to him. He thought of Dahlia, how she'd walked through his door one night, and now he struggled. He debated calling her. His heart begged and his mind cautioned.

He woke up at 6:55 a.m. and walked outside, sat down on the patio, and looked north, seeing the fall foliage next to the ripples on the lake. He reminisced about the calm feeling he got overseas when he looked at the same moon and sun that shone over Minnesota.

He went inside to refill his coffee and noticed a missed call and voice mail. "Ben, this is Arthur. Julia is gone. She passed away during the night. I don't know if you can call, Ben. Please do. Goodbye."

Ben called back immediately.

"Ben, I just didn't know who else to call. We went to bed last night and when I woke up, Julia was sleeping, so I made coffee and brought her a cup. She was gone. I can't believe it. Not a sound, not a goodbye, nothing—my darling Julia is gone. I would die if I could. Life without Julia isn't living. Even after a couple of hours, I already know without her, I am nothing."

"I am so sorry, Arthur. I am leaving in a few minutes. I want to see you. Will you be at home?"

"Yes, Ben. But are you sure? You don't have to come; I just wanted to call someone and picked you."

Still packed from his move, Ben grabbed his luggage and went upstairs. Sarah was walking with a friend, so Ben told Clayton and left.

He topped eighty miles per hour and was in Mankato ninety minutes after Arthur had called. Arthur came to the door looking distraught.

Ben put his arms around Arthur and said, "I am heartbroken and so sorry, Arthur."

"Thank you for coming, Ben. I know people in Mankato but called you because of how much Julia loved you. I guess we always talked about the possibilities of this happening, but there isn't any way to prepare for this. After the time we shared, Julia said she thought of you as a son."

Arthur was shaking. "I don't know how I can live without Julia."

"If it's OK, I want to stay with you for a few days. You and Julia have always been like family to me, and families stick together during difficult times."

"Thank you, it's a day at a time, I guess. I really appreciate you staying tonight. This will be my first night without Julia. I always thought I would go first and tried to prepare her. She was prepared, I'm not. Never expected this.

"It sounds funny to say this today, but that bed you gave us was the greatest gift we have ever received. Julia and I spent every night in each other's arms. I couldn't be more thankful that she left this world with me beside her."

Arthur needed to talk, and Ben listened. "Julia will be cremated, and I will be too. She and I had decided that we wanted to be put together in the same urn. We figured after a lifetime together, it just made sense."

"I will do everything to make your wishes come true. I never knew any couple with a love like yours."

Ben and Arthur picked up dinner and returned to the house. Arthur wanted to talk about the memorial service. Arthur and Julia were members of the Newman Center and had planned a simple service for close friends.

"Julia loved music and wasn't a fan of rituals. I want a service that is just music. That's what she would have wanted. We always thought a memorial service should be a few songs, let people see each other, miss us a little, and go home."

Ben listened and wrote down a few songs that Julia and Arthur loved. He planned to present them to the priest in the morning.

Arthur was tired. "I can't tell you what it means to Julia and me that you came here today. It means the world. I am not sure it is possible to sleep in that bed without her, but I will give it a go. Good night, Ben."

Around eleven, Ben wanted to check on Arthur. He tapped lightly on the ajar door and pushed it open.

Arthur was sitting in the chair facing the bed. "Just don't know if I can do it. Getting in that bed knowing she's not there doesn't seem right. Am just going to sit here a while; you get some sleep, son. Being alone right now feels right. I'm just saying a few words to Julia. I hope she can hear them and understand I would do anything to be with her. You get some rest. Good night, Ben."

Ben respected Arthur's request and went to his familiar bedroom. Lying down, he thought about loving someone for decades and losing them. He wished there were words to say to Arthur, but he understood that there were no words for a man who had lost the love of his life. At least not so soon.

Early the next morning, he got up and went to check on Arthur. He was in bed with his arms around a pillow, probably Julia's. He was quiet. Ben looked closer. He touched Arthur, and his shoulder was cold. On the nightstand was a bottle of vodka and two containers of sleeping pills.

Arthur had gone to be with Julia during the night. His wish had come true.

Ben took the bottle of vodka and sleeping pill containers and put them in the trash. Then he called the mortuary that had visited

Hickory Street earlier that day. The death certificate read, *Heart failure*. Ben would have written, *Broken heart*.

Julia and Arthur got their wings and moved to the other side within hours of each other. Ben remembered talking with them at dinner about the power of the brain and longevity. Arthur left Earth on his terms. He wanted to be with his lovely Julia.

As sad as the day had been, Ben felt a certain satisfaction in knowing that Julia and Arthur lived and died with dignity. There was also satisfaction in selecting a companion urn, which allowed the two sides to contain the ashes of Julia and Arthur. They would be together for eternity.

Their service was as they wished, at the Newman Center, with a simple prayer followed by a brief description of Julia and Arthur's life together. They had chosen five songs, including "Anchors Aweigh," "The Caisson Song," "Over the Rainbow," "Only You," and "I Can't Stop Loving You."

Julia and Arthur had prepared a statement as if they knew neither would be the reader.

Ben read, "Our dear friends, we love you and thank you for the friendship and memories we have shared over the years. Life is precious, so do not grieve for us long—one day is sufficient. Live your life to the fullest, always looking forward. Enjoy the sunrise tomorrow, remembering that we lived a blessed life and are now together for eternity. Go in peace."

Julia and Arthur were buried together at the Fort Snelling National Cemetery in Minneapolis. One side of the marker read:

"Julia Carlson, Nov. 15, 1924–Sep. 2, 2023, Captain, US Army, World War II." The other side read, "Arthur Carlson, Dec. 1, 1923–Sep. 2, 2023, SS3 US Navy, World War II." As they lived, Julia and Arthur died—together.

Returning to Minneapolis, Ben had Ike riding shotgun. They had bonded in grief. Ben talked to Ike about Arthur and Julia during the drive. Ben called Lily. She had brought home every stray animal she found as a child.

"Of course. Bring Ike here," she said. Ben dropped Ike off at Lily's. He heard a growl as he was leaving, and for the first time, he understood that Ike was communicating, not warning. He patted Ike's head. "You are in good hands, my friend."

After reaching Water Street, Ben talked briefly to Clayton and Sarah before retiring for the night. In bed, he reflected on the past few days. The unexpected loss of two lifelong, dear friends hit home. The grief weighed heavily. Heavier than he remembered it being when he lost his parents. *My heart might be learning how to open.*

He took solace knowing he'd been there for Arthur and that Arthur and Julia were no longer apart. He would now honor them by distributing their estate in a virtuous manner.

In the morning, he called Lily to have coffee. She had interviewed for a job with Medtronic and was waiting to hear from Bio-Med Solutions. Ben asked about her mother, and Lily said they were having lunch in a couple of days. This would be their first conversation in a while. He was all ears.

"I'm returning to earth slowly," she said. "You know, the news shook my entire belief system. Knowing who your parents are might not matter until you find out your dad is not your dad. My moods swing hourly from anger to sadness. I keep thinking this is a dream. I'm going to need time to sort this out."

"Our thoughts are mutual in some ways, different in others. I am not sure how we will put it all together again, but we will. I will always love you and be your father."

He wanted to say more, but he was running on empty. The loss of Arthur and Julia lingered.

For the first time in a while, writer's block returned. It was not so much that he couldn't write but that he didn't want to. He was introspective and grieving the loss of Arthur and Julia. Sarah and Clayton were at church, so he retreated alone to the patio and sat in the sun, thinking about his own belief systems. He felt Arthur had joined Julia.

Do I really believe they are together, or do I want to believe they are together?

Living with two clergy would provide an opportunity to have that conversation. When they returned home, they joined Ben on the patio.

"My dear friends passed away hours apart. I was feeling some relief thinking that Arthur and Julia were together again. But then, I'm not sure I even believe in any afterlife. Thinking of them together feels good, but also crazy. The Bible has many references to life after death. The explanations that work for me may not work for anyone else. There isn't evidence that heaven exists; yet this one beautiful planet exists with human life, and the reasons for that are equally incomprehensible."

Clayton said, "I used to ask why is there something rather than nothing. Most of what we know about our universe is a mystery. I can't tell you why the sun will come up tomorrow either. But I have faith it will."

Sarah said, "There are many faiths on this planet. I welcome more. We are all searching and, if we are honest, without a clue. All ideas deserve our respect."

Ben's sad mind was calmer after their conversation. He was going to believe Arthur and Julia were together. Making that choice was easier because there were more reasons to hope they were together than to wish for the opposite.

The following day, he attempted writing. Chapter 9 was challenging. Issues over Arthur's and Julia's deaths impacted his ability to focus. He accepted that grieving needed time and that, eventually, his energy would return. He decided that a diversion might help.

He stopped by Louie's for a visit and to check on Junior. Louie said, "Maddie told Sheri about the incident with her ex."

"It's no problem. I like Maddie. I hope to see her again. She's not to blame for anything. Life happens."

Ben and Louie shared a Grain Belt on the deck with Junior between them. Louie and Sheri were going strong, and the relationship was serious in the best way. Ben was very happy for Louie. Louie had lived a single life for years, and cohabitation would be a healthy transition. At the end of the conversation, both agreed that living with someone was preferable, until it wasn't.

Ben ran Bde Maka Ska and was about to make a light dinner when Clayton and Sarah invited him to join them. They served sloppy joes, corn on the cob, and sweet potato pie. Ben had never tasted sweet potato pie until five years before when the neighborhood had a block party. Pumpkin had been his favorite, but upon first bite, Ben switched to sweet potato. Sarah remembered. *Like Nathan, another reminder of thoughtfulness.*

After dinner, they sat on the porch relaxing with some hibiscus iced tea. The conversation turned to growing up in Georgia. Sarah and Clayton were children during the end of segregation in the South.

"Everyone sees color first." The evening was like the other talks, and Ben came away a wiser, more learned person.

He remembered Ben Franklin's quote, "We are all born ignorant, but one must work hard to remain stupid."

I have a long way to go.

He tried to write, but he couldn't stop thinking of Dahlia. *How is she? Does she think of me? Am I crazy?*

As a therapist, he had encouraged clients to seek closure. Limbo is not a good place for the human mind. He was immobile with Dahlia, stuck deep, unknowing what to do. Every choice was double-edged.

He walked to his home construction site. The home looked enticing, and he was pleased with the unique design. He still had over two months before he'd be able to live there, but the end was in sight. And so was a beginning.

Easier writing returned. Progress was quick, creative, and thoughtful. For the first time in over a week, he felt inspired again. He was almost finished with chapter 9. "Die with memories, not regrets. Love can open any door."

The last week in September, he spent more time at his property. Watching the construction was invigorating. Whenever he contemplated the year of being without a home, he realized that the experiences had delivered personal growth. So much more than he'd have had living in his old house.

Each month, he had learned from every relationship. Everyone he had lived with was leading a more meaningful life. Each had healthy relationships. He did not. However, knowing this and being able to change were very different things. His baby steps were not enough.

As the month wore on, he looked forward to spending time at his friend Michael's hobby farm just outside Minneapolis. He had horses, goats, ducks, and a donkey named Fred.

Ben received a call from Arthur and Julia's attorney, entrusting him with the oversight of 1.45 million. He acknowledged the responsibility and was determined to honor their wishes and distribute it meaningfully.

Over the past few months, he had learned he'd rather be collaborative than solitary. The more minds, the better. He decided to form an advisory group. He would invite Clayton, Sarah, Louie, Lily, Nathan, Russ, Twila, Caroline, Anne, and Andrew. In addition, he would seek advice from Barbara and José from a distance. Together, they would make Arthur and Julia far prouder than Ben could alone.

Packing for October, he thought about the conversations that had occurred in the Joneses' home. He knew September would be a month of learning from Sarah and Clayton. Indeed, they had not disappointed.

Ben was especially pleased knowing that, in a couple of months, he would be returning to the area for good. Clayton and Sarah would be his first dinner guests.

Waking the next morning, he decided to go for a run. He was going to ask Lily, but it was later than usual. Bde Maka Ska glistened, and the winds were calm.

On the lake path, he saw three men walking toward him. One held an unrecognizable flag; the other two flanked the flag bearer. As they got closer, Ben saw white power on the T-shirt of one. Ben saw them shove a man off the path and circle him.

Walking by, they gave him a sneer. One said, "Nice shit shirt, loser." Ben was wearing a rainbow pride T-shirt.

José saved his life, Sarah and Clayton opened their home to him, and Dahlia had relatives murdered in the Holocaust. He served with soldiers of color in Afghanistan and Iraq. While all this flashed before his eyes, Ben heard his grandfather's words.

Never pass on an opportunity to challenge evil.

Seeing a swastika tattoo on the flag bearer's arm made the hair on Ben's neck stand up. *Never act out of anger or revenge. De-escalation is always preferable.*

As they passed him, Ben just shook his head and looked at them with disapproving eyes.

They stopped, turned, and one said, "You have a problem, old man?"

"You're promoting ignorance."

The three walked toward Ben. When faced with danger, he always asked for guidance. "Grandpa, Grandmother, Dad, Mom. Guide me."

Laughing, the swastika-tattooed one said, "Well, looky here, big mouth is mumbling to himself. Guess he's realizing he is about to get his ass kicked."

Hearing those words, Ben went into a fight-or-flight response.

He wanted to avoid conflict but was trapped by his own ego.

I know better. Violence begets violence.

As the three men came closer, Ben saw a bulge under the white power T-shirt. The one in the middle slipped on brass knuckles. The rules were changing rapidly.

Fear permeated him, followed by an unexpected calm.

This was a familiar game to them. They relished being tough guys with favorable odds.

If I'm going to do something wrong, I'm going to do it right. This was not his first rodeo. His survival skills dominated. Throat, solar plexus, nose, kneecap. His brain was highly active.

The veteran of two tours looked the men in the eyes and said, "I do not want conflict."

If he had to defend himself, defend himself he would. Ben was ranking them first, second, and third. His plan was set. But they were three, and he was one. He recognized there would be no white flag when his brain said, "Perfect."

He looked down for a second, took a deep breath, and stared into their faces.

They were within five feet when he backed up, still open to de-escalation. They laughed, and two began to circle him. The one on the left swung his brass-knuckled fist at Ben, brushing his chin.

Ben attacked straight into the white power shirt, striking him in the throat, leaving him gasping for air. Ben hit him a second time with a left hook and dropped him with a solid right cross to the jaw. The other two rushed Ben.

Stay upright. Sidestepping to the left, he struck one in the middle of his face with a straight right fist. Blood shot out from a crushed nose as the man yelled in pain. Instantly, Ben drove his foot into the screaming solar plexus. Two down.

I've been stabbed. Turning to face him, Ben heard sirens. The last one, knife in hand, took off. Ben gave chase and took him down. The war returned as he slipped him into a ranger choke hold and reached for his KA-BAR.

Ben's world went black.

11

IT IS WHAT IT IS ... OR IS IT?

Ben's world was foggy. He was in and out of reality. He remembered being in an ambulance, arriving at the hospital, feeling pain, and then there was only darkness. His mind floated from his childhood to the fire and back. Bright colors, disturbing moments, then peaceful clouds and calm.

He was in a hospital room when he opened his eyes. Familiar voices accompanied by shooting pain running up his back. He strained to focus, seeing Lily. Others were in the room, but he couldn't see them. Someone was behind Lily. Was it Anne?

Amid searing pain, he felt a pull toward this other person. Finally, the other person came into view, but his eyes only saw their outline against the ceiling light. The person stepped next to the bed and leaned next to Lily and said, "Ben, I can't tell you how wonderful it is to see your eyes open."

A rush of adrenaline entered his body like morphine.

"Dahlia, how on earth did you get here?"

"I had been calling you for a few days, not getting an answer until Lily called me back. Once I knew what happened, I wanted to be here."

Lily interjected, "Dahlia has been sitting by your side for three days."

Ben looked at Dahlia. She said, "I didn't know if you were going to live, Ben, but I wasn't going to let you die on my watch. I prayed to every higher power I could think of."

Ben reached for Dahlia's hand, but the IV stopped him. She put her head next to Ben's and kissed him on the cheek, whispering in his ear. For a couple of minutes, they were in their own world, united again. Dahlia sat up, pulling a chair next to Lily.

Ben looked at both. "What did I miss?"

Lily spoke. "Well, we almost lost you, dear Dad." Tears filled her eyes. "You were in a coma for three days after surgery. The doctors kept saying your chances were fifty-fifty. Your wound in the back had severed arteries, and you were hemorrhaging when the ambulance got you to HCMC. You were in surgery for over four hours. The doctors struggled to stop the bleeding. Last night was the first positive news."

A nurse name tagged Kim Johnson walked in and said, "Hello, Ben. How are you feeling? Would like to check your vitals."

"Thanks for taking care of me."

Nurse Johnson said, "My privilege. By the way, I read your book. Maybe you can autograph my copy."

"Free up my right arm and I'll sign anything."

Ben was in throbbing pain but alive. He asked about the three men. Lily said all three were in the Hennepin County jail, charged with assault with a deadly weapon, along with a slew of other charges, including illegal possession of weapons in their van.

He shrugged. *I regret this. I could have walked away.*

Everyone that had opened their home to Ben had visited him at the hospital. He was surprised to hear that even José had driven to Minneapolis and stayed for two days. Louie had snuck Junior into the hospital. Ben's friends showed up. He believed they may have kept him from dying. *I owe them my life.*

The medical team at HCMC thought that with progress, he could be released in two to three days. The concern about infection had decreased. If he were to stay in the city, he could recover at home. *Where was home going to be?*

Ben was preoccupied with Dahlia. He whispered, "When can we be alone?" He could handle the pain. His priority was to talk with her.

After checking with the medical staff, Dahlia told him that the afternoon looked good for them to have a few minutes alone. He breathed a sigh of relief.

Midafternoon, with his tests completed and pain medication administered, Ben and Dahlia were alone for the first time since saying goodbye at the airport Hilton. The nurse agreed to leave them alone if Dahlia would help Ben eat. Dahlia crushed the crackers into his chicken noodle soup.

"Dahlia, I have thought about you every day. So many times, I wanted to contact you but couldn't decide whether it was the right decision."

Attempting to smile, he said, "Seriously, if it took getting stabbed, almost dying to see you, I'd do it again."

She smiled and tried to laugh but failed. "Ben, had you died, I. . ."

"I didn't die; I'll recover. Since opening my eyes and seeing you, the pain of missing you evaporated. The pain of missing you is worse than the pain from being injured. I know my injury will heal. I don't know if the pain of living without you will ever go away."

"When I heard what happened, I called the airlines without a second thought, but my brain is still reeling with uncertainties. You might be the best and worst thing that has ever happened to me."

Ben said, "For me, our time together has never been long enough to even talk about being together."

Her phone beeped. "Have to take this one." Ben heard, "Oh no, yes, of course."

Dahlia turned to Ben and said, "There was a bridge collapse in Toronto, catastrophic number of injuries. That was my chief of surgery telling me to return immediately. This is unreal. He told me there is a charter flight in ninety minutes with Minneapolis medical workers headed to Toronto, and there's a seat reserved. Ben . . . this is so hard." She kissed him on the cheek. "I love you." She stood up and said, "Goodbye, Ben. I must catch this flight. I am needed in Toronto. I am sorry. I hate this." And she was gone.

Although he understood, Ben's heart ached with physical pain. He felt hopeless, helpless, and cursed, connected to tubes while watching her leave. Sadness crept into every part of him. He asked for another dose of pain medication to escape from reality. It worked.

When Ben woke, Lily was there. She asked about Dahlia.

"Obviously, she isn't just a casual friend. From the moment she got to the hospital, I knew your relationship was special. When I heard, 'I am coming to Minneapolis tonight,' I should have known. I like her, but I am just a little nervous about family secrets these days. Can we work on that?"

"I get it, Lily. I apologize for not sharing more, but who could have thought this would happen? I had doubts that Dahlia and I would ever see each other again."

"Come on, Dad, you're talking to a grown woman here. She jumped on a plane to Minneapolis the moment she knew. I watched her sit by your bed for three days. She's in love with you."

Ben was at a loss for words. "Lily, please forgive me, but talking right now is difficult. I just need to rest. Can we talk later?"

"Of course, but don't forget!"

Dahlia had been in Ben's life just three short times—San Pedro, airport Hilton, and the Hennepin County Medical Center. There was no plan to see each other again.

Maybe he and Dahlia needed to put closure on this painful relationship. Seeing her for a short time opened new wounds. He felt angry and helpless. Consequently, he asked for more meds again even though he didn't need them for his wound. He needed to insulate his mind from her. He slept for ten hours.

In the morning, he had four calls from Lily. He had forgotten to call her back, and she had come back to the hospital. Assured that he was resting comfortably, she had gone home. Emotionally, he was a train wreck, but physically, he was better than any previous day. He began to think about getting out of the hospital. After ruling out Michael's hobby farm, which was forty miles west of the city, he started thinking about possible options. He would find a place to live.

The following day, the doctors agreed to discharge him with the condition he stay within the metro area. Although he was recovering and the doctors were not expecting an issue, they believed that staying in the metro was important. Infections and reoccurring bleeding were concerns.

Discharged, he received a phone call from the Minneapolis Police Department to come to the headquarters to sign a statement and review the charges. Weak and disillusioned, he went to the police station to review the incident. He could tell the meds were working. His mood was elevated beyond reason.

As he sat down to be interviewed, a police lieutenant joined him, and to his surprise, she was another classmate from a small town named Southbrook. He had attended eight different school districts in Minnesota and had gained some exposure.

Lt. Casey Smith said, "Well, Ben Raymond, we meet again under different circumstances. I remember sitting by you in choir. I was bad; you were atrocious. Are you still tone-deaf?"

"I was a new kid, and they needed boys in choir. If I agreed, I could avoid a study hall."

"I was a seventh-grade girl with a voice like James Earl Jones's. That's when I decided to become a cop instead of a singer."

Her voice and humor hadn't changed.

Lt. Smith began reviewing the incident that almost ended his life. She had the facts down as he remembered them, so the meeting was brief.

At the end, she said, "Unfortunately, the knife changed everything. You are fortunate. I am glad you are OK and will recover. All three of these bad actors will be off the streets for a long time."

Ben knew he was on the road back when he spontaneously said, "Casey, can you get me a few minutes with the one who stabbed me? I only need one Minneapolis minute."

In a deeper voice than James Earl Jones's himself, she said, "Ben, if I could, there is nothing I would rather do than watch."

Leaving the police station, Ben's phone beeped. His publisher, John, asked, "Ben, how are you? What a terrible incident. I am so relieved you are discharged and, from what I hear, going to be OK. True?"

"Yes, I think Ben Raymond is on his way back, just going to be a while. Getting out of the hospital is a start. I have lost a week of writing but feel ready to go."

"Listen, Ben, in a weird way, this has turned into a public-relations gold mine. Somebody shot a cell phone video, and it is viral, with a zillion hits. Seeing it myself, I couldn't believe it. Destroying those two and then chasing that dude down after being stabbed. I had no idea you were this badass. Everyone is talking about you. A perfect time to be writing a book. The media all want to talk with you—major networks, morning shows, late-night talk shows, major magazines, they all want a piece of you, Ben. This could send sales through the roof."

"All that is good, John, but for now, I have enough irons in the fire. I need to take care of some personal details before promoting my book. Between you and I, this incident was a mistake. I should have been able to handle the situation better. I'm not some immature eighteen-year-old."

"I get that, Ben, but just agree to do this one local interview. I sort of promised without talking to you. Once that is done, we will talk through any other offers. But remember, this is an opportunity for you too."

"Fine, John. Who is the local one?"

"Liz Joseph, Channel 7 CBS affiliate."

"I just want to get off the phone. Set it up. I've met Liz. She was a correspondent in Iraq. She's a solid reporter. Text me the details. I gotta go, John. Talk soon. Goodbye."

Wanting to be alone, he made a reservation at the Greenway Suites. He stopped by the Joneses' home to pick up his belongings and had a brief conversation with Sarah and Clayton. He was embarrassed about the incident, thanked them for their hospitality, and promised to keep in touch. This wasn't the time to talk. His mind and his body hurt. *I disappointed Sarah and Clayton. Think of all the conflict they faced and handled the right way.*

He checked into the Greenway, went straight to his room, and called Lily. Up front, he confessed a need to be alone. He reassured

Lily that he was feeling good and would call her immediately if anything changed.

"OK, but call me when you are going to bed."

"Yes, my dear daughter, I will."

Ben never touched his suitcase. He lay down on the bed for a minute and then decided to check out his injury in the bathroom mirror. Seeing the six-inch doozy of a surgical scar was somewhat comforting because the healing was visible. The doctors had told him that the internal healing was their concern. That, he couldn't see. Nor did he want to.

He ordered room service. He ate quietly in the room, acutely aware that his underlying emotion was anger. Seeing Dahlia, experiencing strong emotions, and having her leave was an event that he never wanted to experience again. If he didn't know life was precious before, he did now that he'd almost died.

He decided to stop wasting his life. He committed to moving beyond Dahlia. They were not going to be together. He needed to face the music.

Although it was only nine at night, Ben called Lily to tell her good night, agreeing to call in the morning. Lily understood. Ben took two Advil PM and went to bed. A text popped up on his phone. It was from Dahlia. He chose not to read the message, turned off his phone, and went to sleep.

Waking, Ben texted Lily. She responded at once. "Thank you. Want to see you."

"I will be in touch later."

A minute later, he got a call from his publisher. "Hope this works for you. We have an interview set up for three this afternoon at the Channel 7 CBS station. Will that work?"

"Yes, I will be there. Thanks, John. Must run."

A new day, a step forward toward recovery, and warm sunshine gave Ben some inspiration. He decided to read Dahlia's text: "I could not feel worse about leaving you. There was nothing I could do. Please respond, tell me anything. I need to hear from you. Dahlia."

He was not proud of his behavior the previous night. Not reading Dahlia's text was childish. Yes, he was angry. He understood that anger in men almost always masked sadness. He knew how uncomfortable sadness can feel, and being angry was easier. He understood these concepts backward and forward. *Anger almost ended my life.*

Dahlia had come to Minneapolis immediately, and she'd had to leave as quickly to help others. Ben felt foolish, selfish, and childish. She deserved better. *Life should be lived, and neither of us are living.*

He sat down and started to text Dahlia, then stopped. They needed to talk, even FaceTime. However, he knew what waiting for a message was like and texted her, "Dahlia, I am sorry for my late response. Can we talk, preferably FaceTime? Tell me when you're available. Ben."

Hitting the arrow, he felt his message was objective, polite, and lacked emotion. His text did not reflect his true feelings at all. Rather it reflected the direction he would suggest.

Switching gears, he began wondering about the interview with Liz Joseph. Was it live? Audio? Video? Did he need to prepare? Typically, John had given him more information. Rather than call John, Ben called the station directly and asked to speak to Liz.

"Well, hello again, Ben. It's been a while. How are you?"

"Better, Liz; getting out of the hospital was a major step. I feel OK. Am wondering about today's interview. What can you share with me?"

"Of course, Ben, I was going to call you. The interview will be taped, edited, and shown by various venues within our network. You know how this goes—depending on how it looks and how busy a news day there is, it could never air, or it could be on every station nationwide. I can text you the interview questions—there are a few background ones, none for which you would need to prepare.

"I want to introduce you as a Minnesotan, veteran, psychologist, and author. Second, I want to have you briefly discuss the incident. You understand media hype. Third, you can promote your new book. The entire sequence will be ten to fifteen minutes. You will have complete control over what is said, and I will let you have input into the editing too. Does this help, Ben?"

"Got it, Liz; text me the outline. What time do I need to be there?"

"Two fifteen would be great. We can talk. There's makeup, staging, et cetera. Pull up to the main entrance; a valet will be waiting. Thank you, Ben, am looking forward to seeing you again. Goodbye."

His phone beeped. Ben looked down and read. "Ben, I am working until 6 tonight, CST. Could FaceTime at 7. Does that work? Dahlia."

Ben noticed that the tone of their communication had changed. He had initiated the change, and Dahlia had reciprocated.

Needing to be at the station in a couple of hours, he had to think about some clothes. He was going to be on TV. He didn't remember the last time his clothing mattered. Then he remembered. *I was driving to the MSP airport hotel.*

He understood why his publisher was pushing the interview. Most authors would do anything to get airtime to publicize their writing. Hoping to generate some mojo, he began looking at the interview questions. This was one of those life experiences that he seriously disliked. The dreaded necessary evil. For now, selling books mattered.

When Ben arrived at the station, a valet said, "Good afternoon, Mr. Raymond. Welcome to Channel 7. I will take care of your car. You can go inside, and a host will take you to Liz Joseph. Have a good day, sir."

Inside, a young woman greeted him and said, "Welcome, Mr. Raymond. Would you like a coffee, soda, water, or tea?"

"I'm fine, thank you."

She replied, "Right this way, sir. Liz is waiting for you."

Ben was brought to a green room and was told Liz would join him soon.

Momentarily, Liz walked in wearing a black dress with a magenta pattern. Ben had only seen Liz in Iraq, where she wore military fatigues and a helmet.

She offered her hand. "Good to see you, Ben. You don't look like someone who was just in the hospital. Thank you so much for coming under the circumstances. Is it OK if we go to makeup and continue talking?"

"Certainly."

In makeup, a young man named Max introduced himself. "I am just going to do some makeup prep that is necessary for HDTV, OK?"

Ben nodded approval.

Liz began, "Ben, do you have any questions about my text or the format? Since we aren't live, we can stop and restart anytime."

"I am comfortable with the questions, Liz. Would just prefer not to talk about Afghanistan or Iraq and will minimize the incident too."

"Not a problem, Ben." Within minutes, they were on their way to the studio.

They sound-checked and repositioned chairs, and like clockwork, the interview started. "I'm Liz Joseph and am privileged to be here with Ben Raymond, author of the best-selling novella *Hearts on Fire*, with a new release expected soon. Mr. Raymond is a native Minnesotan, army veteran of tours in Afghanistan and Iraq, a practicing psychologist, and a resident of Minneapolis. Welcome, Mr. Raymond. Thank you for being here."

Ben smiled at Liz and lied, "It's good to be here. Thank you for having me."

"Mr. Raymond, may I call you Ben?"

Ben smiled and nodded.

"Ben, you were recently involved in a dangerous encounter by Bde Maka Ska that put you in the hospital. Would you share that story with our listeners?"

"I am a resident of the area and was on a morning run when I entered an unfortunate situation. The situation escalated. Short story—the police arrived, arrested them, and I ended up in HCMC until yesterday."

"A frightening moment, no doubt. So, there was physical contact between you and them?"

"You might say I was motivated by self-preservation."

"Is it a fair assumption that you felt strongly about seeing white supremacists in your neighborhood?"

"Without question, I took offense to seeing white power emblems. In my opinion, they do not represent our country."

"There were three of them. You must have understood the dangers."

"I'm no hero. I detest what they represent, but I would handle the situation differently today. Glamorizing violence is wrong. It has never been the answer and never will be."

Liz changed gears. "Ben, you had success with your first novella, and I am hearing there's a new one on the way. When can we expect to see it, and what can you tell us about it?"

"I expect the book to be out in January. What I can share now is that there will be twelve chapters covering a wide variety of human conditions. Hopefully, it will not be for the faint of heart. Although, you might expect this from an author promoting his own book, I believe this book will be a stimulating, thoughtful read."

Following the interview, Liz and Ben sat in the green room.

"I had heard about your house fire a few months back. Are you rebuilding, staying in Minneapolis?"

"Yes, I love Minneapolis. My daughter, sister, and roots are here. Minnesota is my home."

"When will your home be finished?"

"Not until the end of the year, around the holidays, I'm told. I've been moving around a lot and am currently staying at the Greenway Suites. I still need to find a more permanent place for the rest of October."

"Well, it might seem slightly inappropriate to offer this, Ben, but I have an en suite in Minneapolis, connected to my condo but totally private. If you are interested, it is available."

"Thanks, Liz, appreciate the offer. Having just got out of the hospital, I have a couple of options to check out. But seriously, I appreciate your kind offer. Thank you."

As Ben walked out of the station, the valet had his car waiting. He drove back to Greenway Suites, looked at his phone, and thought, *I have two hours before seeing Dahlia again.* He called Lily and told her about the FaceTime with Dahlia. "Can we take a rain check on dinner?"

Lily responded, "Not a problem. I'm glad you are talking to her."

Ben reminded himself there was no future with Dahlia.

At 7:00 p.m. sharp, he FaceTimed Dahlia. Seeing her face took his breath away. She had just finished a twelve-hour shift yet looked too good to be true. "Hello, Dahlia."

"Hi, Ben."

"I want to tell you that your coming to Minneapolis and sitting by my hospital bed for three days was my greatest gift. I don't think I was able to express my gratitude. Lily so appreciated having you there. But I feel so selfish talking about my life. Tell me how you are and what you faced on your return to Toronto."

"Ben, dear, you look good. Those doctors pulled off a miracle getting you out this fast and recovering. I am so relieved. It is so good to see your face. When I returned to Toronto, my team worked a seventy-two-hour shift, grabbing a few winks whenever possible. There were over two hundred critical-case injuries. The good news is that most of our cases survived."

Ben said, "There is no greater honor than saving someone's life. Doctors are heroes. You are a hero. I am so proud of you. Dahlia, I really don't know where to start. You are a wonderful person and have impacted me like no other. I just don't know how to keep sane. Missing you is miserable. It's no way to exist. Am I making any sense? Tell me your thoughts."

She replied, "Our time in Belize was powerful. When I returned home, I searched for any way to stay in touch. That's why I came to Minneapolis. In Belize, we agreed we were two ships passing in the night. In Minneapolis, we were two ships docked at the same port. Are we doomed for sadness because we're oceans apart? As we have said so many times, our time together is minuscule. I used to be content, and now, I'm not. I have wished we hadn't ever met. The brutal reality of our situation saddens me. You are building a new house in your hometown near your family. I'm in Toronto, which has been my home since I was born. My aging parents need me too. I am all they have now. The situation feels like we are up against immovable objects. My God, I am looking at you through a computer screen. This feels doomed, hopeless."

"I hear you loud and clear. You are a wise woman. You deserve so much more. We must let go, Dahlia. My heart aches hearing my own words. We have both been in difficult situations before and persevered. I trust we will again. What I need you to know is that I have been uncomfortable using the word *love* with you because of the short time we have been together. I don't want to sound superficial. But, Dahlia, as sure as the sun will set tonight, I love you. Time may heal and allow us, using your words, to breathe."

"This reminds me of saying goodbye after our one night together, only worse because I can't touch you. I have no more words, Ben. I want you to be happy, and I am only making you sad. Goodbye, Ben." Dahlia blew him a kiss, ending the call before he could respond.

He understood her need to escape. He stared at the blank screen; he shook his head. It was resolved. A finale he hoped for, but didn't want.

His short stay at the Greenway Suites was over and done too. The hotel room had served its purpose, but he needed to find a bed for the last three weeks of October. He desired privacy and wanted to focus on writing. Briefly, he thought about Eva and the month of November.

He decided to call Liz and inquire about her en suite, mostly because it was easy.

Liz answered, "Hi, Ben. I suppose you were wondering about our interview and how it's playing out. You will be pleased to know that there is a major demand, and we expect that it will play in several states. This is remarkably lucky. The planets all lined up."

Ben had not thought about the interview since leaving the station. "That is great news, Liz. Thank you for all you did to make it happen. Liz, I'm wondering whether your en suite is available until November 1. I know the topic came up as sort of an afterthought, so please don't feel obligated."

"It is available, and I would want you to see it before deciding. I am home now if you want to come by."

"Perfect, Liz. I'm in my car and on my way. All I need is the address."

"It's 318 Groveland. Parking is available on north side of building. Name on my entrance is Elizabeth Wilson. Just need a little privacy. See you soon."

Ten minutes later, Ben arrived at Groveland and rang Liz. She answered and apologized for still being in pajamas, but Ben realized it was only 8:15 a.m.

After a brief tour, he had a new home for the remaining three weeks of October. The decision was easy. He knew enough about Liz, and the en suite was perfect. Liz was on a mission and getting ready for work. She was gone before Ben realized it.

She left a note that read, "Welcome, Mr. Raymond. You are my first move-in following an interview. Haha. Enjoy your day, I am gone until late. See ya when I see ya, Liz."

The en suite overlooked the city. *If I can't write here, I can't write anywhere.* He had a kitchenette and bathroom. Given Liz's work schedule, he thought he may never see her again.

His mind slipped to Dahlia. So many times, in the past few months, Ben would instinctively want to share views, wine, food, conversation, or anything with her. *This has to stop!*

Being the vagabond he was, Ben was moved in after one trip to the car. That was the only good part of living this way. After a few minutes, he was unpacked and at home again. He was especially looking forward to his twelfth bed in the new house. I *don't have any furniture, much less a bed.*

He called Lily. She answered excitedly and said, "Your daughter has her first real job. Bio-Med Solutions offered me a job this morning in their research-and-development department. The company is an upstart and doing some very cutting-edge innovations. I am so relieved. How are you feeling?"

"I am so proud of you, Lily. Congratulations. Your first real job, a big deal. Way to go! Quickly, my health is all right. Every day brings improvement, my wound is healing. Pain is gone except when I did a hundred push-ups today."

"What?"

"It's a joke. Haven't done a push-up for a while now. I have a checkup next week but must believe I am on my way back."

"So, I have to ask about Dahlia. How did it go last night?"

This was not a topic that he wanted to discuss, but he owed it to Lily. He said, "Honestly, painful. Dahlia and I would love to see where the relationship could go, but we don't see it happening, so we are moving forward with our lives."

"I am so sorry and even disappointed. We had bonded quickly over our care for you in the hospital. She is a special woman. I guess all I can say now is I am sorry. Your happiness is all I wish for."

"OK, quick transition, Lily. I moved into a condo on Groveland downtown. Have private living quarters for the next three weeks. Just moved in this morning."

"Wow, good for you. That was quick. How did you scope that out?"

"Did an interview with Liz Joseph from Channel 7 yesterday. Short story, we had met in Iraq, she had the place to rent. So, it was easy. Now, you and I have a dinner date tonight, right? We have a reason to celebrate."

"You betcha."

"Great, pick you up at six thirty."

"Perfect. See you then. Bye-bye."

Ben made a reservation for seven o'clock at Mercado. He asked for a table by the sidewalk. He told the waiter to surprise his dinner guest with a bottle of champagne. Ben was very happy about Lily being happy. In the words of his good friend Louie, a parent can only be as happy as their least happy child.

Ben arrived at Lily's new apartment on time, and the two walked hand in hand to Uptown. It was a tradition that Ben and Lily continued to honor.

Arriving at Mercado, they were seated at a sidewalk table with the surprise champagne.

"You are the best!" she exclaimed.

"A toast to my daughter, a legitimate taxpayer."

The night was perfect for October. Light breeze and unseasonably warm.

As Ben and Lily were sharing a slice of key lime pie drizzled with blackberry sauce, he heard a voice say, "Hi, Ben."

It was Liz, standing next to the table.

"Hello, Liz. I would like you to meet my daughter, Lily."

Liz in turn said, "This is my friend Maddie."

Everyone greeted each other, and Maddie said, "Good to see you again, Ben."

"You two know each other?" Liz asked.

"Yes, we met a couple of weeks ago."

After Maddie and Liz left, Ben gave Lily the short version.

"So, we run into two women, and you are living with one, dated the other, and you just ended another one in Toronto? What else don't I know about my dad? I was worried about you being lonely. Guess I have been a little misinformed . . . I am teasing. You deserve a good life, and I want to thank you for a first-job celebration. Yippee. Now you don't have to worry about me moving back in with you for a while. Based on what I am hearing tonight, there might be too much competition anyway. Feels good to tease you a little. I have been the brunt of so many of your jokes."

Ben and Lily strolled in the direction of Irving. Ben put his arm around Lily and said, "I am so grateful that we're working through everything. We are both going through some undeserved issues." *At least yours are undeserved. I have earned mine.*

"I don't know how healthy this is, but I have put the DNA stuff on the back burner. There is too much going on to try to deal with that now. You almost dying woke me up and made me realize that I am not the only person with problems. I still don't want to talk with Mom about it. Not now."

Ben let it go. He didn't want to ruin an enjoyable evening with Lily. After a hug at the door, he was on his way back to Groveland, looking forward to a good night's sleep in his new en suite.

Entering the residence, he was feeling painful reminders from his wound. His body felt tired from being more active today. Briefly, he thought how perfect Dahlia would feel in his arms, discarding the thought quickly. *When will this stop?*

He put on the pajamas he had bought months ago and had never worn. He thought he'd need them, living with so many different people. Ten months later, he saw the tags. Not having scissors, he put them on, tags included, and walked out on the balcony.

"Hi, Ben." Liz was sitting on the adjacent balcony off the living room. "Interested in some pinot?"

"Why not."

"Come over to my place; the balcony is bigger. There will be a glass of vino waiting."

Ben popped two painkillers and heard Liz unlock the joining door. He walked onto the balcony. Liz joined him and handed him a goblet. Ben appreciated the plush chair's softness on his injured back. Liz was wearing a big white puffy robe. Ben, in his pajamas with tags, envied her robe, remembering the one he'd lost in the fire.

"Isn't life unpredictable? Imagine when you and I met in Iraq, who could have predicted we'd live together and share a vino on a balcony in Minneapolis? Not to mention, not seeing you for years, doing the interview, you moving in, and then seeing you at dinner with your daughter. Ya gotta love it. It's what gets me up every morning. The spontaneity of life."

"Not knowing what's around the corner has always fascinated me." He held up his glass and clinked hers. "To unexpected delights."

Liz laughed, crossed her legs, and her robe slipped, exposing her thigh briefly, which she quickly covered. She had a sultry nature that he hadn't realized when she was in Iraq. Across the board, people described her as a smart, classy, professional reporter, which she was.

She broke the ice, saying, "Ben, why are you still single? By choice? Maddie told me that she liked you. She didn't want to talk about it. You don't have to answer my question about being single. I just slipped into my reporter mode. A minute on the air doesn't allow for small talk, so I tend to get right to it."

"Been asking myself that same question lately. As I mentioned, I have been bouncing around with good friends from my past. I have discovered that all are in meaningful relationships. Closing in on fifty, I'm not sure what's in the cards for me. I have a good life, Liz, but I am realizing that having an interesting life isn't always interesting. Without sounding weird, I don't have enough of these experiences. I have spent too many nights alone. It's a hard habit to change."

"Sounds like you've had some epiphanies lately. As we pass through stages of life, we all learn lessons. When I started reporting, all I wanted to do was travel, be in the action, and be a good reporter. After twenty years of doing just that, I am trying to decide what's next. Seeing you and Lily together tonight made me envious. Never getting married is a life I chose. One never knows the difference without having had the other. When I got my first big job with the network, my boss said, 'You're going places, if you don't do something stupid like get married and have a baby.' I believed him, and even today, I think much of what he said is true. I could name you a dozen top-notch women reporters whose careers dissolved when they got married. I can't think of one man."

"I will never know a woman's life, Liz. But I watched my mother, my sister, and now my daughter struggle with inequities. Women still bear the brunt of parenting more than men. I have yet to meet a man who stayed home with the children. Sounds like you and I are at a crossroad, Liz. Have you decided which path to take?"

"I am grateful for not having made many painful mistakes. I have to admit, though, you are the first person to sit here with me at night, enjoying the view, sipping a glass of wine, and I have lived here for almost two years. How pathetic is that?"

Liz squeezed Ben's hand and held on for a few seconds before letting go. He said, "We're evolving, Liz, and we still have control of our own destiny. You have seen and done more than most of the people on this planet, and you have half your life in front of you. You can make the second half any way you want."

Liz said, "So much of my life is just getting on with getting on. Now, I must deal with my life choice of being at the studio at seven each morning. That means in about five hours . . . I must get some sleep."

Liz walked to Ben and kissed his right cheek, his left cheek, and then his right cheek again. She smiled and said, "Good night."

Ben lay in bed, unable to sleep. Even in her bathrobe, Liz said good night as professionally as if they were in the American embassy in Baghdad. Ben's respect for her had grown.

His wound was more comfortable than it had been at the Greenway Suites. As he passed into sleep, Dahlia was looking at him. His last thought was, *This therapist needs therapy.*

The next few days, Liz worked long hours. Then she was sent on assignment to New York for five days. They communicated by text about housekeeping details Ben could address while she was out of town. He found the time productive but missed her company. He had come to Groveland wanting privacy and now had more than he wanted. He began to think about living in his new house. As comfortable as the home may be, the thought of living alone reminded him of loneliness.

He got a call from his publisher. John was ecstatic about the interview. "Your incident with those right-wing nuts is going to be equivalent to winning a lawsuit. The major network is playing the tape over and over, and I have gotten several requests. This is a huge opportunity, and we should make something of it sooner rather than later. You understand news. Something big happens tomorrow, this story dies."

"You know how I feel about this stuff, John. I really don't like being in the public eye, but I will trust your judgment and do a couple. No more than three. You do the background, run it by me. I am available."

"Can you travel?"

"Yes, not a problem."

"Perfect. I will be back in touch later today, Ben. Bye."

Two hours later, John called. "I have three incredible opportunities, Ben. If you agree, we can get them done in a few days. Here's what I think would be the most beneficial: CBS New York wants to do an on-air interview with you. Be three to four minutes and aired nationwide. Second, a major Toronto media conglomerate wants to do a story that will be printed in numerous Canadian media outlets. If you remember, our Canadian sales from your novella were good. Third, an LA TV station wants an interview too. If we do New York, LA, and Toronto, we will accomplish a promotional blockbuster. I went ahead and arranged all your travel. You will be picked up tomorrow morning at eight. New York is first. Toronto the next day. You'll finish in Los Angeles. You'll be back home four days from now and will have created a marketing windstorm."

Ben agreed. The train was on the track. He sat down and took a deep breath, sighed, and started to pack. He thought, *Toronto. You've gotta be kidding.*

Realizing that he needed some clothes, he called Lily and asked her to go shopping with him. She agreed, and two hours later, Ben was "GQ ready" as Lily described him.

John was impeccable with travel details. A limo was waiting for Ben outside the door at 7:45 a.m. He was wheels up at 7:00 on his way to the Big Apple. Landing at JFK, he was escorted to a limo, and by 12:00, he was in a Manhattan makeup room getting ready for a 1:00 interview.

The interview was classic professional journalism. At 12:30, he received the format and interview questions. At 12:45, an assistant delivered him to a private room to go over details.

The interviewing reporter came in at 12:50 to review the process.

Two minutes before they went live, someone checked his shirt, hair, and makeup. "Good morning. We are here this morning with Ben Raymond, Minneapolis author."

Ben was able to give clear, concise answers about his military service, work as a psychologist, and transition to an author. Most of the interview was focused on the attack, and in standard media format, they dramatized every detail.

"You must have decided that challenging the three assailants was worth dying for," the interviewer said.

"No, I did not expect to die. The assailants made an error of judgment promoting their ideology. The reality is that they have been arrested and incarcerated, and I am doing an interview."

At noon, he was on his way to Toronto, via a limo to JFK. He had two free hours in Dahlia's hometown.

Arriving at the CBC Media Centre he was again escorted to makeup, and the prep began. This interviewer was more interested in his background, writing, and book release. This topic was more appealing to Ben. He didn't enjoy the macho depiction of combat on the shores of Bde Maka Ska.

The interviewer had questions about his past, how being a psychologist played into his writing, how he decided to write, how he chose themes, and what his new book would be about. Because the interview wasn't live, it was thirty minutes long and would be edited for TV and print. The interview was efficient, and at 4:15 p.m., Ben was done. He was being picked up at 7:00 and taken to the airport for a flight to LAX.

Ben knew the Toronto Medical Centre was four blocks away. He had over two hours to kill.

He entered the TMC and found the hospital coffee shop. He sat down in a secluded corner. Unbelievably, he saw Dahlia and another doctor walk into the café. There was one exit, and Dahlia was facing it. Ben stopped breathing; his heart raced.

After a couple of minutes, the person seated across from her stood up, said a few words, leaned over, and kissed her on the cheek. A stake was driven through Ben's heart. He was cold, clammy, and nauseous. The doctor walked out of the café alone. Ben watched Dahlia pull something out of a briefcase and begin reading.

She got up, coffee in hand, and walked toward the exit. She looked directly at Ben as the coffee slipped from her hand. A waitress ran over and started cleaning up. Dahlia stood in shock, staring at Ben.

Ben walked to her. "Is there somewhere we can talk?"

She didn't speak but motioned out of the café into a lounge area where she sat down, still staring at Ben, not saying a word.

"I cannot tell you how awful I feel about this. I was scheduled for an interview yesterday in New York, and today in Toronto, and I am on my way to LA tonight. When I finished my interview, I walked here, not knowing what I planned to do. Then you walked in. I am so sorry."

"How could you not tell me you were in Toronto? I am in shock."

"We agreed to move on with our lives. I made a mistake coming here. All I can say is that I am sorry for you, me, and this dysfunctional relationship. As horrible as these past few moments have been, maybe we have closure. Seeing another man kiss you has given me a cruel dose of reality. One that I deserve."

She stood up. "I am scheduled to be in surgery." Once again, uncontrollable circumstances intervened. "I must leave. Goodbye, Ben."

"I understand. Goodbye, Dahlia."

She turned and walked away. Ben escaped in the other direction.

They both stopped, turned, and looked at each other one last time.

Ben walked in a daze back to the studio and sat in the lobby. He had the limo number and requested an earlier pickup. He wanted out of Toronto. At the airport, he arranged a flight to Los Angeles and was West Coast–bound, emotionally bankrupt, and devastated. *Another terrible decision. Dahlia deserves better than flawed me. Now she has the proof.* It was the worst he could ever remember feeling. *I am a loser.*

Six hours later, at LAX, he was heading downtown to check into his hotel. He lay on the bed, hoping to never have another day like this one. He didn't remember ever before drinking alone in a hotel bar, but that night, he'd had more than one Jameson on the rocks. Self-medicated, he returned to his room and fell asleep wishing for calm.

Drinking whiskey on an empty stomach was another stupid decision. He woke with a throbbing headache. Two Tylenol and a long shower delivered a minimal improvement. The limo picked him up and delivered him to the LA TV studio for an interview that would be taped, not live. *Thank God!*

After New York and Toronto, the LA interview was easy, despite his hangover. Thirty minutes after arriving, Ben delivered what was promised—a hyped-up story line about a veteran who challenged white supremacist ideology—nothing more. Ben promoted his new book as a novel laced with emotion, which delved into the depths of the human mind. *I'm a fraud. It isn't even written yet.*

At 5:30 p.m., he arrived home in Minneapolis, exhausted and hungover. He was despondent, absent of hope. After a quick Uber to Groveland, he stole two sleeping pills from Liz's bathroom, closed the shades, added a pillow over his face to hide his shame, and crashed.

He left a note for her. "Liz, haven't slept for days, stole two sleeping pills from you. See you soon. Ben."

Sometime mid-morning, Ben heard a knock on the door.

"Ben? You up? I heard movement. Want to join me for coffee?"

"Absolutely. Be right out."

Ben put on his pajamas, tore off the tags, glanced in the mirror, washed his face, and, sixty seconds later, walked to the balcony.

"Good morning, Ben. Saw you on TV this morning. Nice job. You made me proud to call you my roomie. Seriously, you did it like a pro. There's coffee, blackberry scones, and watermelon if you want any."

"The last three days were like being in a war zone. OK, not that bad, but difficult. Liz, you are an angel. How can I ever repay you?"

"You could stay here, if you stop stealing my drugs."

"That's embarrassing, but tells you how desperate I was. Not a proud moment."

Liz was caffeinated and upbeat, in a flirtatious mood. "Seriously, I am traveling quite a bit over the next month, so if staying here works for you, I am OK with it. I will be gone about half the time."

"My plan was to move to Edina. Lately, I have been living day-to-day. I will let you know in a day or two. But I really appreciate the offer, Liz. Thank you. And a second thank-you for breakfast."

He couldn't help but notice Liz's body language and behavior. She was happy.

Liz got up, and leaned over to pick up the coffee carafe, exposing herself in an obvious manner. After getting more coffee, she sat down cross-legged on a chair across from him. He admitted to himself, she was alluring. *Maybe a higher power is trying to help me.*

"I want to make you dinner tonight, Ben. Time is flying by, and we haven't even had dinner. Does that work?"

"Absolutely. Wonderful."

Soon the pajama party ended, and they went their own ways.

At dinner, Liz was wearing a short mustard-colored skirt and embroidered white blouse. She prepared broiled scallops, angel hair pasta, caramelized brussels sprouts, and bread pudding with raspberry sauce. She was delighting in their first dinner. Ben was trying to be present.

"Ben, are you going to continue to write?"

"I really don't know. I want to straighten out my life. The last few months—or years, if I'm being honest—have been in disarray."

Dinner was delicious, and Ben opened a second bottle of wine. Liz slid next to him on the love seat. Ben wasn't feeling normal, but he was leaving abnormal behind.

"I'm in a similar place to last time we really talked, Liz. Being alone has become comfortable, which makes me uncomfortable. One can get used to a solitary life. That scares me."

"Would you be interested in dating me and trying to have a relationship? I don't want to make you uncomfortable, but I don't want to pass on an opportunity either. Sometimes, I wonder what you and I might have together."

"I would be lying if I said it hadn't crossed my mind. You are a quality woman. There have been nights when I ask why we are sleeping alone twenty feet apart. But I know it's complicated. Just observing your life, I wonder if you have time for a relationship."

"So true, Ben, some of it I can control, some I can't. I need a reason to slow down. Having a relationship might be that reason. I liked you years ago in Iraq, but war and dating weren't compatible. Interviewing you recently was a reminder, and having you here has clarified my feelings. There is something good about being around you, and I know I will lose it when you leave."

"Honestly, I am surprised, Liz. You would have zero difficulty attracting a man. I have ignored my personal life, and now change is daunting. After being out of a relationship for so long, I'm not that sure of myself. Why wouldn't I want to see what we could have together?"

Liz slid over to Ben and unexpectedly kissed him on the lips.

He reciprocated a tender kiss to Liz. "Let's try."

He held her. They touched, sipping wine, telling stories, relishing each other's company until the wee hours of the morning. They were on the verge of making love, but they didn't, and why they didn't might have answered their question. Both were tired of being alone, but the answer wasn't that simple. After returning to neutral, they shared a platonic kiss and walked to separate bedrooms.

The next day was October 30. Ben called Eva to talk about November. She and Ben had dated for several years. They had almost married until she moved for a job in Washington, DC. She had invited him to DC, but at the time, Lily and his aging mother kept him in Minneapolis.

They had drifted apart amicably and remained friendly. She moved back to Edina three years earlier and opened a law firm that specialized in representing women. When his home burned, she'd responded to his email, offering him a place. They had agreed on November, the last month that Ben would be homeless.

Ben told Liz that he would like to continue seeing her but would be moving out. After the conversation, they knew their relationship was only a convenient fantasy. Staying would have become uncomfortable. Avoiding another painful breakup, he told Eva he would move in on his fiftieth birthday, November 1. He ended chapter 10 with, "Joy and sorrow are often lovers."

12

UNCOMFORTABLE SILENCE

Beginning his final month without his own bed was mildly uplifting. Thirty days from then, Ben's new dwelling would be ready. The trials and tribulations of each month had taken their toll. In December, he would have more control over his life. Driving to Edina from downtown Minneapolis was a fifteen-minute trip. He was compelled to swing by 10 Water Street.

This fall season had been a spectacular mosaic of color. Uncharacteristically, many trees still maintained their leaves, spurring Minnesotans to discuss climate change. He had remembered several snowfalls during October, but this year, there were only sunny days and green grass. The weather had been a boon for home builders, and his home was ahead of schedule. A December 1 date seemed promising.

Stopping in front of the construction, he watched the hustle and bustle of a half dozen workers. The outside structure was complete. He admired the castle-like architecture and the wood-and-stone exterior. He had chosen a rich, deep, caramel tone with cherrywood accents. The home was encircled by rustic, stone sidewalks. It had two archways. He'd made unconventional requests and was a little apprehensive and relieved when he saw the result. *At least I did something right.*

He relished the exterior appearance. The round tower on the side of the house was especially unique. Surrounded by windows, the tower resembled a lighthouse that begged to display the view. Driving away, he was at peace with the progress. With completion of the book and home, he could address the areas of his life he'd long neglected. *Thirty more days.*

Moving in with Eva would be an easy transition. They knew each other very well, having lived together for five years. After she'd moved to DC, they had continued to talk, anytime one needed a listening ear or second opinion. Ben and Eva respected each other. Consequently, they relished the simple life and laughed about how boring they were.

Arriving at 4 Red Oak Lane, Ben was struck by the natural beauty of the groomed lawns, trimmed trees, and eclectic architecture. Nary a home had a sibling on the block. Each was sui generis. Ben parked in the driveway, rang the doorbell, and waited.

Walking back to the car, he heard, "Ben, so sorry. Taking a quick shower." Eva, in a bathrobe and wet hair, gave him a hug and said, "Welcome, birthday boy!" He had almost forgotten the date was November 1, and he was a half century old.

Eva invited him in. "Make yourself at home. Be right back." She was dressed and back in ten minutes. "It's your birthday, big guy. This day is for fun and frolic." Then she winked. Ben had always liked Eva's sassy attitude. She knew what mattered and what didn't. "We have a day to celebrate, and time's a-wasting. I just need to grab a couple of things and we are off."

He still found her attractive. Her long black curly hair, black jeans, and black cashmere sweater complimented her skin tone. Like Ben's dad, she'd often been asked about her heritage. *Eva is unique in every way. How did I mess that up?*

He had given little thought to his birthday, but Eva was on top of the occasion. She was the ultimate planner. They had dinner at the Capitol Grill—a peppercorn-crusted filet mignon—and then they went to see Aaron Neville, Ben's favorite voice, just down the street at the Dakota.

Eva had gotten seats a few feet from the stage. Ben's fiftieth birthday was an unexpected, smashing success and so timely for his heavy heart. Unbelievably, Eva had passed a message to Aaron: "A lifetime fan is celebrating a big birthday and requested his favorite song, 'Can't Stop My Heart from Loving You.'"

Aaron approached the table and whispered, "Name?" to Eva. "Happy birthday, Ben! I dedicate this song to a stand-up man and veteran. Veterans Day is a few days off. Make sure you give some love to those who served."

Aaron sang Ben's favorite song and walked to their table and clapped. Amazingly, the entire Dakota applauded. *We're all looking for a reason to celebrate.*

At home, Ben said to Eva, "You are so thoughtful. Thank you from the bottom of my heart. I have always loved you, and tonight was unforgettable. Would you agree to plan all my birthdays?"

Eva laughed in the way Ben remembered. A throaty contagious laugh that would make anyone smile. *Eva is a gift of joy to my dismal life.*

He had hardly been in Eva's house, and his luggage was still on the living room floor. For the first time, he saw her home for what it represented. Coming from humble beginnings, Eva was determined to have a nice house. She would only buy high-quality furnishings. Once, she slept on the floor for months waiting for the perfect bed. Each room demonstrated her good taste. Every aspect of her home, floor to ceiling, represented her personality. Eva had achieved what her family was denied. She refused to settle.

"Where are my living quarters, Eva? It seems the butler forgot to move my luggage."

"I told him we didn't know where you were sleeping yet. No use moving them twice. Given our history, odds are, one of us will wake up somewhere else."

This adorable woman hasn't changed. How did I ever let her slip away? I didn't. She left town.

Having a bruised heart already, he was cautious. *Is she involved with someone?* Eva was someone who lived in the present and believed in the concept of loving the one you're with.

"Let's get you to your bedroom for some birthday sleep."

They walked to the lower level. The room was big enough to be a gymnasium. Ben's bedroom had a king-size bed with corner posts. Eva invited him for a nightcap.

Moments later, they were sitting outside. Eva changed into her pajamas. The crisp evening was made comfortable with a glowing red heat lamp. The contrast of the cool air, warm lamp, and soft chairs couldn't have come at a better time.

They clinked glasses, and she said, "Together again, if only for a month."

"If tonight is any indication of what life will be like here, you will need a SEAL team to force me out."

They laughed in unison.

Having shared everything during their years together, there was no need to impress. They knew most of each other's secrets. The night was a comfortable reunion of lost lovers.

"Like this wine, Ben? It's from the South of France. Remember when we used to drink the cheapest wine available? We never owned a corkscrew or needed one."

"I remember that any wine shared with you was delicious. However, this is excellent. Quality is your trademark."

"That's why I lived with you for five years. You get it."

Then you took off. You wanted more.

"So, tell me, Ben, what have you been doing since the fire? We've been out of touch. At least with the details. All I know is what I have seen from your interviews on television. When I read about the conflict by the lake, I said, 'That's my old boyfriend.' Remember the first night you slept over? I slept like a baby. Being a small-town girl in the big city, I was a little spooked about living alone. Selfishly, I wanted you to move in the next day. I used to think you just talked tough to make me feel safer. I was wrong about that. You can be fierce. Back then, I fell in love with every side of you. You reminded me of a wounded puppy, and I wanted to protect you. But in those days, there was this other side that few knew; now the world knows, and I'm a little jealous.

"I remember you saying, 'Courage is being able to do something when you're afraid.' You taught me how to defend myself. I gained confidence from your faith in me. Now, there's a lot of fight in this little dog.

"Lily used to tell me you were the only man she ever knew with a feminine side to match your masculine side. I didn't know what she meant until we lived together. You are a Renaissance man. I have yet to meet another like you." Suddenly, Eva said, "Kiss me quick, now!"

Ben instinctively pulled her close, and their lips met warmly, sensuously.

Eva had done the "kiss me quick" routine on a regular basis when they were a couple. The experience was a sweet relapse into the past.

"Thank you for your kind words. I know it's my birthday, but you must stop." Stuttering, he tried to finish a sentence. "You still make me nervous." He could feel his heart throbbing in his temple. Quickly, he took a gulp of wine. "When I met you, you seemed like the most independent person I had ever met. Nothing could stop you. I used to think I was holding you back. I'm still floundering. You are incredibly successful. Whatever success is, I haven't found it in relationships. Now, I want to embrace what little worth I have and share my life with someone. I'm fifty and alone with no prospects."

"Are you proposing to me, Ben?"

"No, I wouldn't want to be rejected on my birthday. I don't even know if you are in a relationship. Tell me what you want and keep the rest for another night. We have twenty-nine more."

"Maybe when we are fortunate enough to make it to fifty, mortality hits home. We have to consider the possibility that there is more life behind us than in front of us. I talk to myself, ask myself questions, and try to be on the right side of issues. I came from nothing. You and I are privileged, Ben. We took risks and worked hard, but I know that others never had the same chance. You can't take a risk unless you have a risk to take."

She kept talking. "You know my history. Growing up in an abusive family where my mom took the brunt of my father's rage, I still have emotional scars. You remember how afraid I was of noises? It's better, but never gone. Living alone in DC, I bought a pistol."

She looked down, contemplating a decision. "I want to show you something." Leading him into a walk-in closet, she pulled on a shoe rack, and a portion of the wall opened. She took Ben by the hand and led him into a small room. She pulled the door shut and turned on a light. There was a completely made-up bed in the room next to a picture of her grandparents.

"They adopted me when I was ten after the county took me out of the home. This is where I go to feel safe." She put her head on his shoulder, and neither spoke for several minutes. "You are the first person to see this. I built it myself. Knowing I have this allows me to sleep when I'm afraid. I don't need it often but would never give it up."

Ben held Eva close, whispering, "The beginning of your life wasn't fair, but you never made excuses. You've faced every fear and won."

"I am glad I showed you, but let's get out of here. I will tell you more before you try to refer me to a shrink."

They popped a couple of IPAs and sat on the living room sofa.

Eva said, "There is a method to my madness. Crazy as it seems, I have more reason to be concerned for my safety than ever. I am pissing men off daily. My distrust of men that began with my dad is still with me, even though he's gone. I have never hired a man in my law firm. I have nine outstanding litigators, and so far, I have only represented female clients. We never turn down a case where a person is living in fear or needs a restraining order. I'd do the same for a man, just haven't found any men needing our services. Ben, you would love to see these lawyers in action. I only hire lawyers with fire in their eyes. Together, we've opened a center in Minneapolis that will subsidize any single working mother's childcare needs too.

"I want to make a difference. I understand their issues because I've lived them. When we find men that are downright jackasses and abusers, we take them on. We are women's best friends and these deadbeats' worst enemies. No angry man's hand will ever hurt me again. As sick as this sounds, I will shoot to kill."

Ben was and wasn't surprised. Eva would help anyone, anytime, and she was relentless.

"I admire how passionate you are in your work. You are amazing. How about the other part of your life? Are you seeing anyone now?"

"Isn't vocabulary interesting? Am I 'seeing anyone' really means am I 'sleeping with anyone,' and sleeping has nothing to do with sleeping. What you really want to know is if I'm in a relationship. We've both had relationships since ending ours ten years ago. I think that topic is best saved for another night. As you said, there are twenty-nine more."

Skipping topics, she added, "This is your birthday, and we shouldn't be so serious." She slid next to him and snuggled into his neck. "I have missed you. Ten years ago, I didn't fully understand what we had, and now it's glaring me in the face."

With the biggest question unanswered and the time being 2:45 a.m., Ben suggested they get some sleep.

Eva nodded as they stood up. She put her arms around his neck and squeezed him close, kissing him softly, then she stepped back and took a deep breath. "Happy day-after-birthday, Ben."

"Best birthday ever. Good night, Eva."

As his head hit the eleventh pillow of the year, he felt grateful to have lived fifty years. He knew several who hadn't. *Eva never answered my question.*

That night, he dreamed of Dahlia and their time together. He woke up after watching a man kiss her. Ben decided a long run might be the best medicine for his mind. After running a block, a sliver of pain reminded him of his injury, so he walked. This had been his first exercise in a couple of weeks.

Eva was enjoying breakfast in a sun-filled room and invited him to join her. He sat down next to her.

"Good morning, Ben. How are you this beautiful second day in November?"

"As you articulated last night, we are blessed people. We are nearing the top of Maslow's hierarchy. Now I need to fix my head."

"What's going on in your head, Ben? You seem preoccupied."

Ben hesitated before telling Eva about Dahlia. Dahlia wasn't in his life, and he wasn't in Eva's life either. *If I'm going to be a stand-up, honest person, I must start somewhere. Why not today?*

"I met this woman, Dahlia, last January in Belize. Our lives were both complicated at the time, but we had this special connection. It's been a rough year emotionally. Honestly, I am crazy about her, and we just ended it. I'm an emotional wreck."

Ben laid it out in detail, including every tidbit right down to the last time he saw her walk away in Toronto.

"Ahhhhh, that sounds so awful, Ben. I am so sorry. What a painful ending to a special love."

She moved to him, put her arms around his shoulders, and held him in an almost motherly manner.

Ben said, "I can't believe that story just came out. I don't think I have ever shared a story quite like that. Maybe I am evolving. As a therapist, I have listened to people say how good it felt to let it out. I feel such relief sharing my story. Dahlia deserves better than I. But I regret we never had a chance."

Eva said, "Loving relationships are simply the best. Being apart is the worst, especially with no end in sight. Did you ever discuss being together in Minneapolis or Toronto?"

"No, our relationship began with such a confusing fury of emotions that we never considered that option. It would have been like telling someone you are in love with them on a first date and asking them to marry you the next morning. We were forced to give up."

"I get it, Ben, but the relationship sounded so damn genuine. I mean, you had strong feelings for each other without even kissing. You fell in love with each other's thoughts. If someone loved me before they kissed me, I would run away with them tomorrow."

"This is so good for me. I trust you, Eva. I just realized that I've lived with you longer than anyone else. That's big life stuff. As strong as my feelings were for Dahlia, our relationship couldn't survive. That closes the door for me."

Ben leaned over and returned the kiss to Eva that she gave him on his birthday.

There are kisses, and there are *kisses*. This one, he wouldn't forget. Soft, sensuous, and never ending. A life-changing kiss, the kind people reminisce about in old age.

He held her face with both hands. "Thank you, Eva. I have to be at my homesite in ten minutes to make some decisions with my builder." He rushed away.

Eva sat stunned by the last hour. Looking down, she noticed goose bumps on her legs.

Driving to 10 Water Place from Red Oak Lane was a hop, skip, and a jump. The builder and interior crew were waiting to get the final approval for paint and tile. Ben made the decision within minutes. Afterward, he walked the house, imagining the final product.

Returning to 4 Red Oak Lane, Ben saw a black Jaguar in the driveway. He went downstairs to shower. Afterward, Ben did his standard fifty push-ups and decided he would add one from now on each year. He chuckled thinking about doing seventy-five at seventy-five.

When he came upstairs, Eva had company. "Ben, I would like you to meet someone."

Ben walked into the living room.

"Ben, this is Ross. Ross, this is Ben."

The two shook hands.

Ben said, "I am meeting Lily and doing some furniture shopping this morning, so have to run. You two have a good day."

Ben got into the car wondering if Ross was a fellow lawyer, her financial planner, her lover, or some combination of the three.

Lily met Ben at the Galleria. She was wearing a black business suit and had her hair up. This was a first for Ben. He had seen Lily dressed up many times for prom, homecoming, and weddings, but never as a professional.

"You're hired. Lily; you look marvelous."

"I am going to meet with the company bosses after lunch. Signing my contract and doing the official stuff, not even sure what that means. I mean, this is my first job."

"Lily, you are the real deal. They are lucky to have hired you. I would give anything to sit invisibly in the corner and watch."

Lily laughed. "I expected you to say you would be outside in the car if I needed you."

"I would be if you ask, but I know you don't need me. You have done this all on your own. Honestly, you have always done it on your own."

After shopping for home furnishings, they sat down for lunch. Lily said, "I was so impressed and proud watching you on TV and thinking, *That's my dad.* I must ask, how's your back? Any pain?"

"No, not really, Lily. Had my first short run today, all good. Pretty sure I am almost healed."

"How's it going in Edina? When you guys were together, I was so young and into being me, I hardly got to know Eva."

"Very relaxed. Her house is big. I feel like we could go days without ever seeing each other."

"But given your history with her, what's it like? Is she alone or with someone?"

"Funny you should ask, but honestly, I don't know. Like I said, the house is big."

"You were in Toronto. Did you see Dahlia?"

Ben's stomach sank. He took a deep breath. *If I can tell Eva, I should tell Lily.* He told Lily the story, feeling both good and bad. Good that he was sharing his personal life with his daughter and bad for the sadness the story held. Ben knew that hurt between parents and children was powerful, either way it traveled. Lily felt his hurt.

"I am sorry, so very sorry. I liked Dahlia and hoped the two of you could figure something out."

Ben changed the subject. "Have you seen your mom recently?"

"No. I can't get myself to see her. With the new job, I want to stay focused. I probably should be doing something different with her, but I don't want to, not right now."

Ben understood. He felt similar but worried that their lack of contact would grow into a bigger problem if left to fester.

"Lily, we both have issues with what has happened. If I set up an appointment with your mother's therapist, would you go with me? If after the meeting you never wanted to go back, we could say we tried and let it go?"

"Do I want to? No. But if you agree I don't have to go back unless I want to, maybe. I must go to work now. Thanks for lunch."

Lily had to go be a grown-up employee, and Ben had to begin the finishing touches for his novel. Hugging her goodbye, he knew telling her about Toronto was the right decision. Sharing would open the door for more real conversations from that day forward.

He wanted to help Lily and Alison heal before the window between them closed. He called Alison, who called her therapist immediately, and the appointment was set up for Saturday morning at ten. He shared the info with Lily, who reluctantly agreed.

Back at 4 Red Oak Lane, the black Jag was gone. Eva said, "How was Lily and shopping?"

"Productive, followed by a lovely lunch. I am constantly reminded that she's a grown-up."

"She will always be your little girl, but Lily is a lovely young woman."

"Thank you, Eva. She had similar compliments about you this morning."

"Ben, do you have a couple of minutes now, or are you on your way somewhere?"

"No, I have time. What's up?"

"Ross is someone I have been seeing for the last couple of months. Because he is recently divorced, I have been guarded. When you asked the other night, I didn't know how to respond. After you shared your Dahlia story, I feel like I needed to be up front with you too."

"Does he know about our history? What does he think about me living here?"

"Was sort of funny. He recognized you and said, 'Isn't that the guy who got stabbed down by the lake?' So, I gave him the short version of why you are here for the month of November. He knows we were together years ago and isn't comfortable with you living here. The conversation annoyed me. I told him, 'I've slept with him, and now I'm sleeping with you. Get over it.'"

"I appreciate you telling me. As much as I would like to talk more, I have some authoring and have a deadline staring at me. Can we talk later?"

"Absolutely, Ben. We can make dinner together for old times' sake."

Finishing chapter 11, Ben wrote, "We must learn to let people go!" He knew the last chapter was important. He wanted an unpredictable ending that would lead the reader to ponder. He had a rush of adrenaline closing in on the finish line because he would be free to take a hiatus from writing, perhaps for a couple of years, maybe forever.

Eva and Ben both loved Indian cuisine, and they made chicken tikka Kashmiri with jasmine rice. She had bought a few Taj Mahal beers. They enjoyed a dinner they had shared a few times in a previous life. They had always loved random weeknight celebrations. Ben was not someone who lived for vacations, weekends, or holidays. He believed that any day could be a time to celebrate.

During dinner, Eva asked, "Have you ever thought about how our life would have been if we had got married and had a couple of kids?"

Ben smiled. "Gee, I don't know, maybe a couple of thousand times."

They both laughed and clinked beer mugs.

Dinner was delightful. They laughed remembering wonderful past times and trips they'd taken, including the one to Buenos Aires where they almost got married and were thwarted by not having their birth certificates on hand.

Eva's cell rang. "It's Ross. He is in the neighborhood and stopping by."

Ben said, "The unpredictability of life."

Before saying another word, the doorbell rang, and Eva's boyfriend was in the house. Ben looked for an escape hatch.

Ross gave a brief hello, and the three sat in the living room enjoying the last glasses of Taj Mahal. Ben had to admit that Ross was a good guy, even though he would have preferred to dislike him.

Several times when Eva and Ben's eyes met, they both knew neither wanted Ross's interference. Their history was long, and their time in November was short. Neither had a clue about the future of their relationship, but both understood that Ross didn't fit in with them that night. After an hour, Ben faked being tired and excused himself.

Ben lay down, and the song "Sleeping Single in a Double Bed" began playing in his head. Alone again, feeling some self-pity, he was reminded that talking to himself was becoming too common. He thought of the numerous relationships that had gone south for some reason and knew they were his own damn fault.

He had told Liz he would call her, so he decided to use the moment to be a man of his word.

"Hello, Liz. How are you? Is this too late?"

"No, Ben, I'm a night owl, as you know. How's living in a different home?"

"Everything is fine, but I can't wait to move. I have a high need to have my own place after a year of bouncing around."

"I get it. Even when traveling for a few days, hotel to hotel, I can't wait to get home."

"Liz, could we have dinner sometime?"

There was a brief silence, and Liz said, "I'm not sure it's a good idea, Ben. I played all my cards with you. I know you understand when I say that I am beyond dating. I want a serious relationship and need someone to be crazy about me. Someone to adore me. I am pretty sure that is not going to be you, Ben. I just don't think you are emotionally available, at least not to me. So having dinner wouldn't make sense. Do you understand?"

"Guess I must, Liz. To be honest, I am concerned too. I need to work on myself. You don't need me to stroke your ego, but you are a beautiful human being. I can't even think of a fault in you, whereas I have a page full. I am somehow inept at moving forward with a relationship. This past year has taught me that I need to change. Finishing my book and getting my home back is a priority. After December 1, I can only hope something works."

The call with Liz ended. Ben lay on the bed doing some serious self-talk. He knew Liz was right. She deserved someone better too.

Almost a year after the fire, Ben was alone and as Liz so accurately explained, "emotionally unavailable." Ben accepted that something was wrong with him, and that if he didn't fix it, he would not only be alone that night but always.

He went to sleep confused about so many aspects of his life. Dahlia was everything he loved, yet Ben had an inability to move forward with her. For now, he was grateful he'd seen her with another man. It was clear evidence they were done.

He had never been comfortable competi⸱ ⸱⸱⸱ an, mostly out of fear he would lose. Like Liz had so ⸱ ⸱⸱⸱ ulated, Ben wanted to be adored too. *I'm not adorable*

The next day, seeing Eva was more th⸱ ⸱⸱⸱ uncomfortable. He wondered if Ross had spent the night. Ben ⸱⸱⸱ited to get out of the picture pronto. He wasn't going to wait for his house to be ready.

He had a doctor's appointment. He had hardly thought of his injury. The medical news was good, so he went for a run around Lake of the Isles and ran into Lily and a friend, William. The three agreed to meet at Isles Bun and Coffee.

He watched her interact with William across the table. Lily was clearly experiencing love.

Driving away, he hoped Lily hadn't sensed any sadness in him while she took another life step. *It is healthy to be happy for Lily. I am happy for her.*

Ben stopped by his home. He would move in now if he could. The closing date was set, and he would be doing a walk-through soon. Seeing the house was the uplift that he needed. Glancing at his watch, he saw November 25.

Prematurely, he began to pack. Knowing he could get everything together and be out in thirty minutes felt good. He hung on to the idea that having his home back would bring his mind some peace.

"Eva, my home will be ready in a couple of days, and my book is almost done. I need to be alone to complete a couple of tasks. So, I am moving across the lake into the Beach Hotel. That way, I can be there for deliveries and final issues before moving in December 1 . . . but I want you to come visit. I will always want you to be happy. We are forever bonded. And if your house ever burns down, you have a place to live. Ross will have to find his own place."

"Be careful with your words, Ben. Don't make promises you can't keep. I'm glad we have reconnected in the middle of our life story; our souls are worn, but wise."

Ben got in his car and drove to the north side of Bde Maka Ska and checked into the hotel. Don't make promises you can't keep. I'm glad we have reconnected in the middle of our life story; our souls are worn, but wise."

Ben got in his car and drove to the north side of Bde Maka Ska and checked into the hotel.

He declined Thanksgiving Day invitations. He chose to be alone. The next night, he sat alone in the penthouse of a twelve story building overlooking the city of Minneapolis, eating a turkey dinner from Boston Market and watching old movies. He took an Advil PM and went to bed at ten thirty. His move-in date was December 1. In two days, he and Lily had a meeting with Alison's therapist.

As Ben pulled into the parking lot that Saturday, his sister, Anne, called.

"Hi, Ben. Do you have a minute? All our family talk in July inspired Andrew and me to research our family tree. I feel a little creepy saying this to you, but I sent our DNA in for analysis. I was doing mine and saw you left your toothbrush, so I included yours too.

"You won't believe it. We are only half-Norwegian. We are half–Iberian Peninsula. Unbelievable, huh? Guess we know where Dad got his olive skin and black hair. Your and my DNA were the same, of course, but still! Who knows what else we don't know?"

Ben was shocked. "Text me the results. I am late for an appointment, Anne. Will call you later. Thank you so much for doing this and including me. I can't tell you how important this is. Gotta go, love you."

His phone beeped. Reading the text . . . Ben was 50 percent Norwegian, 50 percent Iberian Peninsula. When combined with Alison's 50 percent French and 50 percent European Jewish, the result matched Lily's outcome perfectly.

Ben was exhilarated. Lily was his biological daughter! He laid his head on the steering wheel, unable to move until Lily knocked on his window.

Lily opened the car door and said, "What's wrong? Are you OK?"

"Not only am I OK, I'm better than ever. I can't wait to tell you." He hugged her and couldn't hold back. "I just found out that you are my biological daughter. My family history was incorrect. Our DNA matches. Here's the proof!"

Lily grabbed him, holding his face in her hands. There were characteristics that mirrored hers.

"I'm speechless. I knew it. I knew it. I even look like you. Our smile, our eyes, they're the same. I knew it."

They hurried to the therapist's office. Once inside, they found Alison.

"Sit down. You are going to want to hear this. Lily is my daughter. Here is the proof!"

After reading the report, Alison could hardly speak. "When Portuguese and Spanish were indicated, I assumed . . . I assumed . . . but I was wrong. All these years, the suffering. Trying to protect both of you. But I was wrong. Oh my God, please forgive me."

The session was not what Ben had expected. It was so much more. The three of them released some of their pain with each other and pledged to move forward. The mistake had been rectified by Anne, who never even knew.

Driving away in their separate cars, Alison, Ben, and Lily were relieved. Ben and Alison knew the blame for the affair was mutually owned. Ben had failed Alison, and ultimately, the marriage crumbled. That was on him. But now, Lily could return her mind to what she'd believed for twenty-one years.

Over the next few days, Ben isolated himself to fine-tune his book. He used room service, exercised, and visited the sauna. Other than calling Lily several times, he didn't use his phone.

His book was finished four days early. "Out of the ashes, a soul was found. In essence, love is fire."

13

THE PINNACLE

The clock read 2:27 a.m. It was officially December 1. Ben was still awake, only a few hours from moving into his home. It had been twelve months. A long year of trial, tribulation, and growth. He was fifty, only a year older than when the fire destroyed his home. He believed he was ten years wiser. At least he hoped so.

He created a cup of below-average coffee by mixing white powder to brown powder. A hot shower moved him out of his roller coaster of emotions. After a less-than-restful night, he was slowly becoming alive. *This is the day I thought would never come.*

He opened the shades to check the weather on the horizon. His phone beeped. The furniture was on its way to 10 Water Street. His energy surged knowing he would be sleeping in his own bed that night.

He had circled Bde Maka Ska hundreds of times, but this morning was different. This time, he was going home. He pushed his birth date into the keypad. The front door unlocked.

Even though the rooms were empty, he had a sense of relief. He explored his home, seeing skylights and a stone fireplace with one charred brick from the fire placed in the center. Walking up the curved stairway, he was certain his refusal of straight stairs had been the right decision.

The grand prize was the third floor. The sun was shining through the lighthouse windows onto curved walls. The brick circular interior looked as he had envisioned, just high enough so he could see the Minneapolis skyline, Bde Maka Ska, and Lake Harriet. Ben concluded that this would be his go-to destination for weather-watching.

His doorbell, or more accurately, his door song, "Greensleeves," began to play. Ben had chosen the music personally. He used the technology on the wall to see who was outside his door. Lily! He ran down the curved stairs. "The best surprise ever!"

"Congratulations on your new home! I had to come over. I want to see everything. My boss insisted that I come in a little late today. I brought you some bananas, scones, Sumatra coffee, and cinnamon cream."

Ben hugged Lily a second time.

Lily looked around the kitchen and said, "I am going to try to make us a coffee without hurting myself. This machine looks like I need a heavy equipment license."

Shortly after, Lily delivered two terra-cotta cups. Father and daughter were the first to break bread in this home. The absence of furniture didn't diminish any pleasure from their breakfast on the floor.

"Before we talk about this grand abode, I am so happy this DNA stuff is behind us. I was really feeling crazy the last few weeks. The news was so hard to believe. I mean, I even walk like you. Duck-like. So, what are your first impressions of the house?"

"Honestly, I am just pleased to finally have a home. I might add, *we* have a home. This is your home too, Lily. For now, we are close, can hang out, and can run the lakes together. What a gift!"

After a rapid breakfast, Lily said, "Better get going or I'll be moving in for sure. Don't want to get fired before I get my first check."

"Thank you so much for coming by and bringing me the essentials for my first morning." He pulled Lily close and whispered in her ear. She was off.

Ben hardly had time to say goodbye when the furniture movers arrived. The delivery people's efficiency was perfect. They were in and out in less than an hour. The home on Water Street was beginning to look cozy.

"Greensleeves" again.

Hitting the nearest wall button, he saw Clayton and Sarah. Opening the door, he grabbed both. Clayton and Sarah said, "Welcome home." Ben said, "My favorite neighbors, please come in!"

Ben offered coffee and scones without napkins, and together, they sat on plastic-covered furniture. "You are the first to sit on this furniture. How fitting and appropriate that it is you."

"Don't forget the promise of that first dinner either," Sarah said upon leaving.

Ben looked at the time. Eleven fifteen, and his house was partially livable. Only the sound system and television installation remained. He'd missed a few messages throughout the morning.

Anne asked if he needed help.

There was also a text from Dahlia. They hadn't communicated since the nightmare in Toronto. Ben sat down. Although he knew Dahlia's intention was well meaning, he guessed what the message would say. She would be wishing him well and congratulating him. Ben knew what he needed to do. He hit Delete.

Then José called. "Hola, amigo. If I have my dates right, you must be in the midst of moving into your new home!"

"You are correct, mi amigo. How good of you to remember. How are Barbara and that younger version of yourself?"

"Both are great, thanks for asking."

After a few pleasantries, Ben heard "Greensleeves."

"More deliveries, José. Can I call you later?"

"Of course, *paz, miho*, adios."

The electronics were installed, and Ben put on some music for the new home. Ben chose the Platters. "Only You," "Smoke Gets in Your Eyes," and "The Great Pretender" reverberated through the house, changing it into a home.

He wondered about his failure in relationships. He was a wiser man, and the year had been a great teacher, but he wasn't sure he could apply his learning to life. *Deeds, not words.*

His phone rang. It was Maddie.

"Hi, Ben. I was just visiting Louie and Sheri. They told me you were moving into your new home today. Congratulations! I am wondering if you have any interest in hanging out sometime. It seemed we might have started something nice and never got to see it through."

"Why not?" Ben said. "Why don't you come see the house?"

"When works for you? I am sure you have a lot to do, having just moved in . . ."

"Maddie, I have never been one to worry about that stuff. It will take a while to get everything in order. If you want, tonight works. Come by, we'll share a glass of wine."

"Really? What time?"

"Does seven o'clock work?"

"Great, see you then."

Good decision. Inviting her felt like being an adult again.

Ben knew a wine and hors d'oeuvres run was necessary and went to France 44 to solve both problems. Returning with bruschetta, cheese, stuffed olives, and Malbec, he had just enough time to run the lake and be ready for Maddie.

He unpacked a couple of dishes and two wineglasses for Maddie's visit. "Greensleeves" played. He opened the door, and Maddie's energetic self was a pleasant sight. Her long curly hair, black eyes, and rose-colored dress with matching lipstick looked elegant.

"Welcome, Maddie. So glad you were able to come over. So far, you're my favorite guest!" Both laughed. "Would you have Malbec, or is there something else you'd prefer? Hope you're up for a whirlwind tour."

"Malbec is perfect, Ben, thank you." Kicking off her heels, she said, "Let's do the tour!"

Handing Maddie a glass of vino, Ben began showing her the kitchen, deck, living room, office space, a guest bedroom, and an undefined room. Walking up the curved stairs, he looked back at the shimmering chandelier.

Maddie said, "Wow, that chandelier really sparkles."

Upstairs, he showed Maddie a workout area, guest bedroom, and the master bedroom.

Maddie sat on his bed, saying, "I could enjoy this view in the morning."

"You're welcome to stay over." Both laughed with a little tension. "I didn't even know that view existed."

Ben enjoyed seeing Maddie on his bed. She seemed to belong. He was tempted to say that she was the most beautiful woman that had visited his bedroom, but he didn't.

Next, they went to the lighthouse room, sitting down in plush, mustard-colored swivel chairs to enjoy the wine and gaze at the view.

"I have never seen a room like this. Where did you get this idea?" she said.

"Who knows? I've always wanted a round room with windows. The goal was to be up high with surrounding windows and a concave ceiling."

"With a wall fireplace. This is a special place, Ben."

Because the view, chairs, and wall fireplace seemed so cozy, Ben retreated to get the appetizers. He thought that the combination of wine, food, and skyline could facilitate something, but what, he wasn't sure. He couldn't believe how comfortable he finally felt, in his own home at last.

Passing the time, chatting, listening to music, and sipping on wine, Ben asked Maddie to dance. They slow danced to Boz Scaggs's "We're All Alone." At one point, she laid her head on his chest. Feeling her warm breath on his neck was soothing. When the song ended, neither wanted to stop, but the next song, "Bad to the Bone," began, and they both laughed and sat down.

Ben's first evening in the house was a smashing start. However, all good things must come to an end. Maddie said she didn't want to wear out her welcome on the first night, and she had to be up early to pick up a birthday cake for an office party the following day.

"Greensleeves" played again, and Ben saw a package being delivered on the monitor.

"Since I have to go, maybe you can walk me to the door and get your package. I hope we do this again soon." She kissed Ben lightly on the lips.

Ben opened the door. "Close your eyes, Maddie. You have something on your eyelash." When she did, Ben kissed her softly on the lips.

Maddie opened her eyes. "Sure you got it?" and closed her eyes again.

When the second kiss ended, she laughed and said, "Gotta go. I have a business to run in the morning." Her smile spoke volumes.

Maddie touched Ben's hand, turned, and walked to her car.

Ben picked up the package on the porch, walked into the house, poured another Malbec, and sat down by the fireplace. The package had an unfamiliar return address: "3D Images, New York City, NY," addressed to "Major Ben Raymond."

What is this? He decided whatever it was, it could wait. Laying the package on the coffee table, he took his wine upstairs.

The next morning felt to Ben like a genesis. The book was finished, his body was mending, he was moved in, and most importantly, Lily's life was more settled. So many issues were resolved, he could finally focus on his long-neglected pursuit of happiness. On his first morning, still in his own bed, he committed himself to being a better person.

He started the day with a personal tour of the lower level. The walk outdoors offered a brick patio, outdoor fireplace, and veranda, followed by a grove of leafless trees on a sloping lawn. He imagined the spring . . . green grass and budding flowers.

On the main floor, he saw a balance of openness and quaint privacy. The furniture blended into the house as if they were built together. The skylights gave an appearance of being outside. He could see the blue sky from every room. Entering the lighthouse room, he sat in the chair facing the lake. The sun glistened through the skeleton of trees. He cherished the quiet moment. For almost a year, silence and quiet had meant loneliness. Today was different.

He began to wonder. *Is living alone a viable option, or am I simply appreciating being alone after living with others for almost a year?*

Feeling something sharp, he looked down and saw an earring on the chair. *Maddie marked her territory.* His thoughts remained with her. *Sipping wine, listening to music, dancing. Those pleasures have been missing for years.*

Ben's phone was beeping. It was his publisher. "Good morning, Ben. Hope I didn't wake you. Sometimes I forget that you are outside EST."

"No problem, John. Did you receive the first draft?"

"Sure did, and the review-and-editing process has begun. We are hoping to start the printing the last week of the month. The promotions have already started, so we can offer preorders for the holidays, promising deliveries the first week of January."

John continued, "I am already hearing positive comments from the team that have started the first reading. That is great news from people who read for a living. You should fly out for a couple of days so we can brainstorm your next work."

"I am going to take the rest of December to put my life in order. We'll talk in January."

"Remember, Ben, you are in the sweet zone right now. Don't wait too long."

"Understood, John. I need to run. Thanks for the call."

Ben understood how the trappings of success could derail his goal of focusing on his personal life. Money wasn't his priority for the immediate. *Money only matters when you don't have enough. I'm all right.*

He held Maddie's earring and remembered how he'd loved dancing with her. *Might Maddie be that special someone?* After just one night, he was upbeat thinking of her. Now that he had her earring, he had a reason to contact her.

"Good morning, Maddie. Thanks for coming by last evening and especially for the dance. Found a gold earring in the lighthouse. Must be yours! Hope you are enjoying the birthday party. Ben."

A minute later: "Love your house, Ben! I had a good time, such a sweet dance, so nice! Yes, my earring. Now we must see each other soon . . . I only have one pair of earrings . . . XO, Maddie."

Maddie is so warm, fun, and kind. Could life really be this simple? One date, more dates, fall in love, live a happy life.

Ben regretted not reading Dahlia's text. He regretted thinking of her too.

He called Maddie.

"Good morning, Ben. Sleep well last night?"

"I did. Almost felt like a grown-up, waking up in my own home. This was long overdue. Listen, Maddie, I was wondering if you would be willing to help me with a second opinion for some home furnishings, and then we could have dinner tonight or tomorrow night?"

"I would love to. Either night works. Why not tonight?"

"Perfect. Shall I pick you up around six thirty?"

"Actually, I will be in Uptown for a meeting that ends at six, so I could just come by, if that works."

"That would be great. Looking forward to seeing you, Maddie."

Ben looked forward to spending time with her and getting her opinion on rugs, towels, and lamps, boring-but-essential items for his home. On the kitchen counter, he noticed yesterday's delivery and opened it. His heart stopped, then began beating rapidly. There was no note, no card, just a photo.

Four feet, twenty toes. Ten magenta toenails and ten boring ones, with a blue Caribbean backdrop. There were two frozen mojitos in the foreground and palm trees glistening in the sunlight in the background. A spectacular picture. One that Ben had been attempting to erase.

The picture was a beachfront bar, sipping delightful drinks, feet up, and loving life. Today, the picture was a setback. Ben took the beautiful picture out to the garage and put it behind closed doors. He was moving on and returned his thoughts to Maddie.

That evening, "Greensleeves" played, and the monitor illuminated Maddie's charming face. Ben opened the door, and they shared a casual hug before Ben offered her a water, soda, or whatever her heart desired. Maddie requested a water.

Coming directly from work, she was dressed professionally in a burnt-orange top and dark brown slacks. Ben thought she looked lovely and told her so.

"You are always so kind, and I love that you notice. That's nice!"

Ben leaned over and kissed her cheek. She smiled again. He handed her the earring and said, "You left this here on purpose. Thank you for giving me a reason to call you."

Maddie blushed.

Soon after, they were reviewing household additions that he had selected but was more comfortable buying after Maddie's approval. Shopping was short-lived, and they were having dinner at La Boca Chica in an hour. LBC was a casual Mexican restaurant with authentic food. After ordering enchiladas, blackened snapper, and guacamole prepared table side, Ben and Maddie began investigating each other's past.

"I can't believe you were in Afghanistan. What do you remember about being there?"

"My experiences were different than a tourist's. Mostly, I have euphoric recall of my time. Majestic mountains, honorable people, aromas of fantastic food, and smiling children come to mind. Afghanistan was a dichotomy. The best of humankind amid the madness. Would you like to visit there?"

"It is a dream I hope comes true, but my dreams aren't as important as peace. I am so sad that war has become the norm. Afghan people just want to live. The wars are heartbreaking."

"Every year, I hope there will be a breakthrough. Now that the war is over, I hope there will be less violence. Time will tell. How did you get you name, Maddie? I'm curious."

"My name is Madeleine, named after a Polish nurse who delivered me. My parents still talk about her. She is a wonderful person who helped so many people."

"Can I call you Madeleine? It's so beautiful."

"If you like, that will put you in a small circle; only my parents call me Madeleine."

"Thank you for that privilege. I like that, Madeleine." Continuing their exploration of their past, Ben asked about Chad. "How did you meet him, how is he, and do you still communicate?"

"We met in Central Park in NYC at a Paul Simon concert. In the middle of thousands of people, five people from Minneapolis ended up standing next to each other. We just jumped into a relationship too soon. My life is much calmer now.

"Ben, is being single a chosen path, or are you open to having a serious relationship?"

"The past year has been a multitude of lessons. Living with different people forced me to evaluate my life. I want to share my life with someone. One of the lessons from the past year is that a shared life is a better life."

"Why do you think a shared life is better?"

"Almost all my memorable experiences involved being with someone. I want that every day. For example, tonight with you is delightful, sharing our thoughts, dreams, not to mention delicious food. Without you, I would be at home by myself, in my new house, wishing someone were there. I want to stop wishing and start living."

"Are you asking me to move in?"

Both busted out laughing.

"We could try tonight and reassess in the morning."

Madeleine smiled at Ben in a way he hadn't seen before. She was tantalizing, and he was reveling in every moment.

They left La Boca Chica hand in hand and returned to his home. Driving into the garage, he thought of the hidden picture behind the door.

Taking Madeleine's hand, he said, "One of my best decisions was the tunnel to the house. Because of the lot size, I didn't want to give up home space for an attached garage, so I asked the builder if they could install a tunnel."

Moments later, Ben and Madeleine were walking through a beautifully sconce-lit muraled tunnel. In the middle of the tunnel, Madeleine stopped and looked at a section of the painting. "Interesting. What is this about?"

"I asked an artist to create an abstract painting that represented my ancestors' journey from Bergen to Liverpool to NYC to Minneapolis. I have the painting upstairs, waiting to be displayed. Because I loved what she did, I asked her to do a larger version here. Now, I can walk by this every day."

Finding each other's eyes resulted in an embrace and tender kiss. Although underground, Ben and Madeleine were connecting on a new level. Soon after, they entered his home.

Sitting by the stone fireplace, he asked, "Do you have an early-morning obligation, Madeleine?"

"No, I don't have anything until the afternoon."

Ben proceeded to light the fireplace for the first time. In five minutes, they were looking at a crackling fire on a December evening. Again, he wondered if he would ever forget the crackling fire sound. Ben offered Madeleine a hot chocolate or coffee. She chose chocolate, and he succeeded in having his machine deliver two marshmallow-covered delights.

"What makes you happy, Ben? I mean, day to day, what makes life meaningful for you?"

Madeleine wasn't someone desperate for a man. He knew that she had opportunities and, for some reason, had never married. He wondered if the reason was that she had a good life, strong family ties, a career, and just never met that special someone. He savored watching her drink the hot chocolate, flicking her tongue in the marshmallow, and sighing.

"Curiosity, I suppose. I'm fascinated by what I don't know or don't understand. Day to day, I try to continue learning. I heard someone say, 'Every person you meet knows something you don't.' I enjoy variety, the more the better. Sleep patterns, diet, exercise, clothes, conversations, sunshine, clouds, rain, wind, warm, cold are simple daily examples of things I embrace. For example, on a cold winter day or in a rainstorm, I run the lakes. Am I making sense or talking to myself?"

"I was just thinking you live in the perfect climate. Seems like you need stimulation."

"What matters to you, Madeleine?"

"I love realness. I need genuineness. I run from superficial experiences. If I see artificial ingredients in food, I won't eat it. If someone talks about money, I'm bored. If they don't know where Afghanistan is, I'm gone. Friends must be someone I can call anytime, anywhere, and I know they will answer. I'm not easy to please, Ben."

Ben and Madeleine talked into the wee hours of the morning.

"Ben, it's 2:20 a.m. I think I need to leave."

"Another option is I could offer you a toothbrush, pajamas, and your own bedroom."

"That sounds great. I am exhausted, been up since six."

Ben returned with a new pair of his pajama bottoms, a white T-shirt, a new toothbrush, and some toothpaste. "The bedroom is upstairs, and the bathroom has most anything you need. If I forgot anything, tell me. I'm staying next door."

Madeleine smiled again. "Thank you, Ben."

Ben got ready for bed, put on pajamas, and went to say good night. He gently knocked, and Maddie giggled.

"Who's there? Come in and say good night quickly, Ben, because I will be asleep before you get to the *night* part if you hesitate."

Ben entered. Madeleine was sitting up, pillows all around her, wearing his T-shirt. He went over and sat on the bed. "There can't be any ghosts because you are the first person to ever sleep here. See you in the morning unless you need something."

Ben kissed Madeleine softly for a few seconds, sighed, got up, and closed the door.

He got into bed thinking of his first sleepover, Madeleine. He was a little bothered that having her sleep next door was an easy decision. *Why didn't I ask Madeleine to sleep with me?*

Ben let it go and, on his second night in his new home, slept perfectly.

Waking, Ben went downstairs to make breakfast. With a bakery in the neighborhood, he decided on bagels. He would be back before Madeleine was awake. After her long day, she was sleeping in, and Ben was pleased.

Arriving home with fresh warm bagels, he made coffee and went to ask Madeleine if she preferred breakfast in bed or wanted to join him downstairs. He quietly went to the bedroom door and listened. No sounds. Deciding to crack the door, Ben slightly opened it, seeing the bed was made. Ben thought Madeleine was in the bathroom, but the door was open.

"Good morning, Madeleine." There was no response. He called louder. "Good morning, Madeleine."

Ben walked into the bedroom. She was gone. He was puzzled until he saw a note by the bed.

"So sorry, Ben. Will call you this morning."

Ben was concerned and perplexed. *Why would she leave?*

He wanted to know she was OK and that there wasn't an emergency. It didn't make sense. However, Madeleine had left a note, so Ben assumed she would call.

An hour passed, and he was feeling a need to know that she was OK. He texted her and said, "Please call me." He received a text within a minute saying, "Sorry, Ben, call you at nine." Feeling reassured that Madeleine was all right, he waited.

At exactly nine o'clock, his cell rang. "Ben, I am so sorry for leaving in the middle of the night."

Ben said, "First, tell me you are OK."

"I am home and fine. Let me try to explain. Since being a little girl in Afghanistan, I have struggled with PTSD. I've taken medication for it for years. I didn't plan to spend the night, so I didn't have my medication. I woke up about 4:00 a.m. feeling anxious, so I decided to come home and take it. I am so sorry for leaving like that, but I didn't want to wake you. My PTSD is effectively controlled by medication, and I was so tired last night, I never expected what happened."

"I am so relieved that you are OK. Last night was so perfect, I was worried and confused about what had happened. I kept wondering what I had missed."

"I am sorry. As I think about it now, I should have woken you. But a few hours ago, I was anxious and not making the best decisions other than to get home and take my meds. In fact, I am running on empty now, having hardly slept."

"Listen, Madeleine, I understand. Get some rest. Call me later if you're up to it."

"Thank you, Ben. I have an important meeting now, call you later. Bye for now."

Ben sat holding his phone for a few minutes.

Lily called. "Wanna run with me, Dad?"

"Absolutely."

Halfway around the lake, Lily suggested a little detour and pit stop. They spent the hour catching up by a warm fireplace.

Ben asked about William.

"So far, all good. He's so laid-back. I've known him for two months, and I am amazed how grounded he seems. Never seen him in a bad mood. He's upbeat, and he loves to talk about anything. William is a sweet ingredient in my life."

"I am happy for you, Lily. Your life puzzle is being put together. I love watching the pieces fit in—a job, living on your own, now William. I hope we always have these talks."

"Hanging with you will always be special. By the way, Dahlia called me asking how you are. She is a good person. I asked about her life too. Sounded like she is dating someone."

"I didn't know you talked with her but am glad she is moving on too. She deserves to be happy. Our situation was hopeless." *Dahlia is the most wonderful failure of my life.*

"We have only talked a couple of times. When you sit in a hospital room with someone for a few days, you get to know them. Got lots of good vibes from her."

Soon after, Ben was leaving Lily on her doorstep and jogging back to Water Street.

Back home, he was in an upbeat mood. He considered that maybe being alone was his destiny. Even the Maddie experience didn't turn out great. However, for today, he was going to focus on being content and finally in control of his life. The holidays were enough to give him optimism, at least for today.

He appreciated Dahlia's call to Lily. He understood their connection and how adversity could form a powerful bond.

Madeleine called later that afternoon. She sounded tired, and Ben guessed she didn't feel well. Consequently, their phone call was brief. He was feeling like the night he'd met Chad, believing that Madeleine needed time and space. *PTSD, she was an innocent child.*

Ben focused on putting his home together and buying holiday decorations over the next few days. Between tasks, he spoke with Madeleine. She was having a busy week. She had returned to her normal self.

Buying a tree was a reminder of being alone. He asked Lily to come over and decorate it.

"Would love to, but is it OK if William comes along?"

"Of course."

In the middle of the week, they came over and decorated the tree. However enjoyable the evening was, their leaving left Ben with a sad feeling. Sitting alone in front of a warm fire was a reminder that a home without anyone is just a place to live.

He contemplated inviting Eva over but quickly ruled it out. The idea was selfish and self-serving. He had to reach out to his friends, not old girlfriends.

Remembering his promise to Clayton and Sarah, he invited them for dinner. He had one date on his calendar. Second, he called Louie to invite him, Sheri, and Junior over for a happy hour. Two dates on his calendar. *Progress.*

The following two nights were baby steps in the right direction, beginning with Louie, Sheri, and Junior. They announced plans to marry next summer. Louie asked Ben to be his best man and Junior to be the ring bearer. At the end of the evening, Junior resisted leaving, running, and sitting on Ben's lap. The decision was made on the spot. Ben surmised that Junior was jealous of competing with Sheri for Louie's time.

Ben and Junior Walker followed them to Laurel Avenue and collected all his feline essentials. Going to bed that night, Ben laughed, thinking, *At least I'm not sleeping alone.* Junior was right next him, and both appreciated being together again.

The following night, he had dinner with his favorite neighbors. Ben prepared a classic Minnesota cuisine of pot roast, carrots, and potatoes. He cheated by buying a sour-cream-and-raisin pie, Clayton's favorite. The evening culminated with Ben thanking them for their friendship. The night was one of neighborly perfection.

Junior loved being back on Water Street. He'd already found a perfect perch in the lighthouse.

Ben decided to host a holiday party for the people who had allowed him to stay at their homes. He wanted to have all of them under his roof for New Year's Eve. Even if he had to take out a loan, he would provide a complimentary room and transportation to and from the Stavanger Hotel. He was taking steps to rebuild his personal life.

The next day, Madeleine called and wanted to stop over to talk. She looked sad. "I feel like I am one big disappointment after another to you. Ben, I am moving to London. I have been trying to grow my business by forming a partnership with a relative and just got the approval this morning. I am flying to London on Friday. I have been working on this merger for over a year. I am excited about the opportunity but very sad about you and me."

"Unbelievable, Madeleine. I'm at a loss for words. We haven't had much of a chance, have we?"

"You just never know about life; there is a surprise around every corner. I am going to stay in touch with you, if that is OK. Don't rule out any possibility. You'd love London, come see me."

Ben faked a smile. "Goodbye, Madeleine." Days before, he'd thought she may have been the one. Life was still uncertain, and too often disappointing.

Realizing that getting invitations out for a holiday party was borderline urgent, he composed an email using the same addresses from a year ago, only adding Alison and Ted. *Nathan taught me the true meaning of forgiveness.*

My Friends,

I know you might be hesitant to open an email from me. Don't worry about this one.

A year ago, I was desperate. Each of you opened your home to me. Because of your kindness, I had a roof over my head, but that was just the beginning. I learned from watching your meaningful lives and am grateful beyond words.

As a small token of gratitude, I want to invite you to a New Year's Eve soirée at my home. To make the evening enjoyable and convenient, I have reserved rooms at the Stavanger Hotel in Minneapolis and arranged transportation to and from the hotel. This small gift is in return for all you did for me.

The soiree will begin at 8:00 p.m. and will include food, libations, and music. Please bring nothing but yourselves.

Dress for dancing and expect celebratory kisses at midnight.

Ben

Ben knew that Lily would be a great resource. She was well connected in the food, music, and planning scene. He was not. After texting her, she agreed to come by to lay the groundwork.

He started a to-do list. Lily showed up at 6:30 that evening, and the father-daughter show began. She already had catering and music options penciled in and just needed his approval. She had three friends in a Costa Rican combo called *Los Gatos*. Second, she had called her friend who had catered the party at Nathan's house. Food, beverages, and music were finalized by 7:00. Ben requested the bartender, Jeff.

With invitations out and food, beverages, and music decided, they relaxed and munched on Korean barbecued chicken pizza and Mexican Cokes by the fire. He asked Lily about her new job.

"My head is spinning. I am excited about eventually getting into R&D. That's my goal. I know it's only been a few weeks, but so far, I love going to work."

"That's what it's about, Lily, loving what you do and doing what you love. How often do you talk to Dahlia?"

"Since the hospital, I guess we have talked maybe five times, the last time I guess three to four days ago. We like each other. Sometimes, you don't even come up in the conversation."

"Don't make a special call, but the next time you talk, tell her I am seeing someone. You might think that is dumb, but if she is trying to move forward with her life, it might be easier."

"OK, but seriously, you are adults and should be able to communicate with each other. I don't want to compromise my friendship with Dahlia by playing telephone."

Ben nodded. "Sometime down the road that may happen, but for now we are both trying to get our lives on track. Maybe she will invite me to her wedding next year."

Lily gave her dad a puzzling, disapproving glance. Ben regretted sounding sarcastic.

"Listen, I have to go to work tomorrow and want to be sharp and rested. This party will be so much fun. By the way, are William and I invited?"

"You and William are the guests of honor."

"Plan on it. With bells on."

The email responses were coming in. Russ and Twila were in, as were Nathan and Natalie. So were Anne and Andrew. Rachel and Caroline said, "Yes, but don't need a room." Ben really wanted José and Barbara to come.

Louie called. "Wouldn't miss it for the world. Wait till you see Sheri dance. You'll know why I am marrying her."

Clayton and Sarah confirmed. Michael responded that he was coming too and would be bringing Fred, the donkey Ben hoped he was joking. The party was taking shape. Ben was relieved. In the back of his mind, he worried that all of them had seen enough of him. There was a cloud of sadness in the air thinking of Arthur and Julia. Thinking outside the box, he invited them, saying to himself, *Don't pretend to know what you can't.*

The question of Eva loomed in Ben's head. *Should I invite her? Is it appropriate?* Ben called Louie, his moral guru, for guidance.

"Louie, regarding the New Year's Eve party, I want your opinion. Should I invite Eva?"

"If you are uncomfortable having her there, absolutely. Invite her. You're at your best when you're uncomfortable. Besides, the hell with your comfort level. She should be there, and if you're a nervous wreck, all the better. I hope you are inviting Alison too."

Laughing, Ben said, "I invited Alison. Always been able to count on you. I will invite Eva. By the way, Junior thanks me every night for taking him back. He said the bed got too crowded for him. See ya, big guy."

He forwarded the email to Eva with a special note at the bottom saying, "I hope you can attend. Bring Ross, a friend, or come single. Hope to celebrate another New Year's Eve with you."

He wished Eva would come alone.

That evening, Ben was pleased when Eva RSVP'd. She didn't specify alone or with a companion. Alison surprised him, saying, "Ted and I will be there."

He decided that José deserved a phone call. Barbara answered.

"Hi, Ben. José and I were just going to call you. He's in the shower. We have a couple of details to work out, but our intentions are to be at your party. Pretty sure we'll make it."

"That's great, Barbara. I want you to stay at the Stavanger too, but know that you are welcome to stay here afterward if you want to hang out for a couple of days, up to a month."

"Thanks, Ben, we will be in touch soon. On my way to work. Must run. Love you. Bye."

"Give José my best. Tell him I will call. Bye, Barbara."

Ben heard an email beep on his phone. Liz's response was a polite decline. "Regretfully, Ben, I am unable to attend. I am going to London and will be spending New Year's Eve with Maddie. Next year, have another one, and send an invite earlier."

Ben wasn't sure if there was a hint of sarcasm in the email. If there was, he understood. *Control the things you can, and understand the things you can't.* Ben let it go. His focus was on New Year's Eve.

He began thinking about whether to make any comments to the group. They were the people who had been with him through hell and high water. He wanted to be short, sweet, and on target.

Thinking about his message, he was certain that his experience was rare. He had never heard of anyone moving to a different bed every month for a year. Twelve beds!

His year taught him that the most extraordinary events can happen in the most ordinary places. There was a time when he believed that one should explore the world. At fifty, he realized that living in his friend's homes had taught him more than all his travels.

Lily called. She was spending Christmas Eve with her mother and Ted, adding that William had invited her to his family home for Christmas Day. She hadn't committed and wanted to know if Ben had any plans. They could all go to William's family in Stillwater.

Even though Ben wasn't fond of holidays with strangers, he valued time with Lily and reluctantly agreed. Another baby step. A year ago, he would have declined and spent the day alone. He was different from a year ago.

"Dahlia called me yesterday. We spoke about her plans for the holidays. Her parents celebrate Hanukkah and Christmas. She's spending Christmas with her parents on Marco Island. She didn't say whether her new beau was joining her. As you requested, I told her you were seeing someone. Dahlia told me she wasn't surprised. She said you deserve a good life, and with a home and your book finished, you should be more relaxed. She said to give you her best."

Dahlia hadn't brought up the housewarming gift that was still in the garage. Ben didn't either.

Ben spent Christmas Eve with Louie, Sheri, Clayton, Sarah, and two other families on Water Street. Clayton and Sarah hosted, and since Louie and Sheri didn't have family in town, Ben invited them. The evening was a stereotypical Minnesotan Christmas Eve. Large snowflakes were falling.

Louie and Sheri insisted on bringing Ben to the Basilica for midnight mass. Louie confessed that the bishop had agreed to perform their wedding at the Basilica if he saw their faces a few times. The mass was the ultimate connection with Christmas.

Christmas morning, Ben got a call from Lily. They would be by to pick him up at eleven for the drive to Stillwater and Christmas dinner. Reluctantly, Ben was fulfilling his obligation as a father by putting on his big-boy pants and showing up.

Craig and Shelley Lund were gracious hosts. Craig was from Iowa and had met Shelley at the University of Minnesota. After marrying, they started their veterinarian business in Stillwater and never left.

The Lund's family Norwegian heritage was prevalent. Lily smiled when the conversation turned to heritage. Only a few months ago, she was shocked she wasn't half-Norwegian, then relieved to find out her dad wasn't either. The smile and the wink indicated Lily was at peace.

After dinner, the Lund's had gifts for everyone, including Ben. When Ben expressed his regret in not being a bearer of gifts, Shelley said, "An autographed copy of your book would be a perfect gift whenever available."

Ben said, "Like money in the bank, count on it."

Privately, Ben and Craig shared a scotch by the fire. Ben hated scotch but sipped slowly.

"Shelley and I simply love Lily. You must be very proud of her."

"Thank you, Craig. All I hear are compliments about William. We are fortunate."

When William and Lily dropped Ben off around eleven that night, he was reminded of his hesitance to go and that his obligation had resulted in a rewarding evening. He was still learning about life at fifty.

On New Year's Eve, his house was ready. The buffet of food was laid out, the band was setting up, and the dance floor was ready for company. Jeff, the bartender, was there. Ben sought him out.

"Hey, Jeff, good to see you. Thanks for being here. How about coffee next week?" *Deeds, not words.*

At about 8:15 that evening, guests started arriving, beginning with Louie and Sheri. Clayton and Sarah followed. The chartered limo delivered everyone from the Stavanger Hotel, including José and Barbara, Nathan and Natalie, Anne and Andrew, Caroline and Rachel, Russ and Twila, Michael and Robert, and Lily and William. Last, Eva brought Ross, and Alison brought Ted.

Everyone was in the house by 9:00, and the music began with Ben's request, "Samba Pa Ti." Couples were dancing. Next, they played "Soul Man."

About 9:30, Ben decided it was time to deliver his little talk. Everyone had enjoyed a few libations and danced a few numbers. He went to the foot of the stairs, walked up three steps, and held up a glass of champagne. Like clockwork, Lily clinked her glass with a spoon.

"I want to thank all of you for coming. Last December, in the wee hours of the morning, Louie Larson took me in from the cold. From February through November, I was welcomed into your homes with hospitality and love.

"You would think having a roof over my head would be enough, but I gained so much more. Before the fire, I was existing. You showed me how to live. I learned that *being* was more important than *doing*. I learned about myself from each of you.

"I was forced to look at who I was. Much of what I saw was difficult to accept. The lessons learned from watching and living with each of you are priceless. Inviting someone into your home might be the kindest gift possible."

Ben paused; he was speechless. Hesitating, he didn't understand. He thought he saw Dahlia in the back of the room. *Am I losing my mind?* Composing himself, he looked again, and she was gone. He continued, "Finally, I want you to know that I will always cherish your friendship. We have about two hours left in the year. Enjoy every second. I love each of you. You are my people."

The room exploded with applause, followed by the band playing a rendition of Bob Marley's "Redemption Song."

Ben walked to the back of the room. Of course, Dahlia wasn't there. *The brain is amazing,* he thought. *How strange to experience a dream while awake.*

"Great job, Dad. I saw a lot of emotion while you were talking. There is a lot of love in this room tonight. Come over here. I want to share a moment with you."

Lily sat down by the glowing fireplace. "After talking to Dahlia and listening to you, I saw the writing on the wall. Neither of you were seeing anyone. You were each making up a line to make the other feel comfortable. I leveled with her, and she leveled with me. She hasn't been with anyone since you. You are in love with each other. You should be together. Tonight, you will be. Dahlia is standing behind you."

Ben turned around. The love of his life was standing in front of him. He couldn't believe his eyes. Taking her hands, he said, "In San Pedro, I knew you were the one. I have loved you since the very first night. We must try to make this work."

Dahlia said, "No one ever found a place in my heart like you. Being with you makes me alive. I had to come here tonight."

Ben said, "We'll try?"

Dahlia said, "With all my heart."

Ben and Dahlia shared a soft kiss that lasted until everyone noticed and began clapping.

Dancing accelerated up until the countdown began. "Auld Lang Syne" played, and everyone hugged and kissed to the sound of horns.

Dahlia's kiss was the sweetest of Ben's life. They had been given a chance.

"We should have done this months ago. My mom insisted I come here tonight. Mothers know their daughters!"

"I am so grateful to be looking at you, Dahlia. I admire your courage to come here. I owe it to you and your mother to prove it was the right decision."

Lily, Dahlia, Dahlia's mother, and Anne had rescued Ben from despair. *Women, the givers of life, have the wisdom and courage to do whatever it takes.*

By 2:00 a.m., people were ready to return to their resting places. The party was a success. Dahlia and Ben were at peace in the lighthouse room looking at the moon and stars.

"Dahlia, being together seemed impossible, so I tried denying my feelings, yet all my thoughts returned to you. I know you are the one for me for the rest of my life."

"Ben, I said this to you in Belize. This only happens once in a lifetime. My heart made a choice, and my heart chose you. I fell in love with you when your hand touched mine. I kissed you long before I kissed you. If you ever ask me to leave, I will burn your house down."

Ben said, "My house is safe."

Ben got up and opened a drawer. "I have something for you to read. This is the final paragraph of my novel. I wrote this in San Pedro the day you left. In fact, I wrote it on the side of the road after watching your plane lift off. Because of you, I wrote the end of my book before the beginning and spent February through December making the story fit."

Ben handed the handwritten page to Dahlia. She read, "My heart aches for this woman. This is real and pure. My heart, mind, and soul have been unified by a woman named Dahlia. Is it possible to fall in love before kissing someone? Before her, I would have said *impossible*. Now, I must find a way."

Dahlia said, "You have found me, and I have found you. We belong together, and finally, we are."

On a cold Minnesota night, Ben was surrounded by warmth. He kissed her hand and looked into her eyes, knowing so much more than before the fire.

This night was the beginning of a lifetime together. Ben's mind was calm, and his heart was at peace. Dahlia was finally in his arms. After she had fallen asleep, Ben went out to the garage and brought the picture into the bedroom. Dahlia would see the picture when her eyes opened.

I love her. That's the beginning and end of everything. Fate struck a fire, and her love keeps it burning.

ABOUT THE AUTHOR

David Knudson lives with Dawn Marie near the shores of Bde Maka Ska in Minneapolis, within walking distance of his two daughters and their families. His life career as an educator began in Mexico City, was delayed by a period in the US Army, and was followed by decades as a counselor at Eden Prairie High School. David's next chapter of life spanned the globe as he worked at the International School of Vienna and as a cast member of *Alt For Norge*, a television show in Norway.

The author considers himself an ordinary man trying to live an extraordinary life. An avid Letterman fan, David emulates the phrase, "Fun follows me around." *Twelve Beds* is his first novel. Fascinated with the human condition, David's goal was to write a novel that touched upon an array of emotional relationships. During one fateful conversation on a balcony in Belize, David wondered what a person would do if their home was lost in a fire. Thus, *Twelve Beds* was born.

ACKNOWLEDGMENTS

Thank you to my family and friends who supported my writing with kindness and optimism.

Thank you to Dawn, whose energy, creativity, and love ensured that *Twelve Beds* became a reality.

Thank you to those who selflessly built bridges along my path: Luke Toft, Susan Hamre, Dr. Daniel Ihnat, Senator Steve Cwodzinski, Norris Comer, Dr. Tony Moulton, Carrie Augst, Arthur Himmelman, Frima Karon, Hillary Ross, Dr. Gerry Timm, and Susan Timm.